Africa on Fire

The End of the Beginning

Bruce Capner

Wendüleu Publishing

Published by: Wendiilou Publishing
Wendy Brown

Photo credits to:
Bruce Capner

Cover design: Craft to Cover by Wendiilou
Wendy Brown

For more copies, contact the publisher.
212 Glenburnie Rd
Rob Roy NSW 2360
wendiiloupublishing@gmail.com
0468 998 268

Africa on Fire

The End of the Beginning

Chapter 1.

The spitfire went into a steep dive hot on the tail of the German ME 109 Fighter. The Pilot did his best to get away, ducking and weaving to try get out of the spit's gun sight. A burst from the spit took away the 109's tail fin and damaged the left wing. Klaus Benz, the pilot, knew the aircraft was doomed, but no further fire came. Had the Spit run out of ammo?

As the pilot of the spit was about to fire another burst, the radio crackled, "All aircraft to suspend all hostilities immediately and return to base."

The pilot, Flight Lt Ian Smith, a Rhodesian, acknowledged; "Flight leader Roger!! Returning to Base."

Klaus Benz' 109 was losing height and out of control. He looked over his shoulder and made a mental note of the spit's number SP 171, he opened the canopy, undid his harness, put the 109 on its back, and dropped out. His parachute opened and he landed in the channel. All the spits had assembled and were flying west towards the Kent Coast, the white cliffs shinning bright in the midday sun. The radio crackled again; it was Frank Munro. He was the first to ask what was up?

The Dover Cliffs whisked past as the five spits roared over the unmistakable drum of the Rolls Royce Merlins.

"We will soon find out, Frank, the airfield's not far."

The radios crackled one after the other, the same question "What's up?" Then came the answer, "The war is over. To all personnel today, Germany unconditionally surrendered, the war in Europe is over".

***

Frank and Ian were best friends and had met up at flying school and joined the same squadron in 1940. Frank had fought in the Battle of Britain; both had earned the distinguished flying cross. Ian and Frank were twenty when they joined, now they had finished the war flying sorties up and down the Kent Coast, often on a daily basis. They were both weary of the war, as everyone was, and wondered when it would end. Now it was over. The airfield was now in sight, and they could see people scurrying about.

The aircraft all landed safely and taxied to the edge of the airfield. The flight crew came running over as the spits switched off their engines and the pilots disembarked. A flight Sergeant shouted, "Have you heard, Sir? It's over."

Ian, with a huge grin on his face, replied, "We all have, it came over the radio." They could hear the cheers and laughter coming from the main hangar.

Then, from the Sergeant, "Meeting in one-hour, main hanger, Sir."

Ian turned to Frank, put his arm around his shoulder and said, "Well, Mate, we both made it. I had my doubts for a while, about you especially, such a shit pilot and all".

They laughed and made their way to the mess tent. Ian told Frank he was going to clean up and would see him in the hangar in one hour. The whole air crew were fell-in at the far end of the hangar, pilots to the left, other ranks on the right Everybody was chatting loudly when the Commanding Officer walked in with the Adjutant and the Second in Charge. The chatter began to die off and eventually went silent as the Commanding Officer stepped up on a small stage and began his speech.

"Well, as you all know, the war is over. Well done to all. I will make it short and sweet; we are looking for pilots and air crew to take on the Japs. Anyone interested is to report to the company office tomorrow at 0900. All other ranks will be discharged within twelve weeks. Again, well done. I will see all ranks in the officers' mess this evening at 1900 hours for a bit of a piss-up".

Laughter broke out, no one knew the Commanding Officer had a sense of humour.

***

When Ian and Frank met that night in the mess, the conversation turned to what they were going to do now the war was over. Frank began with "Well, Mate, what does the future hold for you?"

"Well, all my family are in Rhodesia, so that's where I am headed, farmers all of them. We have 45000 acres of good land, plenty of water near Gwelo in the Midlands. What about you, Frank?"

"Well, I did three years of law at Edinburgh University until the war started, I'll have to see what's on. My family live in a little place called Gullane, not far from the city. As you know, Dad died, and I couldn't get away for the funeral. So, I will see what Mum is up to as she's on her own."

***

It was nine weeks before their discharge papers came through. Frank and Ian met at the local, The Dog and Pheasant. Sarah, the barmaid, said, "Hello," and pulled them each a pint. It was August 1945, and there was a chill in the air. So, they settled by the fire next to the Jack Russell who belonged to Sam, the local poacher.

Then Ian spoke to Frank, "You have my information and contact details? I hope to hear from you often."

"You will, mate", replied Frank, "You can depend on that. You know the war has changed me. You know, I have family in Kenya."

"Yes, you did mention it." replied Ian, "Great country, a lot to offer."

"I will give it plenty of thought," was Frank's reply, "might make the move myself." They had a few more pints.

Ian finally said "That's enough, I'm off to Tilbury tomorrow, booked on the "Union Castle Uganda" headed for Durban, South Africa. Set sail on Wednesday, stop at Port Said, Mombasa – Durban, then by train to Rhodesia and home. I'll miss you, Frank, but I feel we will meet again."

They shook hands and made their way back to the barracks.

They rose early the next morning, had breakfast, and reported to the guardroom for the last time and signed out. There was a RAF Vehicle waiting the take them to Dover station. Frank was the first to leave, he was heading north to Edinburgh. They shook hands for the last time, Frank gave Ian a shove and said, "Look after yourself", and jumped aboard, gave his mate a wave, and went to his seat.

The train pulled into Kings Cross, London. The platforms were packed with soldiers, sailors, and airmen heading home. Frank found the right platform and boarded the train. Fortunately, he was entitled to a first-class carriage, and made his way to the front of the train. It was standing room only at the rear. He found a compartment, entered, put his kit above his seat and sat down. There were three others, two by the window and one opposite. Frank then said "hello" and they each expressed their feelings about the war being over.

They stopped at Birmingham where half the train emptied and took off again. Frank looked at the carnage the bombing had caused. Brum and Coventry had taken a terrible hammering. He and his squadron had done their best to get as many of the bastards as they could, but a lot got through.

The train chugged along, blowing black smoke, and moved into greener farming country. Of all things, Frank found himself daydreaming and thinking about elephants. His father, Tom, used to take him and his twin brother, Brian, to the zoo in Edinburgh quite often. Both the brothers had looked in wonder at the huge grey beasts as they sauntered to the edge of their enclosure and stretched their trunks over the top for a piece of bread or a carrot. Brian had died when he was ten in a drowning accident, but Frank knew he was still with him.

Frank drifted off into a deep sleep and was suddenly shaken awake by a loud bang and a jerking motion. They had reached Crewe. He knew they would be here for an hour, so he got out and walked down the platform and ordered tea and a Rock Bun at the Café. It was all they had to eat.

He walked back and sat back down in his compartment. He was on his own now. He was remembering a letter his mother, Rita, had received from her brother-in-law, his uncle Jack. He said in the letter that he was doing well on the farm but, because of his age, felt he needed a bit of a hand and would Frank be interested in taking on the job as manager.

Frank had replied and said he would think about it, then the war started, so it all went out the window. Now, he was turning it over in his head again.

It was 9 in the evening when they pulled into Waverly Station in Edinburgh. It was still as dreary as ever, but a lot of people were coming and going in lots of different uniforms. He disembarked and made his way to the stone steps that led up to Princes Street. He climbed the steps and stopped at the top. There would be no buses at this hour, so he made his way to Leith Street, where he knew he would get a bed for the night. He walked down the street and stopped outside an old tavern painted black with red and gold stripes on the sign. It read: *The Black Douglas Tavern.* It was after hours, so the door was locked but he knew the landlord would still be serving drinks and he could see a slight glimmer of light under the door. So, he made his way to the side entrance, opened the iron gate, and went in. He went to the back door and lifted the huge iron knocker: bang, bang, bang. It echoed through the other side of the door. Seconds passed and a voice called out from inside "Who is it and what do you want?"

"It's me, Frank Munro, Tom's Son. I'm home and I need a bed for the night." The huge door opened with a creak. Standing in the doorway was a huge man, Jim Gillespie, he and Frank's father had been at school together, so Frank called him Uncle. Uncle Jim had played Rugby for Scotland in his younger days. He spent most of his life as a policeman in Edinburgh but had lost an eye in a fight while clearing a public house. He now wore a black patch over his left eye. To say he was an intimidating figure would be understating it. He looked at Frank then reached out his right hand and put his left arm around Frank's shoulder. "Come in, laddie, so good to see you." By now his wife had arrived and gave him a hug and a kiss on the cheek.

"Hello, Aunt Maggie. Nice to see you again."

"Come in," she said, "come in, let's go through to the bar and have a drink."

They all went through. Half a dozen locals were sitting by the fire. Everyone said "Hello." Jim poured three whiskies on the bar, giving one to Frank. Frank took a pound note from his pocket and offered it to Jim.

Jim, with anger in his voice said, "Put that away, you'll pay for nothing in this house."

Two of the local Scotsman fell from their chairs but regained their composure after a few minutes. The others gaped in astonishment and continued to drink. One said in a broad Scots accent, "did you ever hear such a thing?" The conversation was about the war and how well Britian and the allies had done, and how touch and go it had been for some time.

Eventually, Aunt Marge asked, "So, Frank, any plans?"

Frank replied, "Not as yet, Aunt Marg. Mum doesn't know I'm home yet. I'll surprise her in the morning."

They put Frank in the spare room where he slept soundly. The next morning, he was awakened by Aunt Marge. She had with her a tray. On it was a cup of hot tea and a sausage sandwich with tomato sauce. Frank felt guilty because of the rationing but gulped down the tea and sandwich. He got up, shaved and dressed, said his goodbyes, and promised to drop in when in town.

They all went to the front door, as Frank was leaving, Jim said, "I went to your dad's funeral. I understand you couldn't make it with the war commitments and all. Go and see him, he's buried next to your brother, Brian."

Frank walked into Leith St. and over to the bus shelter. It was eight in the morning, and he could see a row of green and yellow buses lined up. There was a morning chill and a slight drizzle of rain. He looked at the buses, one read Haddington, one Dunbar, and then one, North Berwick. This is the one he wanted. Gullane was only 15 miles from Edinburgh, so the journey wasn't long and there were only a few passengers. They followed the winding road through Preston pans, Aberlady, and then Gullane. He passed the cemetery and church yard with its stone wall and stopped at the bus stop outside Pat McCall's, the Baker. He got off and as he did, Pat came running out, a look of amazement on his face "Frank, Frank, what a surprise. Your mother will be over the moon. Does she know you're home?"

"No, Mr McCall, she doesn't.

"Well, away with you as quick as you can. Rosie's just been here for the rolls and bread."

Rosie was a black Labrador that Frank's dad had brought home one day as a pup. He had found her in a sack on the golf course. He untied her and took her straight home and returned to work. He had been the head Green Keeper at Gullane Golf Course. He had been there all his life except for four years in the 1st World War when he served with the Cameron Highlanders. He was fourteen when he started as a green keeper. He had died in 1942 at the age of sixty-four. They found him on the 11th Tee, heart failure, they said. Something to do with the mustard gas in the war.

Frank made his way up the road, past the goose green and the timber yard. It was about quarter of a mile then, as he turned the corner within sight of the house, he saw her sitting at the gate. It was Rosie. His mum had written about her in every letter. How she sat at the gate, waiting, only coming in to be fed then back to the gate. When it got dark, she would make her way to his bedroom and climb onto the end of the bed until morning, then return to the gate.

Every morning, Frank's mum gave her the straw basket and sent her off to McCall's Bakery for the bread and rolls she shared with her neighbour. Then she was back on watch, waiting for Frank. She recognised him immediately, her ears shot up and she bolted off towards him. Frank went down on one knee and braced for impact. She slammed into him almost bowling him over. Her tail whacking against him. Frank made a fuss of her, then stood up, "Come on, girl, let's go, Rosie". She fell in at his side and they entered the front gate.

The house was a typical, stone-faced tenement with a small front yard and a small yard at the rear. Frank banged the brass knocker that was shining so brightly he could see his face. He had no response, so Frank tried again. He heard a shuffle from inside and the door opened. It was his mum, Rita. She stared at his face, then her jaw fell open, she put her hand to her mouth in amazement. "Franky, oh Franky, you're back safe. Why didn't you tell me you were coming?"

"I wanted to surprise you, Mum." Said Frank.

"Well, you have done that" and she threw her arms around him.

They went inside, Rosie at their feet. It was still early on, just ten in the morning. Rita asked if he had eaten, Frank said "yes, I stayed the night with Uncle James and Aunt Marge. They fed me before I left."

"Bless them both," said his mother. They went into the kitchen and sat down. Rita put the kettle on, and they began to chat. She asked, "Well, Frank, now that it's over, do you have any plans?"

"Well, Mum," replied Frank, "I kept thinking about Uncle Jack's letter with the Job offer in Kenya. Things are pretty grim here by the looks of it."

"Well, Franky, you could do a lot worse."

***

The next morning, Frank and his mum rose early as they had spoken about visiting his father's grave. They sent Rosie off with the breadbasket and she had just returned. They drank tea with a bacon roll and chatted about what was going on in the village. Most of the young men had been away at the war and quite a few hadn't made it back.

They dressed and made their way to the cemetery. Frank's mum in her best hat, and Rosie alongside. It was only a twenty-minute walk, and in no time at all they were at the iron gate. They walked inside, it was a dreary place, and the morning was cold. They found the path and walked to the grave. It was neat and well-kept but there was no headstone for his father. He was buried next to his brother, Brian. They both sat on Brian's grave and Frank spoke softly, "Sorry, I couldn't make it back, Dad, but Brian is here." Rosie had her head in his lap, and she looked up and put her paw on his arm and pulled at it to get a pat.

She had been at the funeral for the old man and remembered the big brown box carried by the six villagers, Pat McCall, had been one. They placed the box over the open grave. She knew the old man was in there. She caught his scent as they walked by, and she knew now he was still here buried in the earth. Frank's mother brought her here every Sunday morning with fresh flowers. She remembered watching the man in the black frock standing at the top of the grave, opening the black book, and speaking the words, "Dust to Dust" she remembered the big man with the black patch with his arm around the woman who was crying.

After the service they made their way to the local pub for the wake. A few of the locals spoke about Frank's dad, and how he never missed a day at the greens. All ended well, everybody drank too much, laughed, and joked, and started to disperse late in the evening. James and his wife, Marge, saw Frank's mother home as they were staying the night, accompanied by Rosie. As they went in through the back door, the house was in darkness, and it was cold and dreary. Rita began to sob uncontrollably. Marge took her into the front room, sat her down and spoke to her.

"The war will be over soon, Rita, Franky will be home, and Rosie is here."

Rosie was at her feet looking up into her eyes. Rita reached out and gave her a pat and Rosie snuggled in closer. Marge said, "Rita, sweetheart, I will stay on for a few days till you feel better".

Her husband who was standing in the door agreed, "That'll be fine, Rita. I'll go back in the morning."

The weeks passed and Rita accepted the fact that Tom was gone. She visited his grave regularly and sat and spoke to him. Frank sent money home every month with extra this month for a headstone, but she would wait until he returned.

***

In the weeks that passed, Frank felt obliged to stay with his mum and applied for a job at the Clydesdale Bank in Edinburgh. At the interview, he had impressed the panel of three with his war record and maturity, and he was offered a job in the foreign currency department which involved transfer of funds to different parts of the world. Mostly people immigrating and transferring their funds. His salary was fifteen pounds per week. Frank was at his desk at 0800 hours every morning, the doors opened at 0900 and in came a stream of folk asking about rates and how much to transfer their money. Frank closed his desk at 1500 and then began on the paperwork. It seemed that everyone wanted to immigrate, and he thought to himself, *you couldn't blame them, jobs were plentiful, but money was tight, and rationing was still in place.* Every day, applications came in for transfers to Canada, USA, South Africa, Rhodesia, Kenya, Australia, even New Zealand. He thought to himself, *New Zealand? Why in God's name, New Zealand?*

***

He'd been at the bank now for nine months and was growing restless. He knew this was not the career path he wanted. His uncle Jack wrote every couple of months, confirming all was well and still hoping Frank would accept his offer as manager.

Frank made his mind up on the bus that night. He would speak to his mum this evening at supper. He got off the bus, walked up the road and round the corner. It was dark, but there she was, as always, Rosie. She sat wagging her tail, waiting. They went inside, Frank closed the door quietly behind them, his mum was in the kitchen cooking supper. He sat down and she asked him, "Well, Frankie, what sort of a day?"

Frank replied, "Same old, same old, Mum. I have made my mind up. I'm off to Africa."

"Oh, Frankie, that's wonderful, Uncle Jack will be so pleased."

Frank spent the night writing to his uncle, telling him the good news but he was worried about his mum. He decided that he would post the letter in the morning in Edinburgh.

***

At the bus depot in Edinburgh, taxis would meet the buses and offer lifts to Princes Street for sixpence. Because of fuel shortages, as many passengers would pile into each Taxi as possible to keep the cost down. Frank had stopped availing himself of this practice as, the previous week, two Taxi's had crashed head on, and thirty-eight Scotsman had been injured. Two of the passengers, who were uninjured, ran off without paying but they were suspected of being Englishmen. Probably from Yorkshire. He preferred to walk, if only for the exercise, but today was a special day, only, he didn't know how special as yet.

As Frank walked towards the bank, he noticed a shapely young woman in a tight dress walking not far ahead of him. He caught the reflection of her face in a shop window and recognised her instantly. It was a school friend, Janet Sinclair, from a village nearby called Aberlady. They had been close friends, Frank one class above her. He called out, "My goodness, but you have got a big bum."

She recognised his voice and spun around with a wide grin, "and you, Frank Munro, have a funny nose."

17

They had always teased each other. Frank about her bum and she about his crooked nose. She hurried towards him and kissed him on the cheek, and he held her for a brief moment.

Frank whispered, "It's so good to see you again, Jan".

She replied, "And you too, Frank. I heard you were home. A proper hero, I heard."

"Well, that part's true, Janet, I saved the R.A.F and then the country."

They both laughed. Janet was the first to start with questions. Frank gave her a brief rundown, the bank, back living with his mum, but he didn't mention Kenya.

"And what about you, what are you doing?"

Janet replied, "I'm at the hospital, a nurse, just qualified as a theatre sister, and I'm enjoying it."

Frank asked if they could meet for lunch, but Janet said she couldn't as she had a busy day, but could Frank come to her parents' house for Sunday lunch. Her parents would love to see him again. Frank agreed. Janet kissed him again and said, "One o'clock Sunday then." She turned and was off. Frank thought to himself, what a beautiful woman she had turned into, well dressed and confident. He couldn't wait for Sunday.

When he arrived home that evening, Rosie was waiting as usual, and they made their way inside. Frank couldn't wait to tell his mother. "Mum, you will never guess who I bumped into in Edinburgh?"

His mother replied, "No, Frank, you will have to tell me."

"It was Janet Sinclair, you remember her?"

"Of course, Frankie, she used to come here while she waited for the school bus." She looked at Frank and sensed a change, slight but a difference nonetheless, "And what is she up to?"

Frank blurted out "She's a nurse in the city and looks really well, terrific in fact."

"Well, Franky, she certainly seems to have impressed you."

***

That night, Janet lay awake thinking about Frank, she had only known two men in her life, and they had both been short term because of the war. Her first love had been killed in the war, the other just a fling. This was not for her. She was now in her early twenties and wanted someone stable to settle down with and start a family. Frank fitted the bill to a tee; she could hardly wait for Sunday. Janet was the eldest of four sisters, the others being Morag, Debra, and Helen.

It was just before one on Sunday when Frank knocked on the door, Janet made him welcome and invited him in. They went through to the front room where the whole family were seated. Janet's father rose, shook his hand, and offered Frank a glass of whisky which Frank accepted. They all made Frank very welcome, and they settled down to conversation about politics and what the future would hold. Janet's father, George, was the local blacksmith and was doing well. The war had been over for nearly two years now and he had had to put on three men to help out. They were busy doing gates, railings, and all the replacement steelwork for that which had been taken away for the war effort. They sat and had a nice meal.

At around six, Frank said his goodbyes and arranged for Janet to visit his house the following Sunday. Frank had still not mentioned Africa to Janet as he wanted to get to know her better.

***

A month passed, and Frank had decided Janet was the one he would like as a partner. So, he decided now was about time to see what she thought. They were having lunch in Edinburgh when Frank started, "Janet, I need to tell you something."

"Yes," said Janet, "Go on."

Frank hesitated a little then blurted it out, "I am going to Kenya, and I want you to come with me."

Janet looked at him with a look of shock on her face. "Well, Frank, is that some kind of proposal and why didn't you mention it before?"

Frank replied, "It is indeed a proposal, and I wanted us to get to know each other."

Janet looked at him, "I will tell you right now, Frank Munro, yes and yes. I have always wanted to go abroad.

Frank laughed, "You have made me a very happy man".

He began to outline his plans and told her of the offer made by his uncle. The weekend came, and Frank arranged to speak to Janet's mum and dad. When he arrived, everybody was grinning from ear to ear, so he knew it was all out of the bag. The three sisters were there. There was a seven-year age difference between Janet and Morag. All three were only teenagers. Morag was the cheekiest and most brazen. When Frank walked through the door, they all started, "and what do you want, Frank Munro?" They made kissing sounds and pursed their lips.

Frank said "Away you go, the three of you. You especially, Morag, with your skinny, hairy legs."

She replied, "I haven't got hairy legs, Frank Munro."

"Oh, yes, have a good look lassie," and everyone laughed, except Morag.

Janet's mother ordered them into the kitchen and Janet, Frank, and Janet's parents went into the front room. Frank opened the conversation, "So, it looks like the cat's out of the bag."

"Yes, it certainly is, son, and we couldn't be happier."

The weeks passed and Frank and Janet laid out the plans for the trip. They were not going to take any furniture or large items, only bedding, crockery, and clothing. While all this was going on, Rosie lay around listening. She knew something was up.

Janet's engagement party was small, about fifteen of her friends from the hospital and Aberlady. They all met in a small pub in Edinburgh. They had a good time, drank a lot, reminisced about men and the good times they had. At closing time, they all climbed into taxis and made their way home.

Frank and Janet had fixed a date for the wedding, 12ᵗʰ June. They were married in Gullane Church, just over the road from the school they had attended. Half of the village turned out and they set up a beer tent for the guests at the golf club. There were pictures of Frank's dad and all the other greenkeepers from over the years.

Janet and Frank moved in with his mother. Rita was so excited at the prospect of grandchildren. She was only in her mid-50's and had been a schoolteacher in her youth. Now she worked from home, keeping books for the local businesses and people around the county and did quite well.

It was the middle of June and a beautiful summer; the shows would be here the following week. It was like a small travelling carnival that set up on the goose green every year. Now the war was over they were returning to normal.

Everybody turned out for the show from all over. So, the first night he told his mum, Janet, and Janet's family to meet them at six pm on the road at the timber yard.

While Frank was waiting, he looked at the old timber yard where they used to play. It was closed now, and he recalled how it used to have a steel spiked fence on the outside but that had gone for the war effort. He remembered that, when they were nine or ten years old, he and four or five of his mates would sneak in and play hide and seek or cowboys and Indians. They used to run around the racks of timber.

One night, Billy Henderson disappeared. They looked for him but couldn't find him. They thought he must have just gone home, but when he didn't return, his parents told the police, and they went to look for him. They went out with dogs and torches and found him dead. He had fallen or tripped onto the steel spikes, and one had pierced his heart. They said he must have died instantly.

The following year, Brian, Frank's brother was washed off rocks at the beach by a freak wave and drowned. They found his body the following day.

Janet's family arrived with the three sisters in tow. Her father had driven up in the van he used for the business, an Austin. He parked and they all jumped out, staring at the bright lights of the show, the music so loud, you could hardly hear yourself speak. People were moving about with fairy floss and hot dogs.

Frank thought about how things were getting back to normal. He took out his wallet, called the sisters over and shouted "Here, you three," and gave them a pound each. "Go" he said, "and don't waste it."

They ran off giggling and squealing and shouted back, "We won't, Frank, thank you."

The four made their way over the road onto the green, Frank and Janet's favourite ride when they were kids was the jungle ride. A huge circular ride, all green and gold that whipped around in a circle in a wave motion. It stopped, Frank paid the man and he and Janet jumped on. Frank said to Janet "for old times' sake, Jan, it's probably the last time."

"Yes," she replied.

Janet's parents gave them a wave. They would content themselves with the games, the clowns with the turning heads where you dropped ping-pong balls into their mouths to see if you could win a prize, or three balls for one shilling to see if you could dislodge a coconut, although Janet's father was convinced that they glued the coconuts in or shooting ducks with an airgun.

Anyway, when he returned it was with a ginger teddy bear. It wasn't long before the night was over, the sisters were waiting at the car, Morag, with Fairy Floss in her hair and all over her face. The other two not much better, with tomato sauce all down the fronts of their dresses. They thanked Frank and took off home. Frank and Janet walked home, hand in hand. As they turned the corner, there she was, Rosie, sitting as usual, tail sweeping the pavement. They went inside, mum was still up and asked if they had fun. They both replied that they had, had a cup of tea, and went to bed.

***

Frank received regular letters from Ian in Rhodesia, telling him what a great time he was having. The farm was doing well, and he was thinking of going into politics. His chosen party was the Rhodesian Front.

Frank had given notice at the bank, and it was agreed he would go on ahead and make sure all was well in Kenya. He wasn't happy about leaving his mother and had convinced her to accompany Janet. Jack was so pleased when he heard the news, he telegrammed saying he was so looking forward to the family getting together. The next-door neighbour agreed to take Rosie, but Frank didn't know if it was the right thing to do.

Frank had booked on the same ship Ian had left on, the "Union Castle Uganda". It was only twelve days journey to Mombasa, and he looked forward to seeing the sun again. The day arrived and Rosie saw the two suitcases at the front door. She knew this might be the last time she would see her master. She lay down flat on the carpet, listening and watching. She watched Frank kiss his mum and give a big, long hug to Janet, then it was her turn.

"Well, my girl," said Frank as he knelt to pat her and say goodbye, "you have been the best, most loyal friend anyone could ask for". Frank was choking, holding back tears.

Rosie never moved, not even a wag of her tail, then she raised her head and licked his hand. Frank stood up, took a suitcase in each hand, walked through the open door and then he was gone. Rosie rose from the floor, made for the corner, and took her seat to wait for her master to return. Both the women were crying and called her, "Come in, girl" but she stayed at her spot. Janet and Rita left her and then they heard her bark once, then twice and she was off. It was him; her master was back. He hadn't left her.

Frank saw her take off and, as usual, braced for impact. "Come on inside, Rosie, we can't leave you. You are coming to Africa as well."

Frank gave instruction to Rita and Janet on how to transport Rosie. They had to have a crate made with wire on one side and a fixed water bowl. Arthur, the carpenter in the village would make it and Rosie would accompany the two women on the train and aboard ship. It was late in the evening before Frank had finished, so he stayed the night. They decided that his mum would put the house on the market. She was quite sad as the home had been handed down from her great grandfather, but she had made her decision.

The next morning, they all travelled to Edinburgh to see Frank off on the train. Uncle James and his wife were there to wish him all the best. Janet and his mum were both in tears as the train left.

Frank looked out the window as the train chugged along, the whistle blew, and he finally dozed off. Then a sudden bang and it was Crewe Station. After another four hours, they began to hit the built-up areas. He could see a lot of construction had started. It had been two years since the end of the war and things were moving ahead again.

He dozed off and the next thing he remembered was "tickets please, tickets please, Sir". Frank handed over his ticket; the conductor clipped it and thanked him. "Kings Cross station, London, in thirty minutes, Sir."

He didn't have to change; this was the boat train. It went straight through to Tilbury docks. The train had been quite full but now he enjoyed the compartment with only one other, a gentleman in his thirties who smoked a pipe. They introduced themselves, Andrew was his name, from Newcastle. He was a surveyor and was also off to Kenya.

***

The trip to Mombasa was uneventful, a bit rough in the Bay of Biscay but once through there, it was plain sailing. It was two days to the entrance to the Mediterranean and they arrived at first light. As they sailed in, Gibraltar was on the left.

It was September, beautiful and warm, lights flashed from shore, the ship had identified herself and she was given the okay to enter. Ship life was pretty humdrum, however. Frank spent the morning with a crisp walk around the deck after breakfast and then a bit of a catchup with Andrew. They discussed their expectations and got to know each other very well. It turned out that Andrew had served with the Commandos while he was away. His girlfriend had run off and married a Canadian. Frank was travelling first class, Andrew, second. So, mealtimes were segregated. Frank had to dine with an annoying woman and her three children, two girls, and one boy, he found all four of them to be a pain in the backside. The woman was the wife of some government big wig, Secretary to the Governor, and she insisted on being called *Her Ladyship*. She and her offspring seemed to look down terribly on the working class and made the stewards' life a living hell. Her view was that any person of colour was just meant to be a servant, even though she admitted to having never seen a black person and had never left England before. So, Frank avoided her, as did everyone else, as much as possible.

In the afternoons, Frank would visit the ship's library and take out books on the history of Africa. It made for interesting reading. He found a book on the Boer War, and the Zulu War.

In the evenings, Frank and Andrew met up for a pint and discussed Kenya. One night, Andrew said, "You know, Frank, I heard a rumour about a bit of trouble, something called Mau-Mau."

Frank replied, "Yes, mate, my uncle, Jack, has mentioned it in his letters. He says it's nothing too serious, mostly amongst their own people. Quite savage at times, I believe, the government have sent in the army and settled it down a bit."

They said their goodnights and went to their cabins. Frank lay awake thinking about Kenya and the farm. He was excited to get on with the job. He missed Janet and his mum and, of course, Rosie. They would be following on in eight weeks. Frank eventually fell asleep until six in the morning when a knock on his cabin door awakened him. It was the steward, a Welsh lad with a cup of tea. "Morning, sir,"

"Morning, Taff, what's the weather like?"

"Fine" was the reply, "be in Mombasa in forty-eight hours, Sir."

Frank drank his tea, shaved, and dressed, and made his way to the dining hall. As usual, Lady Muck and her offspring could be heard dressing the stewards down, so he elected to eat at the other end of the dining hall.

Frank finished his breakfast and made his way onto the deck where he leant against the rail. It was a beautiful morning. Since they left the Suez Canal, Frank was amazed at the number of Arab Dhows he could see with their distinct white triangular sails. He counted twenty-three this morning, all sailing south, probably sailing to Mombasa or Zanzibar. Must have spices on board to trade for gold and ivory, he thought. He was getting bored now and welcomed the idea of leaving the ship as soon as possible.

He fell into his normal routine, chat with Andrew, library, sleep. Two days passed slowly, then on the eve of docking in Mombasa, he couldn't get to sleep until one am. When the morning came, he found himself on deck watching the African coast pass slowly by on the horizon. When he was awakened the steward had informed him, "Well, sir, we are here".

Frank heard a lot of shouting and people running about on deck.

"Alongside in thirty minutes," said Taff.

Frank had packed the night before and was ready to go. Uncle Jack had arranged to meet the ship and Frank was excited to see him again. They had always gotten along well. Frank glanced out the porthole just as they passed Fort Jesus, a beautiful, old, fortified, castle-type structure built by the Portuguese back in 1593 as a place of safety from the Arabs who raided up and down the east coast, something Frank had learned in his reading on his way out. It had served as a base for forays into the interior, a prison, a place to hold slaves, and a watch tower out to sea. It was designed by the Italian,

Giovani Battista Cairati, and the cannons were visible and painted black. It looked quite beautiful.

The ship had now tied up and people were milling about on deck with suitcases, dogs on leashes, and cats, of all things, in baskets. People were waving and shouting as Frank made his way up on deck. He put his suitcases down and stood by the rail. It didn't take long to spot Uncle Jack standing on the wharf dressed in a kilt and large hat and pressed Khari shirt. They saw each other immediately and waved in recognition. Frank made his way down the gangway, Uncle Jack waited at the end with an African who took Frank's cases. They shook hands, Uncle Jack and Frank first, then Jack introduced the African. "Frank, this is Benjamin, your new house boy and cook. They shook hands but Frank was surprised at the African handshake.

"You'll get used to it, Frank," said Jack, "shake the hand, then the thumb, it's their way."

They walked to the vehicle Jack had driven up in, a fine-looking truck. Jack explained he had bought it from a rich American who had it specially built for him after the war. It was a Studebaker Army reconnaissance car, converted for hunting game, and green in colour. At the rear, for standing and viewing, it was open but had a canvas top which could be pulled down and fastened to keep the weather out. It had 2 axles with double wheels at the rear to give traction in the wet ground. Frank commented that it was a fine-looking vehicle, Jack said he paid four hundred pounds for it, and it was Frank's to use on the farm.

"Jump in, Laddy", said Jack, "I'll give you the quick tour."

It was ten in the morning and all three of them were sweating already. "It's all right, Frank, it's because we are at the coast, the humidity is terrible, I know."

They started off, left the port area into what, Jack said, was the red-light district, even at this early hour the ladies were about, not a lot were African, there were a lot of light-skinned women, a lot of very attractive coloured girls. Uncle Jack explained that these were the leftovers of the Royal Navy, Army, and Airforce, and Merchant Seamen. None of them knew their fathers but were loved by their African mothers and forced to make a living selling themselves to support their families. The Europeans had created a new race in Africa with nowhere to go.

They drove on through markets selling all kinds of produce, bananas, fruit, green vegies, trinkets of ivory and gold. There were carpets, chickens, ducks, pigs, and geese of all sorts. Uncle Jack said "Lie back, Frank lad, it's three hundred miles to Nairobi. We'll stay the night at my hotel, spend a day in the city and head for the high country the next day." Frank was excited and knew Janet was going to love her new country.

"It's about five to six hours driving," Jack continued, "so you can give me a spell when I get tired."

They drove out of Mombasa and the people and buildings became more and more sparse, it was September and officially the start of the wet season, the road was dirt and freshly graded, so they were making good time. Frank looked up and saw there were clouds in the sky. The land was flat with hills in the distance. When they were about fifty miles out, game started to appear, the odd zebra, and wildebeest which Frank could identify. Three large antelopes ran across the road with beautiful horns, three twists on each horn, brown with white stripes. Frank asked Jack what they were, and Jack replied "Kudu bulls, a lot of them around. I should tell you, Frank, we are staying at the Norfolk, you'll meet a lot of the local landowners. Big meeting tomorrow night about security and this Mau-Mau business. The Army should have it cleaned up in a couple of months."

They were about halfway through their journey, when Jack asked if Frank would give him a breather, so Frank took over. The truck handled very well, and they continued their journey. Off in the distance, Jack pointed out a small herd of elephants. Frank thought this was wonderful, his first day in Africa and he had already seen all this game.

It was after four in the afternoon when Nairobi came into sight and dirt turned into tarred road. Jack gave Frank directions to the other side of town and down the main street to the Norfolk. "We have rooms in the main hotel. You will find it quite luxurious, just down here, Frank." Halfway down the road, Frank spotted a sign 'Norfolk Hotel" with an arrow indicating a right turn. He pulled into the driveway and into the most luxurious gardens he had ever seen, with tall palms either side of the driveway and beautiful garden beds full of exotic plants. Birds and butterflies flitted from flower to flower. He pulled up in front of the hotel where they were greeted by two Africans dressed immaculately in red tailed coats and dark trousers. They greeted each other and the head African opened Frank's door and said, "Good evening, Sirs". Jack recognised them both. The other African said, "Good evening, sir. I will take your bags straight to your suites."

"Thank you, Goodlove," Jack handed him a silver shilling.

"Thank you, sir, thank you."

The other's name was Solemon. Jack did the same and the African saluted smartly. "Your car will be taken care of, Sir."

They made their way to reception, where again they were greeted warmly; "Ah! Sir" said the African "Mr Munro," the Clerks name was Lovejoy, "Welcome back, Sir." Jack introduced Frank, "Ah, also Mister Monroe, Sir, there is a telegram for you, arrived this morning."

Frank opened it. It was from Janet, it read; 'Darling Frank, hope your journey ok, we all arrive in six weeks. Will give date later. Hope you are ready for this, expecting baby in and around July, love and miss you. Janet'. Frank's face beamed. Jack asked what's going on?

"Uncle Jack, I hope you have accommodation for us, Janet is expecting."

Jack took his hand and gave it a good shake, "Well done, Laddy, well done. I had a cottage built for you. It was finished just before I left."

A cottage, thought Frank, he had visions of a ramshackle home. It was all right for him, but would his wife and mother be okay. They made their way to their rooms. All their luggage had been unpacked and neatly put away in the closets. Jack shouted through, "Frank, get cleaned up, we will eat at eight." Frank replied, "OK, Uncle Jack, I will have to telegram Janet."

"That's fine, just tell them at reception, they will sort it for you."

Jack and Frank made their way to the dining room and sat at their table. Jack asked Frank if he had sent the telegram and Frank answered that he had and was looking forward to her arrival and happy about the good news. The waiter brought the menu, and both men ordered a steak, they settled down to eat and halfway through their meal the waiter brought over a note. Jack opened it. It read, 'all farmers and landowners are advised that a meeting is to be held tonight at ten in the main dining room. Signed Lord Asquit'.

"What's it about, Uncle Jack?"

"Ah, some meeting held by this Asquit, another long nosed chinless bastard from White Hall, never done a day's work in his life but we should hear what he has to say."

Just before ten, the men made their way to the hall. At the entrance stood a soldier. He opened the door and they entered. The hall was half full and Lord Asquit was mingling with the people. He saw Jack and made his way towards him. He extended his hand and greeted him. "Evening, Munro" he said in a low-pitched voice. Jack took his hand and replied, "That's 'Mr Munro' to the likes of you." Asquit was taken aback, "Sorry, old man, Mr Munro." Jack introduced Frank "ah" said Asquit, "you are the ex-RAF pilot." Frank replied "Yes, I was a pilot sir, and shook his hand. "Heard you were on your way. Come to give you uncle a hand, I heard."

"Yes, indeed, Sir, and looking forward to it."

"Well, welcome to Kenya young man, hope all turns out okay for you. We've had some bad news from up your way."

"Oh" said Jack, "and what would that be?"

"Well, you know the Bradys, they were all killed three days ago by this Mau-Mau crowd. Quite bloody. Brady, his wife, and both daughters. Their daughters were on school holiday from England, only been here three days."

Jack interrupted, "Christ," he said, "that's only fifty miles from my place."

Asquit went on, "it's been going on for some time but only among the local African tribes. These are the first whites to be attacked and probably won't be the last. The army are ramping up security in the area, so let's hope we can control it."

As they spoke, an army colonel walked over to Asquit and spoke "Excuse me, sir, the meeting is about to start."

Asquit took his chair and began. The meeting went on for two hours; detailing the security force efforts put in place and advice to farmers to improve security on their properties. Most of the atrocities had been made against local Africans. This was the first white-owned farm attack and had proved quite bloody. The family had been caught unawares as they sat down for the evening meal. Brady and his wife had been celebrating the return of their daughters. From what the investigation revealed, all three women had been brutally raped then hacked to death with pangas, and butchered. Some of the body parts were missing. The family dogs were also killed and all their livestock as well.

"God, lad, this is terrible. Let's hope the army nip this in the bud and get it over quickly."

"I hope so, Uncle Jack, I don't know what Janet and Mum will say when they hear about this".

The men went to bed, but Frank could not sleep. He had images of a broken-down cottage at the farm. What would Janet think about the situation. Had he made the right decision?

The next morning, the men rose early and made their way to the dining room. They ate a good breakfast. Jack paid the bill and gave Frank a nod. "Let's be on our way, lad".

The sun was just creeping over the horizon as they drove out of the hotel drive. There was a chill in the air, and the men smiled at each other as they drove to the outskirts of Nairobi and headed north-west towards the high country.

***

Chapter 2

Big Boy, Matengwi, was a huge Kikuyu who hated the white man for hanging his father for killing a Maasai, who had stolen two of his cattle. As far as Big Boy was concerned, his father had done no wrong. He joined the Mau-Mau only two years previously, having been recruited by a powerful headman. He had become very brutal, and it was now time to avenge his father. The group of nine made their way from the thick forest, eighteen miles from the Brady family farm.

They had been told by a farm labourer, a Mau-Mau recruit, that the young girls were also at home. All nine now stood at the far corner of the wire fence. It was eight in the evening, with a new moon, and only the crickets and small animals could be heard. They started to dig silently under the wire and made their way into the compound. They could hear music coming from the house and the occasional burst of laughter. They were all armed, Big Boy with an old Lee-Enfield rifle and three rounds of ammunition, the others with Pangas and short spears. All were barefoot and made not a sound as they made their way to the corner of the verandah.

The generator was switched off and only kerosene lamps had been lit. As they moved closer, Big Boy cocked the Enfield, instantly the four staffies were alert and rushed to defend their masters and their home. They were mother and father with two grown pups, two of the Mau-Mau were attacked by the staffies, and the commotion alerted the family inside. Old man Brady had his side arm instantly in his hand and ran to the front door. The dogs had ripped the legs of two of the Mau-Mau wide open, but the mother and her mate were soon hacked to death. The two youngsters were both beaten unconscious. Big Boy raised his rifle and waited for Brady to show himself. When he came through the door, he was shot in the shoulder and dropped his side arm. The Mau-Mau entered the home and found the three women cowering under the table. They were dragged out and stripped, all three stood naked in front of the Africans. Mrs Brady pleaded for the lives of her two daughters, she was struck across the head and dropped to the floor semi-conscious.

Big Boy gave instructions to his men to rape the girls, they all laughed as they drank the Johnny Walker Whisky they found in the sideboard. The first was the youngest, she was laid spread-eagled on the table and five of the Africans mounted her. She screamed with pain, then it was the second daughter. She fought bravely but stood no chance, her mother begged for mercy, then it was her turn.

When the Mau-Mau finished, Big Boy ordered his men to kill the family. Old Man Brady, badly wounded, tried to drag himself into the home. As he was beheaded with a powerful stroke from a huge Panga, the girls knew their fate was sealed and were quickly dispatched.

Big Boy gave instructions to his men, "cut out the hearts of the whites, we will eat them later in the forest. By doing this we will gain the strength of the white man".

They removed the hearts and put them in a canvass ruck sack, ransacked the house and took all the weapons they could find. As they left, one Staffie lay semi-conscious, but he had the scent of the Mau-Mau and especially, Big Boy. His name was Billie, and he would not forget that scent.

The following morning, the Africans returned to the compound. They had fled during the night when they heard the shot. When they entered the home, they found the Bradys all hacked to death, and the head boy gave instructions to fetch the police.

When the Police arrived, they could not believe the horror they were witnessing. One officer, a young Londoner, vomited and had to leave the scene. He sat on the verandah, holding his head when he noticed one of the dogs was still alive. It was Billie. He turned his head towards the officer and tried to stand but fell back.

The Londoner's name was Colin Brett. Colin made his way over to Billie, knelt and lifted the dog. Just as his commanding officer came over and said, "Colin, take him out the back and put him out of his misery."

Colin took Billie to the rear of the homestead and put him on the grass. He drew his .38 Webley and aimed at Billie. As he did so, Billie looked at him and Colin realised he could not do it. He fired a shot into the air and looked for a container to give Billie a drink and said, "I will be back for you soon, boy."

Billie drank well and over the next hour began to regain his strength and managed to sit and walk a short distance. He made it to the front verandah where his father, mother, and brother all lay dead. He could hear voices from within but now it was beginning to get dark, it had been nearly twenty-four hours since the big black man and the Africans had slaughtered his family and his masters.

No, Billie would not forget the scent or the voice of the big black man responsible for what had taken place.

Very soon, the constable returned, he gently lifted Billy and put him in the back of the Police Landrover.

***

Chapter 3

Frank was at the wheel while Jack slept. Benjamin, the house boy, slept in the back. It was dark now, nine in the evening and they had driven all day, with about another eighty miles to go, by Frank's calculations. The amount of game Frank had seen was astounding, wildebeest, zebra, kudu, impala, even a herd of elephant. Frank counted thirty in all. Now it was dark and only the green reflection of eyes from the side of the road could be spotted. Jack stirred and sat up. "Where are we?" he asked. Frank replied, "Somewhere in Kenya" and gave a chuckle.

"Pull over and let me drive, you take a nap."

Frank pulled over and parked. Jack told Benjamin to build a fire and make some tea, which he did. They sat just off the road on three camp chairs. They had brought a snack which they shared. Jack told Benjamin to refuel the truck from the jerry cans strapped in the back, then Jack spoke "I know exactly where we are, Laddie, another sixty miles and we will be home."

The night was warm, and the moon and stars shone brightly. The air was full of noises, crickets mostly, with the occasional grunt from lions, as Jack pointed out, and the distinctive whop, whop, whop, whop of the Zebra, probably escaping the Lion pride. "All right", said Jack, "let's pack up and move. I would have liked to stop at the local Police station and get the details about the Brady family but it's too late. I'll do that this week when I get the first chance."

They drove on through the night and Frank dozed off. He was jarred awake by a bump in the road, he looked out the open window and saw a sign, it read 'Honey Dew Ranch", Jack's place. Jack looked over at him, "Ah! You're awake. Well, at last we are home. That's my place just up ahead, your place is at the back about three hundred yards."

At the back of Jack's place, Frank made out a thick grove of trees as the stud swung around the corner and the lights caught the front of Jack's house. Frank had worried about what he was bringing Janet and his mother to, but he shouldn't have. Jack's house was absolutely magnificent from first glance, but it had gone dark, and no lights were visible as they pulled up out the front. He told Benjamin to hop out, get some lights on, and get into the kitchen and prepare something for the three of them.

Benjamin replied with a smile "Yes, Boss" and disappeared inside. The lights came on in pear shaped kerosene lamps. Frank looked toward the trees at the side of the house, there was little green eyes everywhere, all bouncing about. "Uncle Jack, what on earth are they?"

"Bush babies and owls, lad, you'll get used to them, they make a hell of a noise."

They climbed the front stairs and entered the open doors. Jack led the way to what, Frank thought, must have been the kitchen. At the far end stood a large black wood stove and oven, the house staff had kept it alight for their arrival. While they waited, Jack poured a whisky from a bottle of Johnny Walker, "Here, lad, have a dram while we wait for something to eat." He beckoned to Benjamin, "Here, you savage, pour yourself a drink. You've pinched half of it anyway."

Benjamin answered back "Ah! No boss, I don't pinch".

"Oh! So, what do you call it?" Benjamin did not reply.

It was late when Frank turned in. He slept well but was awake as the sun was just rising. He could hear noises coming from the kitchen. The lamps were still burning, and he could smell the kerosene in the air. There was a knock on the door, it was Benjamin. "Ah, Baas Frank, I have tea." Benjamin put the steaming hot mug on the bedside table and Frank thanked him. "Breakfast in half an hour, Boss." He left and closed the door behind him.

Frank rose and went outside to relieve himself. He couldn't find the toilet, so he walked to the perimeter fence. As he finished, he turned towards the house and looked, amazed, at the home. It was getting light now, and Frank realised that he couldn't take in the home in the dark when they first arrived. It was beautiful. Six wide steps led up to the verandah, it was mud plaster finish, painted white with pole uprights painted dark brown. The floors were oxblood colour, polished so you could see your face. The roof was thatched, and he could tell it was done by master thatchers, an art the Africans do so well. French doors led into the home and the internal beams of the high ceilings were exposed. It really was beautiful. Janet was going to love this.

Frank had only been in Kenya a few days, but he knew Africa was the place for him. Every African he saw was smiling. He'd never seen so many white teeth. Jack was up and sitting in the kitchen, drinking tea, and talking to the African staff, three in all. Jack introduced Frank. Benjamin, he knew, the other was an African girl, very shy, called Desciple. A strange name, thought Frank, the other was Webster. All were smiling and greeted Frank, then went about their business. "Sit down, Frank, and have some breakfast, then I'll take you round to your place. It's about three hundred yards over there." Jack pointed in the direction of Frank's home. They finished eating and rose from the table, "follow me, Laddie."

The men made their way to the path leading to Frank's home. It led through a thick grove of trees. It was still early, and quite cool, brightly coloured birds and butterflies flitted about in the branches, the birds calling to each other. A couple of minutes passed, and they broke out of the trees. About fifty yards away stood the home. Frank's jaw dropped, "My God," he said, "Uncle Jack, I don't know what Janet and mum are going to say. It's beautiful."

It was bigger than Jack's place, the same pole and Dagga construction with the most beautiful, thatched roof. The floor was black, the poles painted the same. They walked up the six stairs onto the wide verandah and entered the home. On the left were four large bedrooms on the right a huge living area, and at the back, the kitchen. At the rear was the bathroom and another bedroom. It had an outside toilet, twenty yards from the back verandah.

"My god", said Frank, "We'll be roughing it here, Uncle Jack."

 Jack laughed and told Frank to look around and get a feel for the place. "I'm off back to my place, come up when you're ready. Don't get lost in the forest."

Frank made his way to the far side of the house. He looked out across the view; the house was built on a slight hill and about one hundred yards away was a small dam. He could see ducks and geese on a small Island in the centre. This was heaven, what a place to bring up a family. Frank walked back inside to the lounge and sat down on one of the chairs, everything was beautifully constructed, cane and ratan chairs and lounges. In the centre of the main wall was a large dining room cabinet with front glass panels, on the right was a table-height cabinet made to match, with all the cutlery, plates, and serving dishes. All the furniture had small tags saying 'Singh Bros. Furniture Factory, Nairobi' with the address and phone number. Frank had heard the Indian community were great businesspeople and thought to himself, it must have cost Uncle Jack a pretty penny, and hoped he could live up to his uncle's expectations.

Frank spent two hours in the lounge, then rose and started to make his way back to Jack's place. As he looked out over the verandah, he could see a vehicle in the distance but too far away to make out what it was. It was headed down the road towards Jack's place. Frank jumped down the stairs and hurried along the path towards the house. The vehicle pulled up just as Frank reached the front steps. It was a Police vehicle, one of the new land rovers, the driver was a young constable, called Colin, accompanied by two Africans in police uniform. Jack was coming down the stairs and he and Frank greeted the young constable and the Africans. In the back, sitting next to the Africans was a black Staffordshire Bull Terrier.

"Good morning, Mister Munro."

Jack replied, "Hello, going out on patrol?"

"I am, indeed, Sir."

"I would like to introduce my nephew, Frank."

The young men shook hands and Colin said, "I heard you were on your way with the whole family."

Frank replied, 'Yes, indeed, they arrive in about six weeks. Can't wait, they will love it here."

Jack interrupted "You'll stay for lunch, Colin."

"Thank you, Mister Munro, it will give me a chance to tell you what' been happening in the area. I'm sure you heard about the Bradys."

"Yes, we did." Both men replied. Colin turned towards the Staffie. This is Billie, the sole survivor. When Billie heard his name, he gave a yap and his tail beat the side of the land rover like a drum. "He's had a hard beating but recovered well. The boss wanted to put him down, but I managed to save him. He's looking for a home, would you take him, Mister Munro?"

Jack looked at Billie perched with front legs on the edge of the Land Rover. "He's a sound dog, all bone and muscle."

Billie looked as if he understood every word.

Jack spoke first, "I know Billie, I knew the four of them. I'll take him, of course, I need a good dog."

As if by intuition, Billie was out and the first up the steps and into the house. He stopped and turned in the open door and barked as if to say, come on, I'm home. Jack called Benjamin, who came running. "Yes, Baas".

"Ben, get the dog something to eat."

"Yes, Sir. Come, Billie," but Billie wouldn't move. He was still wary of Africans. "All right, Ben, bring something here. He can eat in the lounge. Billie's the new member of the family".

The three men sat down to eat, and Colin began. "As you know, Mister Munro, we have had quite a few incidents in the last twelve months. Mostly Africans being murdered and mutilated, white farmers' stock being butchered, but the Brady incident is the most serious so far."

Jack interrupted "So, Colin, what are the police and army doing exactly?"

"Well, they have brought in two Army Battalions and stepped-up patrols in the areas affected, they have a specialist tracking unit on the trail. It looks as if they went into the forests and are holed up in there."

"Aye," said Jack, "Africa is on fire, lads. It's called Uhuru or independence for the Africans. Do you think we can contain it?"

"Well GHQ are confident it will blow over," said Colin, "but the Mau-Mau are a fiery lot, and it would appear they are being funded by the communist countries Russia and China."

Frank asked, "Do you think we have a future here?"

Colin answered first, "Hard to say, Frank".

Colin spoke for several hours, giving details of the army movements. "I've been told the army has moved in two battalions. One of the Buffs, the other one of the Guards Regiments. So far, they have had no results to the Brady Farm murders but have arrested many suspected Mau-Mau members who are being interrogated as we speak. In a couple of days, we should be getting some feedback. The interrogators are quite brutal, threating the suspects with water boarding, even castration, and I am told, making good on those threats. They have internment camps at the moment, three in all, housing about one thousand prisoners each. So, that gives you an idea of the size of the problem."

When Colin finished it was late evening, so Jack said he could stay the night and he agreed. His two African askari heard him agree and they beamed from ear to ear. So far, they had eaten well and knew the Munros would feed them well again.

* * *

Big Boy led his men into the forest, and they made their way deep into the dark interior. After about ten miles they stopped. He told his men to make a fire and lay out the spoils they had taken from the Bradys'. They obeyed quickly. They had three rifles and ammunition. One old army Sten Gun with one hundred rounds, numerous items of clothing, shirts, trousers, boots, and two handguns. Two of the group had to be left behind because of the savage dog bites but they were with the locals who would look after them.

The fire was burning well, and he instructed one of his men, the youngest, called Sikili, A Kikuyu, to open the canvas pack containing the hearts of the Brady family. "Now, Sikili, cut the hearts and roast them in the fire," instructed Big Boy. The young Kikuyu obeyed and placed the soft meat in the fire. When they had cooked for several minutes, Big Boy retrieved them and gave each of his men a share of the meat. "Now, eat, all of you."

The gang ate the hearts and gulped down beer and whisky taken from the Bradys. When they had finished, Big Boy outlined his plans. "Tonight, we sleep, tomorrow we meet a very important member of Mau-Mau. The most important John Mwangi, our future leader, he will lead us to Uhuru, freedom from the white devils who steal our land."

***

It had been a week since the Brady incident and now the army had become well organised. They had asked for volunteers from the white hunters in the area to contribute their skills in tracking the gang. Two had come forward, an Australian and an Englishman, both had expert trackers, three on each team. The Aussie called Harry Cann had stayed on after the war and made a remarkable reputation as being able to find anything his clients requested. His trackers were three young Maasai, all probably the same age, tall, all over six foot-two inches, slim if not downright skinny. Thay carried shields and spears, dressed only in loin cloth, and had a shoulder strap to carry a water flask.

The other, an Englishman, was called Wayne Frobisher, from Cornwall. His trackers were Wakamba tribesmen, also well built for tracking and they carried spears and shields but different from the Maasai, they were not as tall, and all wore ostrich plume headdresses to give the impression of height. All six had deep facial tribal scars, and looked magnificent, their black skins glistening in in the sunlight, but tribalism flared between them, and it was soon realised that they would have to be separated, or the next morning the army may have had no trackers.

The Aussie, Tin Cann, as he was known, would go with the 1st Battalion of the Buffs. Wayne would go with the Guards Battalion. The hunters briefed their men. Tin Cann began in Swahili. "Alright, you savages, for this job we will be hunting Kikuyu, a whistle went up, the head tracker, Matibi said, "The Kikuyu dogs will pay for this boss, what will be our reward?"

"Two cows per man."

A loud "AHH!!" from all three trackers. Cattle was everything to the Maasai. "We will catch them, Boss."

Wayne was the same to his men only the reward was different, "For yourselves and your families you will each receive one hundred silver shillings each."

The reply from the Wakamba was more subdued, "That is enough, Boss," said the head boy, all three nodded in agreement. The army were on the scene within twenty-four hours, but the hunters and trackers took two days to arrive. The army had made some headway and established the line of flight, it was northwest towards the mountains and their tropical forests.

The tactics they employed were brutal, beatings and electric shock treatment from a generator. Each village took its turn, one by one they eliminated who was not involved. The officers turned a blind eye to their men's butchery. They had established, from the exit in the fence at the Brady Farm, that at least one member of the group was badly injured evidenced by the blood spots and by the blood next to the staffies, so they were searching for a wounded man and on the third day they found him hiding in the grain hut.

He was dragged out, his injuries horrific, the dogs had ripped the flesh from his upper leg to the knee and it hung from his limb. Gangrene had set in the wound and maggots were crawling in and out of it. His other leg was also damaged. The headman was brought out, beaten, and thrown into one of the three-ton trucks. The wounded Mau-Mau's interrogation began brutally, a sergeant took a stick and as he pushed into the wound the Mau-Mau squealed in pain, "Alright, you black bastard, tell us what you know," he spoke through an interpreter.

The Mau-Mau spat at the sergeant and gave a vengeful look,

"All right, if that's the way you want it," the Mau-Mau screamed with pain for over an hour then fell silent.

The Sergeant reported to the company commander, who was drinking tea under a canvas flap, he was sitting in a canvas chair with several other officers in attendance. He looked up and said, "Well, sergeant, did you get what we need?" The sergeant replied, "Yes, Sir, the black bastards are heading towards the forest now."

"Now, Sergeant, you mustn't talk about the locals that way," he replied in a wonderful Oxford accent, "show a little respect now."

"Very good, Sir, do you want me to deal with the headman?"

"Yes, Sergeant, give him and his sons a good beating, and give the women and children the same."

"Very good, Sir."

The sergeant snapped to attention, saluted, about turned, and marched off smartly.

Tracking was impossible because of the local traffic and livestock had all but obliterated any traces, but the hunters had reached the forest and were skirting the edges. Tin Cann was the first to find evidence of where they had entered, about fifteen yards away, blown up in a tuft of grass, he spotted a cellophane packet, red and blue, written on it was 'Smiths Crisps'. This could only have come from one of the Mau-Mau gang. He picked it up and examined it carefully and decided, yes this must have come from the Bradys'. Old man Brady must have bought it in Mombasa or Nairobi for his girls when he picked them up from the boat.

He was carrying a small radio, issued to him by the army. Tin Cann switched it on, and it crackled into life. He spoke into the mouthpiece, "Hello Sunray, hello Sunray, this is team leader one, do you receive? Over."

A second passed, "Hello, Team leader, we are receiving you. Any news? Over."

"Yes, indeed", was the reply, "we have found what we think is the entrance point" and gave the details and location.

"Roger" came the reply "be at your location approximately one hour, over." Tin-Cann replied "We are pursuing on foot, will mark entrance point, over."

"Roger" came the reply, "will follow up with back up. Out."

Tin-Cann's Maasai Moran warriors were excited to get started. It would be easy as the locals seldom went far into the forest, most of their activity was concentrated on the outskirts cutting firewood. Tin-Cann gave the order, "Go, Moran", the Maasai, leapt into action with a whoop. "Now we need at least one left alive,"

Tin-Cann knew it would be hard to restrain them, the Moran took off, their maroon shukas billowing out behind them, spears held underarm for greater speed, Panga's flapping against their thighs. Tin-Cann knew it would be difficult to stay with them as he was carrying the radio and a .415 Rigby Heavy Rifle, and a water bottle the army had issued him with two red smoke grenades. He would struggle to keep up, but he was hard and fit. The Army had a light aircraft at the ready. As soon as any news came through, it would fly over the forest, looking for signs of red smoke.

***

Big Boy gave instructions to his men. They were all young and inexperienced. He had told them to sleep here tonight, and he would return tomorrow. Now he was off to meet John and a new man he did not know. His name was Dedan Omondi, a member of the Amubi clan, the largest of the clans. He was responsible for the armed conflict and many brutal murders of Africans. It was he who planned the Brady murders. It was dark as he left the makeshift camp. He carried the old Sten gun and ammunition and left the others with a selection of four firearms, but they were inexperienced in the use of such weapons. He travelled about ten miles deeper into the forest but became disoriented so decided to stop and rest until dawn.

Tin-Cann and his Maasai stopped at last light, and he spoke softly to his Moran "Well, my askari, how close are we?"

"We are close, master, but we must stop until the sun comes up". Less than a mile away the Mau-Mau band were all asleep. "In the morning, we shall have them", said the lead Maasai.

***

The sun was beginning to rise, and within ten minutes beams of light were filtering through from the top of the forest canopy, it shone on the bright steel of the Moran's spears. A distant screech from a forest bird was the only sound to be heard. Tin-Cann spoke and gave instructions to his warriors, "Alright, you blood thirsty savages", he spoke in Swahili, all the Maasai smiled, wide grins at the mention of blood, "take off, the three of you, slowly, silently, when we are close, tell me."

"Yes, master".

"Yes, and remember, at least one must live."

They advanced in single file for about twenty minutes, it was quite light now and they could see each other clearly. Suddenly, the lead scout stopped and kneeled to the ground. Tin-Cann moved forward and spoke to his Moran. "Are we here?" he asked.

"Yes, master, over there by the large fallen tree in the clearing."

The Mau-Mau had not yet risen. Tin-Cann gave instruction with hand signals, all understood. They had done it so many times before on the hunt for elephant, buffalo, rhino, and lion. They spread out in line abreast about ten yards apart. Two Maasai on Tin-Cann's left, one on his right, spears were now at the shoulder, shields held to the chest. The last Maasai to move stood on a twig that snapped loudly, loudly enough to awaken two of the Mau-Mau. They shouted at their brothers to rise. Instantly they were awake and rose, startled, but it was too late, with blood curdling screams the Maasai charged.

All seven Mau-Mau were now standing. One fired a .38 revolver into the air, six shots. He fired until the hammer just clicked on empty cylinders. Tin-Cann raised the heavy Rigby and shot him in the chest, it threw the Mau-Mau into the air and knocked him back ten feet. As if sensing each other, the three Maasai let go their spears, all three met their targets: the chests and stomachs, and they went down making screaming and gurgling noises. The fourth Mau-Mau raised the Lee-Enfield and fired a shot but could not reload, his inexperience cost him his life. The Maasai drew their Pangas, razor sharp. The Mau-Mau raised the rifle to protect himself but a swift strike from the Panga severed his right hand, only his thumb remained. He lost his grip and the Maasai struck again saying, "you must die, you Kikuyu dog", and spilt his skull in two.

Two remained, Tin-Cann rushed forward to restrain his men, "Stop now, Askari, stop", but their blood was up and there was no stopping them. One Mau-Mau tried to run but the Maasai had retrieved their spears, and he was hit by two in the back, the third only missing its mark because he fell forward. The last survivor was screaming on the forest floor. Tin-Cann got to him first, "We need this one, Moran, if you wish to kill more Kikuyu, let him live."

The Maasai obeyed but poked him with their spears and taunted him mercilessly. Tin-Cann pulled the pin from the smoke grenade and threw it five yards to his front. It made a popping noise and red smoke billowed skywards and sideways. It was minutes before it reached the canopy and escaped into the sky above. He switched on the radio, and it crackled into life, "Hello, Sunray, this is team one, over."

"Go ahead, team leader, over."

"Seven Mau-Mau accounted for, one still alive." The light plane could be heard in the distance as it spotted the red smoke.

"Team leader, we have your location, remain at your loc we should be there by mid-day over".

"Roger, Sunray, out."

The Maasai had failed to see the tracks leading out of the camp. They were still jubilant and busy humiliating their captive.

Big Boy had slept most of the night and woke at dawn. He was busy relieving himself when he heard the shots. Instantly he realised what had happened, he pulled up his trousers and took off through the forest. He had to get to John and Dedan Omondi. They would ensure his safety. No-one knew his identity. He exited the forest late that evening and met the locals sympathetic to his cause. They gave him water and food and led him to a headman's Kraal, where he was made welcome. All the elders in the area were called to a great beer drink and celebration of his escape from the British. John Mwangi and Dedan Omondi were both present and they began to out-line plans to rid their lands of the British forever. It was going to be quite brutal, and they all drank beer and ate fresh roasted meat.

***

The army arrived just before mid-day with two Special Branch Officers in tow. Tin-Cann was the first to speak, "Morning. Over here." He led them to where they Mau-Mau were. The Police Officers cuffed the one survivor and bagged his head with a canvas bag. He had a few bumps and bruises from his captors but managed to stand. They examined the six corpses, one had deep festering dog bites on both legs, one exposing the bone. Tin-Cann asked the question, "How did he manage to get this far?"

"Alright, Mr Cann," was the reply, "thanks for your help. We'll take it from here. Mr Frobisher is waiting to congratulate you at the edge of the forest. Take six cattle as promised from that Kraal where they holed up last. The headman won't be needing them."

As Tin-Cann rounded up his Askari, he could see the army lads putting the six bodies onto litters. He and his men made their way back through the forest to where they entered. It was a half-run, half-walk and in four hours they saw the exit. Waiting at the edge was Wayne Frobisher. His Askari were not with him, he had left them back at his transport to avoid a shit-fight between the rival tribesmen. He extended his hand and said, "Trust an Aussie to get in on the ground floor, well done Tin-Cann, well done. I heard you got them all, but I don't think this is going to be the end. This is just the beginning of the end."

"Well, I hope you're wrong, Wayne, but I am inclined to agree with you."

"Well, I must be off, got some yanks landing in Mombasa in three days' time, want some elephant, they say." The men shook hands again, Tin-Cann said "Till next time then." Wayne nodded.

***

Frank had been at the farm for a week now and Jack had given him the run down and the guided tour. He had introduced him to Tony, the workshop manager, earlier on and Tony had taken an instant liking to him. The ranch's main crops were maize, coffee, tea, and wheat. He also had a dairy herd of one hundred and fifty cows and two thousand head of beef cattle. He had river frontage on two boundaries, so water was plentiful. Jack told Frank that maize was his best earner because the Africans made a paste with gravy which they all relished. They called it Mealie Meal. They also made bread. Jack had done well in the nearly forty years he had been on the land. Only twice did the locust come and clean him out but he quickly recovered, three times the Rinder Pest got into his cattle caught from the wildebeest herds that migrated each year, but he had organised raiding parties to chase the wildebeest west, away from his herds on the other side of the river. The barrier seemed to work, and he hadn't had a problem for fifteen years now. Frank's first stop was the machine shop where he met Tony Johnson, he was a brilliant mechanic and taught the Africans how to maintain and service the fleet of trucks, tractors, and other machinery. He owned a big dog called Rufos Milo. No one knew what breed he was, but he had a fantastic nature with big furry face and a tail that never stopped wagging. Tony had rescued him from the side of the road when he was just a pup, all skin and bone. Tony said he was lucky the Hyena's didn't get him. That was six years ago, and they had been inseparable ever since. Frank got on well with the Africans and Jack had assigned one young man as his guide. His name was Elijah and he never stopped grinning. Jack had issued Frank with a .3006 Garand rifle and an expensive 12 gauge shot gun and told him it was alright to shoot for the pot. The time passed quickly, and clouds were building, the rains would come soon.

***

Chapter 4

Janet and Rita were making their last preparations to leave. Rosie had her crate and was aware something was afoot. Her tail never stopped bashing against what was left of the furniture, and she wouldn't settle down. On the last day, Janet's father, George, and Janet's mum arrived with the Austin Truck and loaded the suitcases and Rosie's crate in the back. In the back seat were Janet's three sisters, all chuckling with excitement. Then Rosie was loaded, the two elderly women sat up front and Janet, although pregnant, had to be content siting in the rear but it had a seat just for her. It was mid-morning and the boat train left at four. That would give them plenty of time for goodbyes. James and Marge from the pub promised to be there along with a whole lot of Janet's friends from the hospital. They drove off but stopped at the cemetery to allow Rita to say her goodbyes. She had a small bunch of flowers for her son and husband, and they let her go in alone. She was only gone for ten minutes and when she returned, they could all see that she had been crying and couldn't talk for some time. They just let her be. They left Gullane behind and made their way along the coast road, it seemed longer this time and they wound their way through the small villages for about forty minutes, then they hit the outskirts of Edinburgh with its stone buildings. They could see the castle now, below was Waverly Station, and they followed the signs: Boat train passengers and baggage straight on. They pulled in next to the baggage compartment and could see a long queue of people and vehicles waiting to unload and board. They waited until a guard with a list came to meet them. "Name please," he said rather gruffly. Janet answered, "The Munros, for Kenya."

"Ah, ok, two ladies, one dog, plus baggage. Please offload onto that trolley and we will load you. As soon as that's done, please make your way down the platform. This is your carriage and seat numbers." The baggage was loaded in no time at all, but Rosie didn't look happy, so, Janet opened the door and gave her a pat. The guard also gave her a pat, "good girl, it's going to be alright," so, Janet decided he wasn't really that grumpy. They walked down the platform, and toward the farewell committee. The majority were women, all crying and determined to hug Janet and Rita. One of Janet's best friends was a Newcastle girl called Liz Craig, a doctor, a little older than Janet, and a brilliant surgeon for her age. When she heard she was off to Africa, she couldn't stop asking her, "when you get there, let me know of any openings for me, please, Janet." And Janet made a solemn promise she would. Liz was married to a Scotsman, an engineer who specialized in building bridges. They had met at university, and he was also keen to get any news. Janet glanced across at the news stand, on the billboard it read, *Kenya unrest, Army called in to Quell Mau-Mau trouble.* Janet thought to herself, what on earth is Mau-Mau? So, she walked over and bought a paper, she would save it for later and read it on the train. James Gillespie and his wife Marge were deep in conversation with Rita and Janet's Parents, Janet and her sister were all in tears. When the call came over the Tanoy, it was a quarter to four. It came; "all aboard for London and Tilbury". The train was full to the brim. It would only stop twice, Carlisle for coal and water, then Birmingham for the same. Rita and Janet climbed aboard, her tears had left her make-up running and she patted her eyes with a handkerchief.

"Last call, all aboard." Then they could hear the doors being slammed shut, one after the other.

"Stand Clear," and everyone moved away from the train. There was a short silence, then a loud whistle and they were off, everyone was waving franticly and, as they pulled away, Janet wondered if she would ever see Edinburgh or any of her friends again.

The train picked up speed as it left Edinburgh and Rita and Janet settled down for the journey. The compartment had eight seats, the girls had the window seats; the other six seats were occupied by a husband and wife and their four children. All the children were very well behaved. After half an hour they plucked up courage to introduce themselves. The man spoke first, his name was James, and his wife, Elsie, the four children just sat there, aged between six and twelve. He was with the railways and was on a five-year contract and very excited about Africa. Janet explained to Elsie that she was three-and-a-bit months pregnant, and her husband was already in Kenya and really enjoying it. Elsie's kids were becoming restless, so she ordered them into the companion way so they could play outside, they obeyed instantly, excited to meet other kids at play. The time passed slowly, and Janet nodded off and slept until jolted awake by the train, they were at Carlisle.

She and Rita decided to stretch their legs and stepped out onto the platform and walked towards the baggage car, the door was open, the guard leaning against it smoking a pipe. He recognised them and said, "Good evening, come to check on the lady? She's fine, just filled up her water bowl." Rosie was so glad to see them, so they asked the guard if they could put her on her lead. He agreed, "just for fifteen minutes, then I have to lock up again." It wasn't long before they were back on the train.

It was about nine in the evening when they reached Birmingham, the same routine, then on to the next stop: the boat train. The women began to feel excited. Janet had forgotten about the newspaper folded up in her bag. An hour passed and she remembered the headlines, she pulled the paper from her bag and began to read. 'Mau-Mau uprising in Kenya' and it went on to outline what had been happening. She read on; the news came as a shock as Frank had not mentioned any of this. She decided not to dwell on it as lots of people were being murdered every day elsewhere, and Frank and Uncle Jack both knew what they were doing. It didn't take long to board the ship and they were led to their cabin by a very nice young man who couldn't have been older than sixteen. They gave him a small tip, he thanked them, turned, and left. The cabin was small but comfortable; the ladies began to unpack and settle in; the ship was due to leave first thing in the morning. It was November when they sailed out of the Thames. Rita and Janet stood at the rail, a lot of the other passengers were there also, there was a lot of shouting and as they left the mouth of river. The tugs pulled away and they were on their own. The weather was bitterly cold, and the women remarked to each other how they were looking forward to warmer weather. They had been told the Mediterranean was beautiful.

***

Chapter 5

Dedan Omondi and Big Boy had been busy for two months now, recruiting and intimidating local tribesmen and their families into joining the Mau-Mau. Their tactics were brutal, and refusal was met with torture, even death. Victims were tied and thrown onto fires, hands and feet were cut off. The women and children were also victims, so far, they had recruited over one thousand Kikuyu and spilt them into over twenty cells numbering fifty plus per cell. Big Boy had been ordered to take two parties of nearly one hundred men and kill an elderly farmer, Ron Blake. Ron was in his seventies; he went out each evening with his African looking for game to feed his staff. As he slowed to cross a dry creek bed, Big Boy ran out of hiding and shot the old man in the upper body, only wounding him. He was hastily set upon by the gang with Panga's and cut to pieces as well as his three loyal Africans. The gang took off into the night. It was three days before he was found, and the hyena's had got to him first. All that was left was blood and some clothing. The army did their best, but it was the start of the rains and the spoor had been washed away but they knew the gang must have come from the thick forest. What they needed was intelligence on numbers and movements, special branch had managed to gain information from the man taken in the forest by Tin-Cann. He revealed the name of Big Boy and a description and the name of John Mwangi but he had died under the brutal interrogation by the Police and army.

The army and police continued patrolling and doing sweeps through suspect villages, detaining many tribespeople, and forcing them into detention camps. Some holding more than one thousand at a time. Still, Big Boy and Omondi eluded the security forces. Big Boy was becoming overconfident and was tasked to seek a job at one of the farms. His job was to subvert the local labour force and gain their trust by either promises of money or ownership of the farm they worked on. Many of the Africans were happy and it would be difficult to convince them. The target farm was Honeydew Ranch.

Big Boy walked into the farm workshop with his two companions and asked to see the boss. One of the Africans went to call boss Johnson. Tony came out and asked what they wanted. Big Boy replied, "We are looking for work, Boss."

"Ok", said Tony, "can any of you drive a tractor. Big Boy immediately responded, "Yes, Boss, I used to drive the tractor at the airfield, cutting grass."

"And which airfield was that?" asked Tony.

"At Nairobi, Sir, long time ago."

"Ok, but you will have to speak to Mr Munro, you two look strong enough. You can work at the brick factory. Ok?"

"Yes," was their reply.

"You will get three shillings a week, a bed, and rations." Their faces beamed as one of the farm hands led them away to their quarters. They had been living in the forest in rough conditions, now they had a bed, money, and good food.

"Ok," said Tony, "What's your name?"

"My name is Samson, Sir."

Well, you're big enough for a Samson. The main house is up there, you can just see the roof. Go on over, I will phone Mr Munro and tell him you're on your way."

"Thank you, Master," replied Big Boy. Tony just got off the phone when Frank and Benjamin drove up in the stud. Frank jumped out and greeted Tony, "Morning, Tony. All well. Just been down at the maize fields. Not that I know much yet, but it looks like a good crop. We'll get the women into the fields in a week.   They can start picking before the rains hit in earnest."

"Yes, you're right. I've got the kettle on. Fancy a brew?"

"Too right," said Frank, "never turn down tea."

***

Billie, the staffy, had settled in very well and Jack and the staff were overfeeding him, and he had put on weight. He was heavy boned and well-muscled. A big staffy, he probably weighed in at around seventy pounds. He was sunning himself at the back of the house, lying on his back, legs in the air.

Big Boy had nearly made it to the house, Jack was waiting on the front verandah. They greeted each other. Jack spoke first, "So, you can drive a tractor, can you?"

"Yes, boss," was the reply.

"Ok," said Jack "if you can do the job, we'll take you on," and Jack began to outline his pay.

A slight breeze was blowing onto the back of the homestead and drifting through the house. All of a sudden, Billie was alert, the breeze carried a scent he could never forget. He rolled over and sprang to his feet. Making no sound, he bounded up the back verandah and skidded on the polished floor. He regained his footing and took off again. Jack was unprepared for the savagery of the attack by Billie. Both men were looking away, toward the workshop, when Billie sprang from twenty feet away. This was him, the big black man who had murdered his family. Billie hit Big Boy with all his force, gripping him in vice-like jaws on the shoulder. He bit deep and ripped muscle and half the shirt from Big Boy's back. Big Boy screamed in agony and turned to run, but Billie had him again by the buttocks. Jack did his best to restrain him, he shouted to Benjamin to bring the dog chain. Tony and Frank heard the commotion and sprang to their feet and began to run towards the house. Jack had Billie by the collar, but Big Boy's wounds were serious. A chunk of flesh had been torn from his shoulder and his arm was limp. His trousers had been ripped off and he was naked except for a piece of shirt. They managed to chain Billie to the verandah post and Jack told Benjamin, "Bring my gun from the drawer, here's the key." Benjamin obeyed, Billie was pulling with all his weight on the chain, and it snapped. In he went again for the attack, taking Big Boy by the leg. Big Boy's screams were of agony and fear. Now Frank and Tony had arrived and looked on in horror. Again, they managed to restrain Billie, but he would not settle. He had the death of this African etched in his brain. "What in God's name happened?" asked Tony.

"Don't know, just went crazy," replied Jack, "I'll have to shoot him. Get that shirt, cover the African as best you can." Tony picked up the shirt as Jack took aim at Billie. He cocked the Webley .38 and was about to pull the trigger when Tony ran over and pulled the weapon away. It went off, missing Billie. "Wait, Jack, look at this." He showed Jack the shirt that Billie had ripped from the African. He pointed out the collar to Jack, "look at this," on the inside of the shirt was the name D Brady. Signed "the Tailors, Nairobi" neatly embroidered on a patch and stitched into the inside of the shirt. "Christ," said Jack, "this must be one of the Mau-Mau bunch responsible for the murders. Where else would he get this shirt? Big Boy lay on the ground very badly wounded, screaming in agony, Billie was still trying to get at him.

"Tony, will you please take Billie inside?" asked Jack "Lock him in the rear bedroom till he settles. Jack gave him a pat and said, "you're a good boy, Billie," and Tony dragged him away. All three of the men were carrying side arms because of the threat of ambush. Tony shouted to Jack, "There's another two down there, they'll be involved as well."

"Ok, tie this bastard up as best you can. Frank, you stay here and look after this one, get on the blower, get the police out here asap, they'll want to speak to him." Frank ran inside and phoned the police. When he returned, Jack and Tony had Big Boy well trussed up. "What did they say?" asked Jack. "Be here within the hour, they are patrolling in the area."

"Good. Alright, Tony, let's go." The men ran off towards the workshop. Jack wasn't a young man but had kept himself lean and fit. They arrived at the workshop. Rufus Milo was waiting for Tony, He had been down at the African compound, sniffing around the girls to see if he could sire any more litters but with no luck. Now Tony spoke to Jack, "We should be able to surprise them, Jack, they have no idea what's been going on. They called the boss boy and asked them where the two had gone. He answered, "They are in the old huts at the far end".

"Come with me," and the boss boy obeyed.

"What is wrong, Sir?"

"Those two are bad ones, we need to take them, come, Rufus." Rufus fell in at Tony's side. It wasn't long and they reached the compound, "where are they?" Jack asked.

"Over there, Sir."

The two were seated at a fire eating Sudza and gravy, both men drew their firearms at the same time. The Mau-Mau had their backs to them, Tony fired a shot into the air, both Africans sprang to their feet and turned, "Stay where you are, both of you."

"What's wrong, Boss?" asked the smallest of the pair.

Rufus Milo growled at them. Tony told him to sit, he obeyed immediately.

"You know what's wrong. The two of you are Mau-Mau." The men both denied the accusation, "both of you shut up, come with us," shouted Tony. They obeyed and were led back to the workshop. When they arrived, they were bound and made to lie face down on the floor. It was thirty minutes before the Police arrived. The Landrover screeched to a halt in a cloud of dust. Colin and another white officer jumped out. Jack didn't recognise him, Colin shouted over to Jack, "What have you got for us, Mr Munro?" but before Jack could start, he introduced the other officer. "Mr Munro, Tony, this is Arthur Trait, Special Branch."

"Nice to meet you both," and Jack began describing the morning's events. They had three African Constables seated in the rear of the Landrover, Colin told them to take their hand cuffs and cuff the two prisoners but give them a bit of clean and brush-up first, the meaning was clear - a good kicking. The constables laid into them and the two screamed and screamed until it was over.

"Right," ordered Colin, "cuff them in the Landrover".

They jumped into the stud and drove up to where Big Boy was lying. He made no sound as Frank walked over. "Hello, Colin." Colin said hello and introduced Arthur. They shook hands, then Arthur turned and walked over to Big Boy, poked him in the ribs with his boot, "so, he's a Big Kaffir, isn't he? And this is the shirt?" He looked at it, "bit damming evidence, this, isn't it?" He kicked Big Boy, but no reply came, he was too badly wounded.

"Okay, we suspected there were nine at the Brady place, we only got eight. We interrogated a captive and he said there was nine, he also gave us a description, and this one certainly fits the bill. We have fingerprints so we'll print him and see what comes of it. We'll take him and patch him up and let you know what happens. We better be off, the sooner we get him looked at the better."

Big Boy was bundled into the stud and Frank was ready to drive off when Colin said to Jack, "Mr Munro, please give Billie a big thank you and a pat from us." Frank took off with the two police officers and Big Boy and headed to the workshop. They pulled up alongside the Landrover and threw Big Boy in the back. He groaned in agony, not from the pain, but from the realisation of what was about to happen. Frank bid farewell to the police officers and wished them well. Colin shouted back, "Will keep you updated."

Frank drove back to Jack and pulled up at the steps, Tony and Jack had disappeared inside. Frank ran up the steps and found the men talking in the lounge. As Frank walked in, Jack turned to him and said, "Well lad, it's been an eventful day, we'd better let Billie out." Jack called to Benjamin and told him to unlock Billie. Billie came out like a steam train straight to the front of the house where he had left the Big African, but he was gone. He sniffed the ground where Big Boy had lain, he smelt the blood and lifted his leg. He took off and did a 360-degree investigation around the house, the big African had gone. Billie bounded up the stairs and ran to the lounge, the three men took turns patting him and he went from one to the other again and again, then Jack shouted to Benjamin, "Ben, will you make up something to eat, we are going to have a whisky, if there's any left that you haven't stolen."

"Ah! No, Boss, I don't steal."

"Oh! It must be the mice then."

"Yes, Baas, it's the mice," Benjamin replied.

Jack shouted at him, "and don't be bloody cheeky."

"No, Baas."

The men laughed loudly and drank their whisky. They all ate and drank, and the conversation went on late into the night until finally Tony stood up and said, "Good night" and stumbled down the stairs. Frank grabbed him by the arm and said, "Come on, Mate, I'll take you home." They climbed into the Stud, it was pitch black until Frank turned on the lights and started the engine. There was a deep rumble in the sky, they noticed huge black storm clouds sweeping about and Tony said, "Well, Frank, looks like the rains are here, it's been a very eventful twenty-four hours, mate."

Frank agreed and drove on. He was at Tony's place in ten minutes and, on the step, was Rufus Milo, waiting for his master. He barked and wagged his tail as Tony climbed the stairs. The house was dark, so Frank kept the lights trained on the house until Tony put some lights on, then he drove off into the night and home.

***

Janet and Rita were sunning themselves on deck as they entered the Mediterranean. It was a beautiful morning and they had just finished breakfast. Janet turned to Rita and said, "I am going down to get Rosie." Rosie came on deck in the morning for one hour and the same in the afternoon. They also saved a snack from breakfast for her, usually half a bacon roll and something from the lunch table. Both women enjoyed shipboard life but were keen to reunite the family. Rita met some of the older passengers for Bridge and Canasta at ten in the morning and she and Janet got into the Bingo in the evening at around nine.

Janet would sneak down to the hold and fetch Rosie. Well, she thought she was sneaking, but the crew knew what was going on and, although officially not allowed, they all turned a blind eye. Rosie was always ready, sitting, waiting, tail beating against the side of her box. Janet would say, "Shh! Rosie," and open her door, put on her collar and lead, and sneak her up to the cabin. At around five in the morning Janet returned her to the hold.

They reached Port Said and entered the Suez Canal. It was early in the morning, and the sun was out. The women stood at the rail, looking out at the sand dunes, and chatting to the other passengers. Once through the canal, they entered the Red Sea, it was beautiful, not a cloud in the sky and the sea a beautiful blue. Dolphins played at the front of the ship and flying fish took off, skimming across the surface of the water. It was only another three days to Mombasa and the women were excited to be back on land and to get their lives back into order.

***

Chapter 6

Frank had been busy doing his share on the farm. The rains had started in earnest, but they had managed to get the harvesting done on time. Uncle Jack said he was very pleased with the numbers he had come home with from the yield of maize. They were still picking coffee but that also looked good. The herdsmen were bringing four hundred head of prime beef cattle in and were corralling them down near the workshop except for about fifty head, they were about three miles away. Jack was a bit worried, because sometimes the odd lion would kill one or two.

Janet and Rita would be arriving in four days, so preparations were being made to drive to Mombasa. Frank didn't want to leave too late in case something came up to delay them, like a breakdown or washouts on the roads. So, they would leave tomorrow afternoon, spend the night in Nairobi, then onto Mombasa the next day and they arranged to stay overnight in Mombasa and meet the ship the following day.

Frank was hardly able to contain himself, it had been two months since he'd seen Janet and he hadn't slept for two days, so Jack was forced to do most of the driving. They stayed the night at the Norfolk as usual. All the Africans were happy to see the Munros and greeted both men with huge smiles. "Welcome back to the Norfolk, Sirs, welcome." Jack and Frank thanked them and tipped them as was their custom. Jack took Frank into the bar and made sure he had enough drink to ensure he got a good night's sleep. The next morning, they were up early, Benjamin took the bags to the stud, while they had breakfast. It was just after six when they left Nairobi and drove onto the Mombasa Road. It was slow going because of the rains. The road was full of potholes and corrugation. The sun was up, but the sky was grey and dark blue as the thunder clouds swirled about. They had the canvas cover up on the Stud, ready for the next downpour.

***

The night before Janet and Rita arrived in Mombasa, the ship ran into a terrible tropical storm, half the ship's population was down with sea sickness, and Rosie was bounced about in her box because the girls hadn't managed to fetch her. Janet and Rita were both violently sick, but it was beginning to subside, and they made their way on deck where they could see bright lights flickering on the horizon. It was raining and the rain had taken the sting out of the tropical heat. Janet asked one of the crew how long it would be before they made landfall and dock. "Ma'am" he replied, "another twelve hours."

Sure enough, as the dawn broke, they could see a small boat making its way towards the ship. The same crewman came over and said, "See, ladies, the pilot boat, it won't be long now," and he pointed towards the shore. Janet looked out and could see the outline of a large stone structure, it looked very old, that must be Fort Jesus, she thought. Frank had described it, and she knew she wouldn't be far from Frank now and a tear crept from the corner of her eye. It seemed like a lifetime since they were parted. As Fort Jesus came closer and closer it seemed to take on a sinister appearance. The sound of the engines and the noisy chatter of the passengers could be heard as they passed below its walls, the ancient cannons were clearly visible, and they knew there was not far to go. It was high tide as they pulled alongside and the crew and the men ashore pulled the long mooring line into place and secured the ship, both women shielded their eyes and tried to make out their men. Suddenly, Janet yelled out, "Look, mum, over there, both of them are standing with that black man." Neither of the women had seen a black man before, now they were everywhere. They could hear a lot of noise below, scraping and banging, then holes appeared in the side of the ship and gangways were wheeled up into them. Over the loudspeaker a crewman could be heard, "all passengers ready to disembark, make your way to the bottom deck".

As it was high tide, the ship sat high against the wharf. Neither Frank nor Jack had seen the women and they started to pace up and down the side of the ship trying to spot them, but they had taken their hand luggage and disappeared below decks. People were everywhere, pushing and shoving, but eventually they managed to get to the top of one of the gangplanks, where a crewman helped them step up, said goodbye, and wished them luck.

They were spotted by Frank who ran to the bottom of the gangplank. He grabbed Janet and lifted her into the air, carried her away from the ship, put her down and drew her close, then kissed her. Not a word had been spoken, then it all came out.

Frank went first, "God, how I have missed you, sweetheart" and kissed her again.

Now Rita stood next to them, she spoke, "What about me, then, have you missed me?"

"Oh, mum, it's so good to see you both here safe and sound."

Then Jack got into the mix, "Well, welcome to Kenya you two," and they both gave him a hug and kiss on the cheek. "Right, Benjamin, this is Misses Munro, times two."

"Yes, Baas, pleased to meet both Madams, Sir." Jack introduced Ben.

"Ben, take the bags to the Stud, we must do the paperwork."

"Yes, Baas."

The ladies had passports at the ready, but the line was a mile long, so they decided to take a walk for half an hour. When they returned, they decided that they'd made the right decision, as the people had mostly disappeared. When they reached the front, they were welcomed by the Customs man and quickly ushered through.

"Baggage is that way, over to your right." Jack and Frank knew the way and the four of them made their way to the office. Benjamin had learned how to drive and now followed on to the office in the Stud. He arrived first and pulled up close to the door, looking very proud of himself. The clerk was at the front desk and asked for the paperwork, Frank handed it to him, and the clerk took it and said, "Ah! You have a dog with you, Sir, all animals are off loaded first, so she should be here. I'll go and look. Rosie was right at the back and very nervous, wondering who all these black people were. The clerk came down and looked at the black Labrador, "Ah," he said, "you must be Rosie. There are people looking for you." At the sound of her name, she barked and wagged her tail.

"Well, my girl, a little wait till you're checked over, then you can go," and she settled down to wait. The men and ladies were talking excitedly about the baby and the time they had ahead, about the rains and the crops, about the game and what a wonderful life they looked forward to in their new country. They laughed, Frank quite loudly. Rosie's eyes opened wide. There it was again, no mistake, she knew that laugh, she rose up on her front legs and listened, yes, there were women's voices too, she gave a loud bark and another, loud enough for them all to hear, then Frank shouted, "Rosie, my girl, is that you?"

It was, it was her master, she scratched at the wire of her box, barking, and howling until Frank asked the clerk if he could go and get her. "Yes, of course, Sir, make sure you put her on a lead." Janet held her lead, and they quickly made their way to the rear of the customs shed. They spotted her and made their way to her side, undid the lock on the door, and out she sprang, howling and whimpering. She ran in circles round them both, then Frank said, "Now settle down, old girl, take it easy." They both knelt and gave her a hug. This seemed to work but not for long. She started again, "Now settle down, girl, settle down."

Janet managed to get her lead on and led her to the large open door, Rita and Jack were also given a greeting, she remembered the old man from long ago, when she was just a pup. The vet came over and gave her a clean bill of health. They thanked him and made their way to a trolley standing next to the Stud, it was their baggage, not a lot, just the keepsakes from times gone by and some cutlery and crockery passed down through the family. Frank's war photos of he and Ian, and the wedding photos. Jack had wandered off to the other side of the customs shed and was admiring three brand new black Mercedes Benz motor cars which had just been offloaded from another small ship. It was a Dutch ship, and on the stern, it had S.S. Messa, Antwerp. As he walked around inspecting the Mercedes, he noticed a tall, slim, blond-haired gentleman making his way towards him, he was accompanied by a very beautiful young woman, both were immaculately dressed in light khaki safari suits. When they got to within earshot, the man greeted Jack with a good afternoon.

Jack responded, "Good afternoon to you both," and asked, "are these three beauties yours?"

"They are, indeed, Sir. They are for the German embassy in Nairobi."

He spoke with a slight accent, "let me introduce myself, my name is Klaus Benz, and this is Ingrid, my wife." Jack extended his hand and they both shook and then to Ingrid, who smiled a beautiful smile, Jack said, "I am pleased to meet you, my name is Jack Munro. I am a farmer up in the highlands. My nephew and I have just picked up his wife and mother, just arrived from Scotland".

"Ah," said Klaus, "very nice." As they spoke, Frank and the two ladies appeared around the corner of the shed. Frank shouted, "So, there you are, Uncle Jack."

"Yes," replied Jack. He introduced them and Frank picked up that they were German.

"So," said Frank, "you are German?"

"Yes," replied Klaus, "I am, but my wife, Ingrid, she is from Austria." Frank had only met a handful of Germans, mostly pilots and aircrew shot down over Britain and captured. He was apprehensive about a lengthy conversation, but Janet saved the day and fell into conversation with Ingrid. Although her English was not good, she could make herself understood. Rosie was at Frank's feet and both Klaus and Ingrid bent to give her a pat. Ingrid said, "I love the dogs, we have four at home. I found it hard to leave them, even for a while."

"I know how you feel, Ingrid, we brought Rosie with us from Scotland."

"That's very good, not many people would do that," then Ingrid noticed the slight bulge in Janet's stomach, "Oh," she said, "are you expecting a child?"

"I am," she replied, "around July".

"Ah, we are trying to make a baby, Klaus says we must do it every day, sometimes twice, maybe three times." Klaus stepped in, "No! No! No! No! Ingrid, people don't want to know our personal affairs."

"What? I say something wrong?" Rita went red and took Rosie's lead and made an excuse that she needed a walk. Jack laughed out loud, Frank and Janet gave a smile, "Well, good luck," they both said, "but it doesn't sound like you will need it."

Jack had booked rooms at the Palm Groves Hotel, rather than drive all the way to Nairobi. Also, Janet and Frank hadn't seen each other for three months, so it would give them time to be alone and catch up. They would spend the night in Mombasa and drive out in the morning. As Klaus and Ingrid knew no one in Kenya, Klaus asked if the Munros would dine with them that evening, but before they could reply, Ingrid stepped in, "Darling, Janet and Frank have not seen each other for two months, they will probably want to do it,"

"No! No! Ingrid you must behave and not talk like that," everyone laughed, they just couldn't help themselves, Ingrid was so open and down to earth. But the Munros agreed just as Rita and Rosie returned, it was a date, nine this evening at the Palm Grove. All the paperwork was completed, so everyone bundled into the Stud, Janet and Frank in the front with Rosie in between, and Jack and Rita in the back. Benjamin was sat in the back. He smiled a broad grin as his brother lived close by, "Ay, a night in Mombasa".

Rosie gave Frank a big lick on the face as they drove out of the main gate. It was only twenty minutes to the hotel and the ladies chatted furiously, "Look at that, look at this, what's that, Frank?" They arrived at the hotel just as the sky opened, neither of the women had seen rain like this and Frank explained it was the start of the rains in Africa. The four of them ran inside leaving the Stud and the luggage to the hotel staff to take care of. Benjamin made off to his brother's, he was wearing a raincoat made from a plastic bag. That evening at nine, the Benzs showed up, the Munros stared at Ingrid, she looked quite different to when they first met her, and Janet looked beautiful with her. Ingrid had brought a camera and insisted on a group photo and Klaus explained she was a top photographer in Germany and her real ambition was to photograph wildlife. They talked well into the early hours of the morning, laughing and joking, the six got along wonderfully, so well that Jack asked them to visit, 'Honeydew' if they were ever in the area and he gave them directions.

They agreed that they would and finalised the night with a large whisky nightcap and they said "Goodnight, we won't see you in the morning as we are pulling out early."

"Goodbye, and good luck. You know where we are, it's been a pleasure."

***

It took Big Boy three weeks to regain some of his health, the interrogators had been relentless with their questions, poking and probing his wounds but he had not uttered a word, only screamed in agony as they went to work on him.

They called him Kaffir, black bastard, nigger; the vilest of names, still he uttered no words. He knew his fate was sealed as soon as his capture and his feet and hands were shackled, he heard the white officers say the evidence against him was overwhelming, just the fingerprints alone were enough, and then there was the shirt of course, but he hadn't given up his leader's name and the other captives just didn't know. But still they persisted, burning his testicles with cigarettes and hot irons, electric shock, covering his face with a cloth and pouring water on it, so he could not breathe, poking sharp objects into his ears, and still he uttered not a word. Eventually they gave up. "All right," the senior officer said, "get him cleaned up and ready for his court appearance." The police Askari obeyed and took him away. He would appear before the court in fourteen days in Nairobi.

As the date of Big Boy's trial drew nearer, he was taken from the local watch-house and transferred to the City of Nairobi's prison. This is where the British murdered the Africans who broke their laws. The day of the trial came quickly, and he was ushered into the court in shackles and handcuffs. Most of his wounds had healed and yet he had not uttered a single word to his white captors, he had spoken to his fellow inmates when he had a chance but was only allowed two hours a day in the general population exercise yard. He spent all this time converting the other Africans into joining the Mau-Mau. It was six in the morning when they came for him, they had clean clothes for him, but he refused them, he was led to the waiting prison van and roughly bundled in. He looked out the window, it had rained heavily during the night and the sky was dark, he could see huge clouds holding back their rain. The journey was short, only thirty minutes. He was hauled out and dragged to the cells below the court rooms, there were other Africans there, awaiting their fate and they knew his reputation. As he passed, he greeted his black brothers, and they acknowledged him. At eight, his cell was unlocked, and he was taken into the court room. It was full, Africans to one side and whites on the other. He saw the police officer who had arrested him, and he met their stare with arrogance and did not move as they dropped their heads and turned away. There was four men in white head dress and long black frocks, shuffling papers and talking amongst themselves.

The court usher walked into the court and shouted, "silence please, all rise." Everyone stood in silence, a door at the back of the court opened and the judge entered and made his way to his place on a large chair. He was wearing a white wig and red robe, he sat, and the usher told everyone to be seated. The judge began, "Does the accused have legal representation?"

"Yes," was the reply.

"Will the defence please rise," an Indian man in a scruffy suit stood, "what is your name?" asked the judge.

"My name is Leo Mahara, your honour. I am representing my client, Big Boy."

"How does he plead?"

"I don't know, your honour, he has not spoken."

"Very well, let's continue. Prosecution what evidence do you have against this man?"

The prosecution began, "the most damming evidence, my lord, are the accused's fingerprints on a whisky bottle at the scene of the murders," and they went on and on, the evidence was damming and conclusive. The defence had nothing, he did raise the question of Big Boy's healed wounds, but the prosecution soon shut him down, "Your Lordship, his scars could have been from before his capture."

"Yes," the judge agreed with the prosecution. There was whispering going on in the court amongst the Africans and the judge ordered silence.

"All right," said the judge, "the accused will stand. Big Boy, you have been found guilty of the murders and mutilation of the Brady family, do you have anything to say before the court passes sentence?" Big Boy looked around the court room. Then he began to speak, "Yes, white man, I want to know the name of the man who said you could come to our country and steal our land, to slaughter our animals, the great herds of wildebeest, of zebra, and the buffalo. You kill the big grey ones and leave them to rot in the bush, taking only their teeth, the grey ones with the long nose because you want to make way for grazing for your cattle. Tell me his name, tell me his name."

"Silence," said the judge, "silence!" But Big Boy went on, "You, white man, lit this fire but you will not put it out. My father's father was a great chief and warrior and my father and so am I. I am a warrior chief of Mau-Mau. Yes, I killed the Bradys and ate the hearts of the whites and the old man and his Askari. You will not win. We are many, you are few." The judge ordered the Kikuyu guards to silence him but neither moved, Big Boy clenched his fist and raised it above his head and shouted, "Uhuru! Uhuru! Uhuru!" The Africans in the court room echoed the chant "Uhuru! Uhuru! Uhuru!"

"You see the power I have, white man, and I am but one." The judge called in white officers, and they cleared the court room. After everything had settled down, the judge continued, "very well, it is the sentence of this court that you, Big Boy, having been found guilty of murder, are to be taken to a place of execution where you shall be hung by the neck until you are dead. Take him away."

Big Boy was transported to the holding cells and put into solitary confinement to await execution.   There were another eleven Africans there also awaiting execution. They were allowed to mix for one hour of each day, all knew of Big Boy and his reputation. There were five other Mau-Mau, the others were murderers, rapists, and violent criminals. They all got to know each other as well as they could. It was December 1953, but it was too close to Christmas to execute them, so their hangings were postponed until January 5th to let them enjoy the festive season. The English were always considerate that way.

***

The Munros had a wonderful dinner with the Benzs and Klaus had revealed he was indeed the great grandson of the founder of Mercedes Benz, and he was here in Africa to do some business. He was on his way to south Africa but had stopped in Kenya to introduce himself to the people at the German embassy and his wife, Ingrid, had insisted she would like to photograph some of the wildlife. Jack gave them all the particulars and they agreed to meet up when they were in the area. It was three in the morning before they said their goodbyes and all made their way to their rooms, a little worse for wear. When Frank and Janet got to their door, a bark came from the other side. It was Rosie, she had sensed their presence before the door even opened.   As they entered, Rosie started running about, jumping up on both of them until Frank said, "enough girl! Settle down." She obeyed. Frank sat in a chair, and she settled at his feet. The next day there was no early risers. Frank took Rosie for a walk and Benjamin was there with some food for her which she wolfed down, "Morning, Benjamin."

"Morning, Sir. The Stud is all loaded, ready to move, I just need suitcases for you and memsaab."

"Right, Ben, we'll go for breakfast and meet you outside."

"Yes, Sir," replied Benjamin. When Frank and Janet walked into the dining room, Jack and Rita were already eating. The four finished their breakfast and thanked the waiters before making their way outside. Rita couldn't get over how lovely and green everything looked and how the Africans were so nice and friendly, the gardens so well-manicured, and everything so clean and orderly. They walked to the Stud, Ben was there with a big smile and a good morning. Frank jumped into the front seat and Janet next to him, then Rosie managed to push her way in-between. Frank began to tell her off, but Janet intervened, "It's all right, Frank, she has been missing you." Jack and Rita climbed into the back and Benjamin into the rear compartment. It was nearly eleven o'clock when they turned onto to the main road to Nairobi. It had been raining earlier and the humidity was a killer. All of them were soaked with sweat. "It will improve when we move away from the coast," said Jack and they all settled down for the journey. Frank shouted back to Jack, "How long do you think it will take us, Uncle Jack?"

Jack replied, "Can't see us getting there before midnight, maybe longer, depending on the road." They started to make good time; the men got used to the questions from the women; "What's that? What kind of animal is that? Oh, look over there, what's that?" They struck one heavy downpour and had to pull over. They were glad, though, as it relieved the heat. The time passed quickly, and it soon began to grow dark. Green eyes began to appear and disappear into the night. Jack told Frank to pull over to give everybody a break, and Benjamin broke out the food they had brought with them. The night was filled with strange noises. They ate a good meal followed by hot coffee Everyone stretched their legs, then climbed back into the Stud, the ladies tried to give Benjamin a hand to pack up but were both told off in no uncertain terms, "Memsaab, this is my job", so they left him to it.

Back on the road again, they drove for nearly an hour when all of a sudden, out of the darkness, they could make out dozens of green eyes on the road. In the headlights, they could make out huge grey shapes crossing the road, it was elephants, Jack estimated about fifty in all. One huge beast stopped and raised her trunk, they were only fifty yards away, it was the Matriarch of the herd, and she moved toward the stud. Jack told Frank to stay still and dim the lights, the old elephant stood her ground as the herd moved across the road. "Everyone, remain silent," said Jack.

All the older elephants formed a perimeter around the calves until they were safe on the other side, then they disappeared as quickly as they had appeared, with the ground seeming to shake as they made off into the night. Janet spoke first, "Well, there's something you don't see every day, aren't they beautiful." Rosie growled, "it's a bit late now, girl, they're all gone," said Frank. Jack said to Frank, "let's swap, I'll drive from here, give you a break." Frank agreed and the five changed places, Rosie settled, pleased that she could stretch out, and gave Frank and Janet a lick. The miles trundled on, eventually they climbed a hill, and at the top they could see Nairobi lying before them, the lights twinkling like stars. "Not long now," said Jack, "probably thirty minutes". It was just after midnight when they drove in through the main gates, the gardens were well lit, and both women were in wonder at their beauty. All the lights had thousands of insects buzzing around them, small bats flew in and out, feasting on their catches. Green eyes stared down from the trees and bounced around in the branches. Before the ladies could ask the question, Frank butted in, "I'll take this one, Uncle Jack. Bush babies and owls."

"Oh," said the ladies "and what *is* a bush baby?"

"Like a small squirrel or monkey," Frank replied.

They checked in at reception and were asked if they would like something to eat but it was late, and they all agreed that they were too tired and wanted to get some sleep.

Frank and Rosie were first to rise the next morning, he looked at his watch, it was seven thirty-five, Janet was still asleep, so he left her. "I'll bring you back something nice for breakfast darling," he whispered. He knocked on his mother's door, no reply, so he went outside with Rosie and took her for a walk. He then made his way to the verandah outside the dining room, where Rosie could sit with them. Sure enough, Jack was already there, and both smiled and said, "Good morning."

"Well, Frank, let's get the women up as soon as we've eaten. I'd like to get on the road asap. They both ate a good breakfast and asked the waiter if they could take a breakfast to the room. The waiter replied, "The Memsaab have just phoned, Sir, we are taking breakfast to them now."

"Ok," Frank replied, "maybe you can put something to one side for Rosie here?"

"Of course, Sir, I'll do that now."

The men returned to their rooms and found the women together in Frank and Janet's room. Benjamin arrived and knocked on the door, he could hear voices on the other side, so he shouted, "Baas, the Stud is ready, I only need the suitcases."

It was another hour before the ladies were ready. Jack had already settled the bill. "Ok," he stated, "this is the last leg." It was an easy drive without any incidents, they passed a few other vehicles on the way, all headed to Nairobi, but they didn't stop, just gave a wave. It was just getting dark as they drove through the gates of Honeydew, everything was beautiful and green. Jack said to Frank, "More rain tonight," Frank just looked at the clouds. It wasn't long before they were at Jack's house and the men could see the looks on the women's faces. The house looked beautiful, the staff had lit the kerosene lights, and there was Billie, tail wagging and sniffing the air. Rosie jumped out, and both dogs came together and looked at each other. Their tails started wagging frantically, then Rosie took off around the stud. The family decided to leave them at it and climbed the steps leading to the verandah. Janet was the first to comment, "Uncle Jack, Frank," she said, "I have seen such wonderful houses in pictures and magazines, this is wonderful, it's beautiful." Rita was also taken aback, "glad you don't rough it out here, Jack."

Frank intervened, "If you think this is nice, girls, wait till you see our place."

Janet looked at Frank, "You mean, we don't live here?"

"No," said Frank, "our place is over there, through the trees" and pointed in the house's direction.

"I can't wait to see it, darling, can we go and look?"

"Uncle Jack, will it be okay, if I take the ladies for a quick tour?"

"Of course, lad, I'll get the supper on."

Frank, Rita, and Janet started towards the grove of trees and called Rosie to come with them. She obeyed, and Billie fell in behind. It was only ten minutes, and they broke out of the trees. The staff had lit the lights on the verandah and inside, they had all gone for the night except for one young African girl, Minnie. She had been told to stay and watch the house. She was standing on the front porch and when she saw them approaching, she smiled the biggest smile, the ladies said, they had ever seen.

Rita said, "What nice people, these Africans are. I haven't seen one that didn't look happy."

Minnie did a polite curtsey and said, "Evening, Sir. Evening, Memsaabs."

All three returned the smile and greeting. Frank spoke first, "Minnie, thank you for everything you have done. It's getting late, so off you go home."

"Thank you, Sir." And she skipped off toward the compound. The ladies were very taken in by the home; not a speck of dust lay on the floor, and they could almost see their faces on the shiny surface. The home, as Frank had said, was outstanding and Rita commented, "Franky, I could really get used to this. Where do I stay?"

"This way, Mum." Frank led her through the house, past the kitchen to a semi-detached building. Frank opened the door and stepped inside, "In here, Mum," Rita looked at the rooms and began to cry. "Oh, Frank, this is wonderful. I just wish your dad could be here. He would have loved it." Rosie went to Rita and lay at her feet; she knew what the tears meant. Both the women knelt down and gave her a pat, Billie moved in, and he was treated the same, both dog's tails were wagging, and they looked at the ladies as if to say, "it's alright". Then Frank stepped in and said, "Ok, let's all have a look around, get the feel of the place, then we are off back to Uncle Jack's." They started back and as they entered the trees eyes began to appear in the branches and both women shouted, "Oh, I know what they are," and they all laughed out loud.

***

When they arrived at Jack's, he was sitting on the verandah, drinking a whisky. As they climbed the steps, he shouted to Benjamin, "Bring the drinks tray," and the four settled down for sundowners and to discuss the coming year. It would be Christmas soon and Jack and Frank were certain the ladies would have something lined up. They soon settled down and ate a good meal of lamb and fresh vegetables, beautifully prepared by the kitchen staff. They didn't discuss half of what they should have because everyone was exhausted from the journey. So, they called it a night and Frank and the ladies made their way back to their house. Rosie followed on with Billie in tow, but Billie was stopped by Jack, "Get back here, Billie," shouted Jack, "this is your place, next to me." Billie reluctantly turned around and sauntered back up the stairs and onto the verandah. "You're a good boy, Billie," said Jack, "now let's go to bed."

That night as Frank and Janet lay in bed, Janet brought up the subject of the Mau-Mau and the article she had read in the newspaper.

"Why didn't you tell me about this darling?" she asked.

Frank replied, "Well, Jan, it really started just as I got here and it was too late to change any of our plans", and he went on to relate the story about Big Boy and Billie. "I wanted you and mum to settle in first, anyway the police and the army assure everyone it will blow over soon, sweetheart, but you must understand, Africa is and always has been a very violent land. But I know we can settle here and make a great life and future together. So far, have you liked what you have seen?" asked Frank.

"Darling," she replied, "I love it, and as long as we are together, I will be happy."

They kissed goodnight and soon fell asleep. This is what Rosie had been waiting for, now it was time for her to creep onto the end of the bed next to Frank. When Frank woke in the morning the bed was empty, he rose, and walked onto the verandah, he could hear the Africans busy in the kitchen and he could smell bacon. He walked to the back verandah overlooking the dam, and there was Janet and Rosie, feeding the ducks and geese. It had rained during the night, and it was quite cool. He cupped his hands to his mouth and shouted, "Hey you two, breakfast is on." Janet turned her head and looked at Frank, "Morning, darling," and she started back toward the house with Rosie in tow. When she arrived, she put her arms around Frank and kissed him.

"Frank, this is such a beautiful place. I love it."

"I feel the same, sweetheart," and gave her a hug.

With that, Rosie forced her way between them, and Janet said, "Alright Rosie, you jealous old thing, let's have breakfast."

Janet spent most of the day unpacking, she had family pictures to hang, one of her favourites was a photo of Frank and Ian Smith standing on an airfield next to a spitfire, Frank looked so handsome in his leather flying jacket and so young.

She brushed away a tear and Minnie asked if she was alright. "Yes," she replied, "we are both so lucky,"

"Yes, Memsaab, we are all lucky".

***

Frank finished breakfast and said to Janet, "Sweetheart, I'm off over to Jack's. I have to pick him up, we're off to do a tour of the compound and workshop."

"Alright, Franky, see you when you get back."

"Come on, Rosie."

Rosie barked and wagged her tail, this was great, she followed Frank to the Stud and watched him get in, Frank shouted, "Come on, girl, in you get." Rosie jumped into the front seat and sat alongside her master. When he got to Jack's place, Benjamin was on the front verandah and shouted to Jack that Frank had arrived. They all drove off towards the workshop. They had to leave Billie behind as he didn't get on with Rufus Milo. Tony was already there, hard at work, and covered in grease. The boys were stripping a tractor as he explained it needed some work done on the engine. While they were talking, Rosie had noticed Rufus Milo making his way towards the Studebaker, she began to wag her tail and made a slight bark. That was enough for Rufus Milo, he was up into the stud, and Rosie was out the other side.

"Right, that's enough you two. Rosie, back inside," but it did no good, they were off around the workshop, Rufus was an instant hit with Rosie, so Frank let it be and rejoined the conversation. Tony spoke first, "You know, while you were away, we had another murder?"

"Oh," said Jack, "who this time?"

"The Keatons."

"Christ," said Jack, "that's next door but one, only thirty miles away."

"One of the sons is left, Tommy. He was away at the neighbour's for the weekend but the rest, all dead. Old man Keaton, his wife, and the other young son, John. Made a real mess of them, I believe. Tommy's away with the police now. Wayne Frobisher and Tin Cann are tracking them. Apparently, they have gone back up into the forest but the army's up there and have had quite a bit of success by all accounts. Raided a couple of camps and killed over one hundred."

"Well, that's good news," said Frank.

There was a queue of Africans standing at the entrance to the workshop, some with bandages, some limping, some lying on the ground, these were the sick, lame, and weary. They were waiting to be taken to the clinic, forty miles away.

Frank spoke up, "You know, Uncle Jack, Janet is a theatre nurse and by all accounts a very good one, give her a couple of days to settle and I will ask her if she would like to set up a clinic here, save all that transport."

"Well, that would work out, Frank, what a great idea", and Tony   agreed that it would be fantastic. Tony cleaned himself up and they all jumped into the stud, Frank gave Rosie a shout and she jumped up beside him. Rufus Milo sat in the back.

"Is this, ok?" Tony asked Frank.

"Yes, of course, its fine, they really get on well."

And off they drove, they toured the newly harvested fields and spoke of Christmas only a couple of days away, then Jack spoke to Tony, "You'll be coming up to the house then, Tony, Christmas dinner, all of us, at my place".

"Of course, thanks, Jack." They finished the tour and Frank dropped Tony at his place, but Rufus Milo was reluctant to leave Rosie and had to be hauled out and put on his lead. Then Frank drove to Jack's and Jack said, "Come in for a quick one, Frank. Is there any whisky left, you black devil?"

"Yes, plenty" replied Benjamin.

"Well, you'd know, wouldn't you?" replied Jack.

They chatted for a while then Frank said goodnight and he and Rosie drove down to his place. Billie followed on and when they arrived, Janet and Rita were seated on the verandah, drinking tea. Frank walked forwards and kissed both women on the cheeks, ensuring Janet was first and then sat down. Rosie and Billie began cavorting around the house, but Frank decided to leave them be and started to tell the ladies about the day and what had been going on. He told them about the latest murders. The women looked at each other and Frank could see the horrified expression on both their faces. Then Rita asked, "Do you think it will get better, Franky?"

"Mum, I don't know, but Uncle Jack seems confident."

As they spoke, Frank could see the police Landrover moving down the road towards Jack's place. He stood and said, "Excuse me, it looks like the police again, I'd better go back to the house." He drove up to Jack's and arrived just as Colin pulled up, Rosie and Billie had stayed with the ladies. Colin got out of the Landrover; Jack was waiting for him on the verandah. "Well, Colin, what's happened?"

"Evening, Mr Munro, evening, Frank, hope you are keeping well. Just doing the rounds, you will have heard about the Keatons. Nasty business again, murdered all except Tommy. He's away at the moment with the police, bloody good lad, good hunter, speaks the language like a local, he'll be a great help. I also have another favour. Look in the back of the Landrover."

Peering over the top were two faces, both Jack Russells, "I'm asking you, again if you will take them, please, their names are Ben and Miranda."

Jack looked at Frank, "Well, Frank do you think you could find room for them?"

"Most certainly, they would be a welcome addition to the family. Mum and Janet will love them, both dog's tails were wagging, and they could tell they had a new home.

"They came from the Keaton place, Tommy can't keep them, he wants to sell up and move on."

"What about the dairy?"

"All the cows had to be put down, the blacks hamstrung the lot."

Frank lifted the dogs out of the vehicle, one under each arm and he noticed Miranda was heavily pregnant, Frank remarked "You've been busy haven't you, young fella".

Jack spoke to Colin, "Colin, you and the Askari's will stay the night?"

"That's good of you, Mr Munro."

The Askari's faces lit up, it meant a good meal and a good bed.

“Okay, Uncle Jack, I’d better get back to the ladies, I’ve been away all day.”

“Alright, lad, see you in the morning.”

Frank put the dogs on the front seat, and they sat there obediently as Frank drove to his house. He stopped at the steps and the Jack russells jumped out and ran up the front stairs.

Janet and Rita were drinking tea on the verandah, “Well,” said Janet, “what’s this then?” as Ben jumped on her knee, Miranda was too fat, so she just put her front feet on Rita’s knee.

“Who’s this then?” asked Janet.

“These are another two orphans, another family has been murdered, not far from here, so I said we would take them in. The Keatons this time. The eldest son, Tommy, is the only survivor. He’s with the police, tracking them now.”

“That’s terrible, Frank,” said Rita, “It seems to be getting worse.”

“Yes, you’re right,” replied Frank, “can we take them in?”

“Of course, the poor souls, it looks like we are in for a few more,” remarked Janet.

Rosie was on the scene and seemed to enjoy her new company.

***

Chapter 7

Dedan Omondi had heard the news of Big Boy's capture and had vowed vengeance against the whites, especially the whites at Honeydew Ranch. But that could wait until the wet season had finished, the next few months would be spent subverting the locals and taking as many weapons as he could, especially firearms. He had been successful at his last attack and the Keatons gave up fifteen firearms and plenty of ammunition, but his men did not know how to put them to use.

What he needed were some African Police constables sympathetic to their cause to provide training on these firearms and now he had another problem, the police were on his trail after the latest murders. But he and his group had made their way deep into the thickest parts of the forest and the rain had covered their tracks and made it impossible to follow them.

***

"Well, let's have some good news, you two. Janet, what do you think about this? Uncle Jack wants to open a clinic and guess who he wants to run it? You, my dear wife." Janet's eyes opened wide, "Oh!" she squealed, "that is wonderful."

"And, mum, if you are willing, he would like you to teach the African children to read and write."

Rita smiled from ear to ear, "Oh, that would be wonderful, Frankie. Janet and I were just asking each other what we would be doing all day. When do we start?"

Then Frank jumped in, "he has agreed to pay you both a salary, the princely sum of fifteen pounds each per week".

The women looked at each other, "that's most generous, darling" said Janet "That's twice as much as I would get back home."

Rita agreed with her, they sat chatting for an hour. As they chatted, Frank looked towards the track leading to Jack's place, he could hear whistling, it was Uncle Jack making his way over for sundowners, a bit of a tradition at five in the evening when families would get together for a beer. As he arrived, he gave a wave and said, "good evening", and sat down. "Well, everyone, Christmas is in three days. What's on the agenda?"

Rita replied immediately "Well, Jack, the African butcher has prepared a lamb, roast beef, and pork, and Janet, I, and Minnie have been busy as well in the kitchen. We have mince pies and Christmas cake."

"Well done, ladies. I am really looking forward to this, Tony will also be joining us. Now down to the last bit of business for the year. Frank, please will you take the stud and trailer out to the far western fence line. The boys have reported a large hole in the fence, everything's loaded, just take four of the boys with you."

"Ok,"

"The hole is being guarded and they have lit a fire so you should only have to look for the smoke."

"That's fine, Uncle Jack, I'll leave at first light tomorrow, shouldn't be hard to fix."

"Good lad," said Jack, "it's great having another pair of hands here. Oh, and take your rifle, the 30.06. Maybe you can bring back a couple of impala or Kudu for the Africans in the compound."

Frank was up at first light, the stud was already loaded, and the trailer hitched up. He made his way outside, picked up the 30.06 on his way plus one hundred rounds. Jack was there to see him off and noticed the one hundred rounds of ammunition.

"We only want two impala or Kudu, not a hundred" and chuckled to himself.

Frank ignored the sarcasm but gave a smile to himself. Rosie was at his feet and jumped up beside Frank, this was great, she was with her master twenty-four - seven. Life couldn't be better. Janet was on the verandah with the russells and waved goodbye as he drove off. The rains had left the boundary road muddy and pot-holed; they saw lots of game, but Frank decided he would collect something on the way home, much to Benjamin's dismay.

"Look there, Boss, Kudu. Look there, Boss, wildebeest."

"Later, on the way home, Ben."

"Okay, Boss, but we may not be lucky."

They drove on for three hours and eventually Benjamin shouted, "look there, Boss, smoke. It must be them." The other boys agreed, Frank drove on for another thirty minutes and eventually, two Africans came into view standing in the middle of the road. He pulled up next to them and jumped out, but they didn't speak English, so Benjamin got the whole story and translated, "Boss," he said, "they say it was an elephant and calf, two days ago, she crossed the river and ran through the fence, she is wounded very badly."

"Ok," said Frank, "offload the gear and let the boys start mending the fence."

They unhitched the trailer and the gang immediately started to fix the fence. Frank told Benjamin to tell them there would be fresh meat for them if it was finished by mid-afternoon. Then he told Benjamin to come with him in the stud and find the two elephants. It was easy tracking as the ground was soft and the tracks were easily visible. They drove for about two miles, and in the distance, could see a small grove of Acacia trees with their umbrella shaped tops. As they drove up, they could see a huge colony of weaver birds still nesting in the branches, all dipping and diving in and out of their nests. Under one of the trees stood the old cow and her calf by her side, as they approached, Frank could see two spears jutting from her body, one in the shoulder and one in her stomach. She was just standing motionless; her wounds had turned septic. She must have been here for at least two days; bird droppings littered her back and sides. Her tusks were huge, she must have been at least forty years old thought Frank as he remembered when his father took him and Brian to the zoo in Edinburgh. The signs said: this is Maely, she is thirty years old; and this old lady was bigger. She made no move, just stood, breathing heavily with her stomach rumbling. The calf moved in closer to its mother, trying to protect her. It raised its trunk and trumpeted a screech as a warning and then ran at the intruders but broke off the attack and returned to its mother's side. Frank could see she was in agony and knew that the only thing he could do for her was to put her out of her misery. But can I do it? He thought. He knew he had to.

"Benjamin, you know I must shoot her, it's the kindest thing I can do."

Benjamin replied, "Yes, Boss Frank, I know, Sir."

Frank retrieved the 30.06 from the stud, cocked it and made his way to the front of the old girl. She had tears running from her eyes from the pain. Frank had second thoughts as the calf looked at its mother, this would be the last time it would see her alive. Frank walked to within ten yards in front of the beautiful old girl and Benjamin heard him say, "I'm sorry, old girl, but I'll look after your child as best I can." As Frank raised the rifle to his shoulder, tears formed in his eyes, and he trembled a little. Rosie looked on from the Stud not sure what was about to happen.

"I'm sorry, old girl," He aimed between her eyes and pulled the trigger. The great grey beast stood for a second, then dropped on all fours, she died instantly. The calf ran in circles, trumpeting, and knew its mother was gone.

"What about the little one, Boss?" asked Benjamin.

"I don't know. What can we do?" Asked Frank.

"We have the trailer, Sir, we can load the small one and take it home."

"Ok," said Frank, Take the stud, go and get the trailer, bring the boys back here. We will load the little one. Rosie, come here girl."

Rosie jumped out and ran to Frank's side. She sniffed the air and looked at the elephants, then walked toward the calf, it had its small trunk gripping its mother and sniffing at her. It stood, swaying side to side, pushing now and again, trying to make her rise again. She had dark stains running from her eyes as if she were crying. Frank and Rosie walked towards it; Frank spoke to it quietly so not to cause alarm.

"Here, now" he said, "you are going to come with us, we will take care of you now."

The calf turned and raised its trunk, then extended it toward Frank. Frank took the small trunk and held it and led the baby away from its mother. It followed on and then it sniffed at Rosie. Frank could hear the Stud on its way back and within minutes it was in view. It pulled up and the Africans all jumped out eager to give a hand. One of the Africans spoke to Benjamin in Swahili and Benjamin translated "Joshua says it is a girl, Sir, he knows the grey ones well."

Frank replied, "So, it's a little girl eh! Ok. Let's get her loaded."

They dropped the rear ramp and began to load her, but she gave a squeal and ran back to her mother's side. After a while they managed to coax her away and back to the trailer. Again, she ran back to her mother's side, then Rosie went to the young elephant and sniffed and licked the end of its trunk, the little elephant put its trunk on Rosie's shoulder, and as Rosie turned away towards the trailer, the little one followed, still holding her shoulder. Rosie walked up the ramp and the baby followed. Four of the boys climbed into the trailer and Frank and Ben closed the ramp.

"Ok," said Frank, "let's get back home". They drove off, the four in the trailer steadying the baby, she still had a hold of Rosie, but Rosie didn't seem to mind. Benjamin turned to Frank and asked, "What about the old one's teeth sir?"

"I don't know, Benjamin, maybe we will just leave them."

"No, sir," replied Benjamin, "that would show disrespect, you killed her, it is your right."

"Alright, Ben. We will send the boys back in a couple of days, how's that sound?"

"Ok, Boss", and they drove on, they passed the mended fence, it looked fine, the boys had done a good job. Frank had decided not to shoot any game as the shots would probably scare the little one. Frank told Benjamin to assure the boys he would be out at first light tomorrow and they could all come. This put wide grins on all their faces.

They drove on, rain was in the air, the dark clouds billowing above them, and lightning flashed all around. They were about one hour from home when the heavens opened, so they stopped and put a tarp over the trailer. The little elephant still had a firm hold on Rosie, but she still didn't seem to mind.

"Good girl, Rosie" said Frank, "we will soon be home."

It had just turned dark as they pulled into Jack's place. He was sitting with Tony having a drink, Jack came down the stairs and chuckled to himself, "well, laddie, I know you haven't been in Kenya very long, but that is neither a Kudu nor an Impala, they have horns. That's an elephant."

Tony laughed out loud, so did Benjamin.

"Yes, Uncle Jack, thank you." And he started to explain but the little elephant became agitated and began to squeal and trumpet.

"Alright, lad, take her around the back and put her in the shed, there's a nice stall in there where I used to keep my horses. Benjamin, take the boys to the compound, get goats milk for her."

Benjamin responded, "There is no goats there."

Jack shouted at him angrily, "I know you were told no goats on the property, but I know they are there."

"Ok, Boss,"

All the noise had alerted the ladies and they appeared at Jack's after about fifteen minutes and looked in amazement at the little one.

"What on earth are we going to do with an elephant?" they both asked.

"Well, first we will try and save her; she desperately needs milk."

Jack went to the kitchen and brought back two large glass bottles with teats on the end.

"Here," he said, "I used these for the foals, the problem is going to be getting her starting to drink, but we will give it a go".

Rita commented, "she seems to have taken a liking to Rosie, she's got a good grip on her".

They dropped the ramp and called Rosie. Rosie obeyed, turning, and walked down the ramp. Billie, the staffy, and the two russells were also present now and just watched on.

Frank spoke to Rosie, "Come, girl," and walked to the rear of Jack's place and into the shed which was only one hundred yards away. The kitchen staff had opened the door and Rosie walked in with the little one following on. It was cool and dry with fresh hay for bedding. Jack had kept it that way in case any calves or foals needed attention.

"Now," said Jack, "the problem begins, how to get her to eat. Someone will have to stay the night with her."

Both women volunteered at the same time, but Jack reminded them that tomorrow was Christmas day and the two ladies had plenty to do, not forgetting Janet's condition, she needed her rest.

"No," he said, "I will get two of the boys to stay with her," Frank decided.

Benjamin organised two young Africans to stay with the calf but when Rosie was called away, she stood by the little one and looked at Frank. The youngster still had its trunk touching Rosie. "Come now, Rosie", ordered Frank, and Rosie obeyed but the young elephant became distressed, so Jack said, "Laddie, it might be wise to leave her here for the night, they seem to have bonded, and it will be the best thing for the baby."

"Alright, girl, you stay here, I'll bring you something to eat." Rosie wagged her tail; everyone was in agreement and made their way back to the house. This night would be critical, and the young elephant would have to drink the following day. Miranda, the Jack Russell had disappeared, but Janet thought she must be back at their place resting. The African cooks had prepared dinner, and everyone made the most of it. Frank sorted a plate of food for Rosie and Benjamin did the same for the African youngsters keeping watch in the shed.

Frank opened the door of the shed and walked inside. The two young Africans put their finger to their mouths so Frank would know not to make any noise. The young elephant was lying on its side, sound asleep, Rosie was resting her head on its neck. She saw Frank and got up and walked to him and licked his hand. One of the boys said, "look sir, she has drunk a full bottle" and both smiled, showing their perfect teeth.

"Well, that's good, lads. Stay with her. Rosie, are you coming home?" Frank turned to leave, and she fell in by his side. Her job was done for the night, and she must sleep by her master, no matter what. The party at Jack's house had broken up, Tony had gone home, a little the worse for wear by all accounts and Janet and his mum had also disappeared, but Jack was still up. "Frank, one for the road?"

Frank said yes and told him about the little elephant.

"Well, that's good news, lad, if she survives the night she's in with a chance." When Frank got home, Janet was already in bed reading, Frank gave her the good news, she was excited and hoped she could help to bring the little one up. They talked late into the night and Janet said, "You know, Miranda has gone missing, I can't find her anywhere."

"Alright," said Frank, "Nothing I can do now, I'll search for her tomorrow". Rosie and Ben, the other Jack Russell, were both sound asleep beside Frank. It made Janet think about the story her mother had told her about a sky terrier called Bobby, a true story, well known in Scotland with a statue that still stands today in his honour at Gray Friars Church in Edinburgh, and an old man, a constable in the police, number ninety, called John Gray.

He and Bobby used to patrol the streets of Edinburgh until one day John, or old Frank as he was commonly called, developed a cough, this cough eventually turned to tuberculosis, and the old man could not be saved, and he died and was buried in the church yard at Gray Friars. Dogs were not allowed in the church yard, but Bobby always found a way to get to his master's grave. Eventually the Minister forgave Bobby and allowed him permission but no matter how the locals tried to coax Bobby away and give him a new home, the little dog would always return to his masters resting place, so eventually the locals gave in and used to take him meals every day. This went on for fourteen years until Bobby died aged sixteen. That was back in 1872, 14th of January. That's where he earned the name Gray Friars' Bobby. No matter what the weather, snow or rain, Bobby remained at his master's side and was buried next to Old Frank and a statue was erected in his honour. The graveside is a popular tourist attraction and Janet had visited it herself.

As she looked at Frank and the two dogs, tears began to well, so she turned away and took a walk outside along the verandah. The night was black, clouds hid the moon and stars, and all was silent. As she looked out towards the dam, she heard a faint squealing from under the house. She went back to the verandah table and found a torch. As she walked down the steps and around the edge of the house, the noise began to get louder, it was under the verandah now. She pointed the torch and could see a hole had been dug, and as she peered inside, she could see Miranda, just within arms-length, lying in a depression.

The noise was from four pups, and they were all struggling to get to their mother's milk. Miranda wagged her tail at the sight of Janet. "Well, Miranda, what do we have here?" Janet reached in and retrieved the pups, one at a time, each squealed loudly at being taken from their mother, Miranda objected but made no effort to bite Janet, just licked her hand and followed her pups out from under the house. Janet carried them onto the verandah and laid them on a blanket and Miranda settled down beside them. Rosie had now come to see what was going on, accompanied by Ben, the father, but Miranda growled and barred her teeth, so both kept their distance. Janet put some pillows around the new family and decided to leave them be for the remainder of the night. She pulled up a chair and fell asleep. At first light, Janet was awoken by a loud crash. It was thunder. She looked out across the open ground and could see a lightning storm in the distance, it would not be long before the heavens opened, so she went inside to find a box to put the pups in. As she passed the bedroom, she could see Frank was beginning to stir, she put her head through the door and said to Frank, "Darling, go and have a look at what's on the verandah. There's also a storm on the way,"

She got to the kitchen to find Rita busy making coffee, Rita turned to Jan and said, "Good morning." Janet replied, "Good morning, mum", it was the first time Janet had called her mum and she warmed to it, she looked at her daughter-in-law and thought how lovely she was and how much she was looking forward to being a grandmother. How wonderful life had turned out, "Coffee's up, sweetheart. I've made one for lazy bones too, is he up yet?"

"Just about," Janet replied, "Oh! And we have four new members of the family, come and look."

The women made their way onto the verandah, Frank had managed to struggle out of bed and was sitting in a chair holding two of the pups. He looked at Janet and asked, "what are we going to do with this lot?"

"We're keeping them. We'll need good dogs to keep the monkey's out of the house and off the verandah. Rosie's hopeless, she just wants to be friends with everyone."

Frank knew better than to object, he just accepted his coffee. "Well, ladies, go make yourselves busy."

***

The Indian tradies had been around to all the white farmers and left a catalogue with each family. It had photos of all the items available, and all they had to do was phone their orders through and they would deliver three days before Christmas. They had all the presents stored in the spare room, all neatly packaged with the names of who they were for clearly marked with a nice card. Everyone was to meet up at Jack's place at midday. Janet found an empty cardboard box which was ideal for the new family, and she packed the four pups in on top of a nice pillow and blanket and transferred them to the back verandah, which was partially covered and more secure, Miranda followed on, and crawled into the box alongside her pups. Janet asked Rita if she would like to walk to the shed and pay the baby elephant a visit, Rita agreed, and they took off towards Jack's place. It wasn't long before the rain started, and both were drenched when they arrived. Jack was there to meet them and asked, "What have we here then? A couple of wet hens?" and laughed to himself.

"Very funny, Jack" said Rita "we're off to see the youngster."

"I've been down, she's drinking, doing fine. Have you thought of a name for her?" asked Jack.

"In fact, we have," said Rita, "we have decided on Jessee. What do you think?"

"That sounds great, ladies, Jessee it is then," said Jack. "I'm going back to my place; you ladies go and have a look at the little one."

Rita and Janet opened the shed door and went inside, Rosie at their feet. Jessee was standing in her stall, the two young Africans fussing over her. She had a blanket draped over her back. Rosie ran forward and Jessee extended her trunk and laid it on Rosie's back, it was obvious that the two had formed a bond. The two ladies approached and Jessee raised her trunk to sniff both Rita and Janet and looked wide eyed at them in recognition, they gripped her trunk and gave her a pat on her shoulder. Janet noticed that Jessee had not a tear, but a bend in her right ear, when she flapped her ear, it was like it folded over, it must have formed in her mother's womb. Then they heard a vehicle outside and Frank calling for Rosie.

"That's Frank," said Janet, "he said he was off to shoot some game for the Africans in the compound." She opened the door and Rosie ran outside and jumped up next to Frank and took her pride of place. Frank said to Janet, "See you around midday, darling," and they waved goodbye.

The ladies made sure Jessee had plenty of milk, then arm in arm, made their way back to Jack's place. Frank drove off with three Africans and Rosie by his side. They drove for nearly an hour; he was thinking about the old elephant and when he could retrieve the tusks. Jack had told him to leave it for a week as it made the tusks easier to extract rather than let the boys chop them out as they could damage them. That would suit him fine, get Christmas over with, pick them up during first week of the new year.

He drove on, then one of the Africans tapped him on the shoulder and pointed into the bush. About one hundred and fifty yards away were a herd of impala quietly grazing, around thirty he estimated. He pulled up and got out of the stud, the 30.06 was already cocked and ready, he leaned on the bonnet, took aim, and fired, the shot hit an impala in the shoulder, and it dropped instantly, the others all raised their heads and before they could take off, he dropped another one. Then they all vanished into the thick bush.

The boys hurtled themselves out of the stud and were on the Antelope within seconds and slit their throats to allow them to bleed out. Frank drove over, Rosie wasn't sure what was happening, so she just sat, looking at what was going on. The boys were beaming from ear to ear and loaded the kill into the truck. Frank had only shot four Antelope since he had been in Africa and he was quite pleased with himself, but he needed at least two more if he was going to feed the compound. He pushed the stud into gear and took off. It was getting late so he decided to head for home, maybe he would pick up something on the drive back. Sure enough, after a while Ben tapped on his shoulder again and pointed to three young Kudu bulls twice the size of an Impala again, he steadied himself, on the bonnet and fired, he hit the nearest bull but it didn't drop and all three took off, he drove to the edge of the thicket and the boys jumped out, ready to give chase, and they took off after it. It was badly hit and left a blood trail; it must have been a lung shot. They ran for three hundred yards, Frank in pursuit as well, when one of the Africans shouted, "There, Boss, kill it." The Kudu was standing under a tree, blood running down its flanks, Frank raised his rifle, it was only fifty yards and fired the fatal shot, the Kudu dropped.

"Ah! Good, boss,"

Frank told Benjamin to bring the truck, which he did. It was a large bull with beautiful, curled horns and tawny coloured skin with white stripes. Loading it was an effort and it took all four of them to get it into the truck. Frank thought to himself, Uncle Jack will be impressed.

The journey back was uneventful. Jack heard the Stud coming up towards the house and was there to meet them. He glanced in the rear of the truck and said, "Well, now that's more like it, laddie, the labour will eat well for a few days. Now, get Benjamin to drop the carcasses off at the compound, wash down the truck, and we will all get on with Christmas. The ladies have rustled up quite a spread, so get yourself cleaned up and back over here."

Billie was having a good sniff at the truck as Benjamin drove off. "See you in about an hour, Uncle Jack," and Frank walked back to his place. They had built a fence between the two houses to keep Billie away from Rosie, if she was to come into season, no more pups was the order of the day. It took an hour, and everyone was ready to go to Jack's place. Rita was already there but Janet had waited for Frank to return. They made their way through the trees, hand in hand and speaking of Scotland and how different it was here and having Christmas without the snow. Janet flinched as thunder and lightning flashed far off, it was going to be wet.

As they approached, they could hear voices and laughing coming from Jack's. Tony Johnson had turned up and was holding a large glass of beer. Everyone had a great time, they shared presents and chatted about the situation in the country and talked about the future.

***

Christmas and new year came and went. Frank had still not retrieved the tusks from the old elephant, Jack had advised him to wait another week, then the tusks would be easy to extract, and now he and his team were ready to do the job. They drove off early morning. It was a three-hour drive. On the way, the boys spotted a lone wildebeest bull grazing by the side of the road, he was quite large and old. The boys said to Frank, "Look, Boss." Frank pulled up and rested on the bonnet, took aim, and fired. Frank had become quite a crack shot, he hit the old bull in the shoulder, and it dropped instantly. The boys were off and onto it in seconds, cutting its throat and letting it bleed out. Frank drove over, Rosie hadn't moved, she just watched on as the old bull kicked its rear legs as it died.

They loaded the bull into the Stud and drove off, the boys chattering noisily in the rear. Frank had noticed that the game he shot, when it was back at home, had the tails missing. Jack had explained it was an African tradition to cut the tails, that way they would gain the strength of the beasts. The old cow came into sight as he drove over, he was amazed the carcass was still in good condition, except that it had shrunk. There was no smell and the hide so thick the Hyena could not rip it open and the rotting meat inside was contained as if in a rubber bag. Jack had told him to put a rope around each tusk and give it a good yank with the stud and they will pull out quite easily. So, Frank reversed. The boys already had one tusk hitched up and they hooked it over the tow hitch, he told them to stand clear and drove off. With a thud, the first tusk came free. Well, that was easy, he thought, now the other. It also came away with ease. The tusks were large. Frank estimated about five feet. It took two Africans to load them. He was thinking about what he would do with them and decided on giving them to Uncle Jack. As Frank stood, looking at the old Elephant, Benjamin could see the look of concern and shame his boss was feeling. He walked over to him and put his hand on his shoulder and spoke to him.

"Sir," he said, "you are to feel no shame, you did a good thing here, when you killed the old one. She was in pain, in three or four days she would have died in agony, you stopped that, and the young one would have died also. You saved the little one, that is her blood, now you honour her by taking her teeth to remember her by. The evil ones are the ones who put the spears into her.”

Frank knew he was right, but couldn’t erase the image of the old elephant, her size and presence now reduced to this, a tuskless old heap of leather. Rosie was at his feet as always, looking up, she knew her master was in distress. They walked back to the stud and drove off back to the homesteads. They drove into the workshop and Tony was there, he walked over and looked at the tusks. “Quite a nice size, Frank. I’ll get the boys to clean them up.”

“Thanks, Tony,” Frank grinned at the Wildebeest, the tail had gone.

***

Chapter 8

The day for Big Boy's execution had been set for January 12th. There was another eleven Africans earmarked for the same day.

Dedan Omondi had been planning Big Boy's escape since he learned he was being held in Nairobi's main gaol. He and his Mau-Mau gang had threatened and intimidated all the Africans at the prison with no exceptions. He had details of the internal layout. All the cooking and admin was conducted outside the main prison, so only a minimum of personnel were inside. The prisoners were fed twice a day, once in the morning at eight and in the afternoon, at three-thirty. All the prisoners were locked in their cells for the night and at four, the night shift took over with only skeleton staff. The main outside walls were eighteen feet high and made of brick. The Prison, thirty-five miles from Nairobi, was built by the British in the 1920's. It held the worst of the worst, it had three layers, the first main gate opened into a courtyard which held the low-level prisoners, the second held the more serious criminals, and the third held the condemned and the death row prisoners. Each gate was guarded by three African guards, supervised by one European who held the keys and only left his locked office at the change of his shift. Dedan Omondi's plan was to enter the prison dressed as prison guards, the main prison compound which housed the guards, and their families, was three miles from the prison's main gate. One week earlier, a group of Mau-Mau moved into the compound and threatened and intimidated the guards and their families. If they did not comply with their instructions, they would butcher the women and children. There were also many guards sympathetic to the cause who openly volunteered to help.

Dedan Omondi had chosen New Year's Eve to put his plan into action. He knew all the whites would be partying until early morning. At four in the evening, the shift was due to change, the plan was to approach the front gate with an African guard known to the whites inside, overpower the three whites waiting to enter, and as soon as the gate was open, storm inside and kill the white guards, then order the captives to telephone the other prison Blacks and allow them entry.

The three guards were so shocked by what was happening they had no option but to comply. The first gate swung open, and the gang stormed in, took the Africans and the white guard by surprise, they clubbed him to death and put a knife through his heart. The others were so frightened that they obeyed without question, and they repeated this until finally they had overpowered all the guards and were in the main death-row house.

The order was given to execute the five remaining whites, who were so terrified that two emptied their bowels. The African guards had agreed to help release the prisoners and took Dedan to where Big Boy was being held. Big Boy had heard the screams of the guards and knew not what was happening. Dedan opened Big Boy's cell door and walked in. Big Boy looked at him in amazement. Dedan ordered all the other prisoners be released at once. The British would be busy for weeks rounding them all up. Then he shouted to Big Boy, "Come, my friend, we must be gone." Big Boy followed, he could hear doors being opened and prisoners cheering as they stormed the main gates and streamed into the open.

Dedan walked calmly to the main gate, discarding the prison guard's uniform.

"Now my friend, we must hurry, we must cross the river and be gone by first light tomorrow morning".

Big Boy's left arm had been badly damaged by the attack by Billie, and he only had partial use. As they walked, they spoke. Big Boy said to Dedan, "My friend, I owe you my life."

"Yes," he replied, "we have much work to do, you and I."

***

It was six in the evening when Mary Higgins telephoned the prison, her husband was always home by five at the latest, but she wasn't concerned as it was New Year's Eve and her husband did enjoy a drink, but when there was no reply, she became concerned. She put the phone down and phoned the governor, Richard Brock. His wife, Ann, answered. They knew each other well and she told her that she had phoned the prison and there was no reply.

Ann said, "Well, that's strange, let me fetch Richard."

Mary could hear Ann explaining what had happened as they made their way back to the phone.

Richard picked up, "Ok, Mary, hang up, I will phone the police and drive up to the prison to see exactly what's going on. I will get back to you as soon as I have some news."

Richard immediately phoned the local police, they were only five miles from the prison and the member in charge explained they had a patrol in the area, and they would meet him at the prison.

Richard was the first to arrive, as he drove towards the prison, he could see there were no lights. This was serious, something was seriously wrong. As he got closer, he could see the double gates had been thrown open. He drove in and parked the Landrover, noticing that all was quiet. Heads would roll over this, he thought to himself, more than likely, his. As he climbed out of his vehicle, lights appeared, it was the police, two trucks full of African constables, and three white officers.

"What the hell happened here?" an officer with two silver pips on his shoulder asked.

Richard replied, "Looks like a prison break, place is deserted."

The inspector gave instructions to his men, "Right, two groups, Sandy take charge of one group, George you take number two."

"Right, Sir," the white constables replied.

"Split up, search the place, when you're finished start outside."

"Right, Sir."

"Governor, you and I, let's have a look inside."

"Right you are," Richard replied.

They entered the first building with only torches, Richard beaconed to the inspector.

"Over here inspector, I'll throw the main switch."

Richard threw the main and the prison lights began to flicker on.

"Ok, let's go."

They walked down the first corridor and found the first white guard, of course, Richard knew him. It was Don Lane, a middle-aged man from Liverpool, who had been with the prison service all his adult life.

"Nothing we can do for him," said the inspector.

His throat had been cut and a knife had been driven into his chest. They moved on into the next section. The inspector asked Richard how many had been on duty.

Richard replied, "Six white officers all up, three relief and three on duty, and twelve Africans".

All the gates had been opened and as they entered the death row complex, they finally came across the remaining five guards, all in a row, knocked unconscious by the looks of the head wounds and then their throats cut and bloody stains on their Khaki uniforms from knife wounds to the chest. The police inspector let out a whistle.

"Come on, let's get back to the main gate and see if my blokes have turned anything up."

They got to the main gate as the first section was returning, "Well, Sandy?" The inspector asked, "anything?"

"Nothing, Sir."

Just as they finished, the second section showed up with the same response.

"Ok," said the inspector, "Sandy, you and your men have a grisly task, all the whites are dead. I want you to remain here with the Governor, retrieve the bodies and take them to the station. I'll take the other section and search the prison compound and see what we come up with."

"Right, Sir," Sandy replied.

"Governor, you had better get on the radio and report this and get them to set up roadblocks for thirty miles as soon as possible".

Sandy interrupted, "Sir, I have already done that, the army are on their way."

"Well done," replied the inspector, "Still I think it would be best if the governor follows up. This is his baby, and his neck."

Sandy and his team, accompanied by the governor, went back inside, and began to retrieve the bodies of the white guards. The inspector radioed the army headquarters and confirmed a battalion of six hundred men were on their way. They would be here within the hour. The section mounted the trucks and drove to within one mile of the compound, it was dark now and the lights in the compound could be seen with Africans moving about, African music was carried towards them by the evening breeze.

Everything looked normal, as if nothing had happened. The inspector had decided to wait until first light before moving in, he had advised the army commander of his whereabouts and to approach with no lights. His plan was to surround the compound during the night and, in the morning, with the army in place, move in and make a search. Surely there must be some of the prisoners still here, especially the ones with lesser sentences. If he could capture some of them, he would get some kind of picture of what went down.

Richard Brook walked over to where the inspector was standing and whispered to him, "I will have to excuse myself for a couple of hours, one of my men was married and I will have to tell his wife the bad news.

The inspector acknowledged the governor and said, "Ok, Sir, I understand. I don't envy you that job. Best of luck."

"Thanks," replied Richard, "I will fetch my wife. She can stay with her and the children. They have two."

It was nearly midnight when Richard reached his home and broke the news to his wife. She held her hands to her face and sobbed, "Oh my god, Richard, what will we do. I have known Mary nearly fifteen years."

Richard replied, "Well darling, we have to tell her. Will you come with me? You will have to stay with her, I have to get back and help the army."

"You know she has phoned here nearly every hour trying to find out what going on," said Ann, "Of course, sweetheart."

They both jumped into the Landrover and drove off in the direction of Tim and Mary's house. When they got there, all the lights were on, and they could see Mary running to the front gate to meet them as they pulled up.

She screamed at them, "Is Tim ok?"

Richard replied, "I'm sorry, Mary, Tim didn't make it, all are dead".

Mary collapsed and started to sob uncontrollably and screamed at the top of her voice, "What will we do now? I never wanted to come here, the blacks will take over and we will all have to leave."

Ann picked her up and they helped her back to her house. Ann asked her where the children were. She had two boys, one fifteen, the other fourteen. They are off in Nairobi staying with friends for New Year and won't be back for two weeks.

Richard asked for the address and said he would send transport to pick them up. He asked his wife to stay with Mary and he explained what was happening at the compound and that he had to return. Richard drove back and arrived at two in the morning. The army commander assured him that his men were in place and the compound had been cordoned off and nothing could get in or out. It was all quiet as they waited for dawn, only the occasional bark of the local dogs.

At six, the sun began to peep over the horizon. The army lads began to stand, every second man slept while the other kept watch. Roosters began to crow, and Richard could see the compound begin to stir. They had two sections, each of nine army men and two sections of equal numbers of African constables. They were carrying knob kerries. The commanding officer gave the order to move in now that it had become quite light.

They moved from house to house and, sure enough, they began to capture escapees. Most had been drinking beer and were still asleep with the local women, still dressed in their prison Khaki. Any who resisted were swiftly beaten into submission by the African constables, bundled outside and made to lay spreadeagled in the dirt. It took only two hours to search the compound and they recaptured eighteen prisoners. The commanding officer and Richard drove down and ordered the eighteen be handed immediately to special branch for interrogation. They had to know exactly what had happened and who was responsible.

The army wound up their operation and returned to base. Other units had been deployed at roadblocks on all roads. For the next few days, reports came filtering in about prisoners being recaptured.

Mary Higgins had returned home with her boys, the three of them were absolutely distraught at the loss of her husband and the father of her children. Ann stayed with them for a couple of days, and they spoke about the future. Mary was adamant she would be leaving Africa on the earliest available ship. Ann comforted her. She said that she didn't blame her, and they spoke about the security situation within Kenya and if she really thought the blacks would win out in the end and take over.

Special branch had over two hundred prisoners and interrogation had revealed the events of the escape. One name stood out amongst all the rest. They knew about Big Boy but the new name, Dedan Omondi, was an unknown and by all accounts a very important member of Mau-Mau.

***

It took big Boy and Dedan Omondi eight days to reach the thick forests on the western border. They had managed to dodge the roadblocks, and locals had supplied them with clothes and information on where the army and police were operating. They travelled on foot and by bus. Twelve of their comrades from the prison breakout accompanied them, the rest had bombshelled and taken refuge in villages around Nairobi or made it to the thick forest close by. The villagers had fed them well and they were offered young women at night. Now it was time to reorganise the Mau-Mau gangs.

They moved deep into the forest. Big Boy knew the area, he had been here before, when the white hunter and his band of criminal Maasi had tracked and killed his group. Now they made camp and discussed their plans.

Dedan began, "Well, my friend, you are free. What do you wish to do now?"

Big Boy replied, "We must train our men, my first attack must be for vengeance. It must be against the whites at Honeydew Ranch."

"Yes, my friend, it would be good to make an example of them all."

They spoke late into the night, the group sitting around the fire eating roasted maize and drinking the local beer. At first light, the group rose, they planned to leave the forest and exit on the far side as Big Boy had done before, as there was no army on that side, only the odd police patrol. They planned to ambush the police and steal their weapons with help from the locals but for the next few weeks they would lie low until the fuss about the prison break died down.

***

A couple of weeks had passed, and the little elephant began to grow stronger and roamed the compound quite freely in the evening. At night, she was shut in the shed with an African boy for company. She and Rosie had become the best of friends and when Janet and Rita went down every morning, Rosie and Billie were both there, and Jessee was up waiting as soon as the door opened. She squealed and ran to Rosie, putting her trunk on the back of her neck then they would all walk down to the dam for a swim. Billie had a bad habit of chasing the ducks but without success. He'd swim out to catch one, but they just ducked under the water when he came close. Billie never gave up and neither did the ducks.

Jessee would draw water into her trunk and spray water over the girls, but they soon got wise and kept their distance. The women spoke about what a great life it was and also the future and the coming birth of Janet's child. Then they would walk back for breakfast which had been prepared by Minnie, Janet's house girl.

"What a lovely young girl, Minnie is", thought Janet. She has a young boy whom she brought with her to work each day. He would sit on the rear verandah and play with the russell family, who had grown big and strong. The rainy season had been late finishing this year; it had lasted into mid-January, the next wet would start towards the end of March and probably last until the end of June. So, Honeydew needed to take advantage of the dry. Roads had to be maintained and fences checked, cattle had to be rounded up, counted, and branded, and the planting gang were on the job with one hundred acres under the plough.

Rosie and the little elephant were quite inseparable except at night. As soon as Frank came home, Rosie went straight to visit Jessee and they would spend a couple of hours together, either down at the dam, or in the grounds of the homesteads. As soon as darkness fell, Jessee was led away to her quarters, gently resting her trunk on Rosie's shoulder, then Rosie was back by Frank's side for the night.

***

Towards the end of March, the clouds began to build, and they knew the rains weren't too far off. Everyone was looking forward to the birth of the new Munro, which was due in July. The jack-russell family had grown and were quite a force to be reckoned with. Anything that came into the perimeter fence was fair game, but all the monkeys and the rest of the wildlife had learned to respect their territory. The pups were nearly four months old now and were very capable hunters, having learned all the tricks of the trade from their parents.

It was Easter Sunday and the Munros had been invited to a party at the neighbour's farm. As they drove off, the rain clouds were swirling around signalling the start of the annual rains. They laughed and joked and were looking forward to catching up at the party. It was going to be quite a do as everyone in the area, including the police, were invited. Rosie had been left at home and was sleeping in her basket next to Frank's bedside. The doors were left open, and the curtains drifted open and shut in the breeze.

A black mamba snaked its way through the fence and onto the front steps, it had been holed up in the kopje of granite boulders four hundred yards from the perimeter fence. The first rains had driven it out and it was looking for dry shelter. The russell family were down at the dam and were slowly making their way back to the homestead. The snake was huge, almost nine feet long, with a girth the same as a man's forearm. It was attracted by the movement of the curtains and made its way towards them. This was the deadliest of snakes on the African continent and accounted for many deaths each year, mostly Africans. One bite could be fatal within hours. It found progress hard going on the polished floors, but eventually, the huge serpent reached the open door, its tongue flicking in and out, testing the air for signs of danger. As it entered the bedroom, it brushed against one of the doors which creaked. Rosie was instantly awake and rose from her bed to investigate. She had never seen a snake before and looked with curiosity at this intruder. She had never killed anything and thought that this thing was something to play with. She sniffed at it and gave it a nudge. The huge snake saw her as a threat and reared up at her in a defensive posture, its neck rose three feet in the air, its rear body coiled, ready to strike. Rosie gave a bark and nudged the mamba with her nose, then the snake struck but because of the polished floor, could not find purchase and missed.

Now Rosie sensed danger. The snake had managed to gain a firm hold on one leg of Frank and Janet's bed. Rosie gave a loud bark of alarm, as she moved forward but she still wasn't the killer she needed to be. The russell family were over halfway back to the homestead when they heard the alarm and took off at a withering pace. Rosie moved closer, as the snake made ready to make another strike, but she was wary now. The snake raised its head, and recoiled, inside its open mouth, it was pitch black in colour. The russell family entered the bedroom, they immediately recognised the danger and attacked without hesitation. In seconds, the huge reptile was in shreds, only a nerve response allowed it to squirm on the bedroom floor. Rosie had cheated death. Minnie, the house girl had heard the commotion and ran into the house. As soon as she saw the snake, she ran straight back out again, made her way to the compound and hid in her room. There are three things, Africans fear the most: snakes, owls, and leopards, all are evil spirits.

The Munros returned home late that evening and found the dead mamba lying in tatters, and the russell family jumping about and barking, they all knew they had done a good thing and were waiting for a reward. It came as a part of a Kudu hock; they each took it from Janet and retired to the front porch.

Frank picked up the remains of the snake and said to Janet, "We certainly did the right thing keeping that lot," and knelt and gave Rosie a pat and her rewards but he knew she would have contributed little to the death of the serpent. He took the body and threw it out in the front garden, he knew it would be gone as soon as it was first light, one of the hawks or eagles would spot it and swoop down and carry it away. Nothing that was edible stayed around for long.

Janet and Frank climbed into their bed and Rosie, hers. They spoke about the party and of course the political situation. By all accounts, things were not improving. Tommy Keaton was there, all on his own since his family had been murdered. He had been working with the army, and he spoke of the difficulty they had tracking down the Mau-Mau gang. They had had some success, killed and captured several hundred, but it was bigger than they had imagined. Most of the Africans wanted the whites out. He had thought of moving to the United Kingdom, but he had been born in Africa. He was African and had decided to move to Southern Rhodesia where he would join the British South African Police. He was leaving in three-months' time. Colin was there also. He and Tom had become very good friends, the best of mates. Colin had signed on with the Kenyan Police for another three years after being promised a promotion to inspector. He would take over as station commander at the end of April, as the other inspector was returning to England.

***

Chapter 9

Janet was putting in a lot of time at the clinic and it had become very popular, but she was finding it difficult to cope on her own with the pregnancy.   The patients at the clinic were becoming more numerous and their injuries more severe and they travelled from miles around for treatment. She had spoken to Uncle Jack, and he came up with the perfect solution. There was a doctor at the African hospital in Nairobi. He was a Welshman, Sam Enfield. Rumour had it that he was returning soon to Britian. He didn't want to leave though, he loved Africa and its people, but he had been having problems with some of the whites. He was married to a coloured woman, something that was frowned upon by the majority of whites and, therefore, he couldn't attend any of the white clubs where the locals were. He was quite outspoken about the English and how they could colonise other people's countries, and exploit their rights, but wouldn't allow locals to join their clubs.

So, Janet and Frank, together with Jack, drove to Nairobi to speak to him. They had phoned him the week before and he seemed keen and listened to their proposal. If he accepted the post, the British government had offered a generous salary. Accommodation would be supplied by Jack and Honeydew Ranch. They would have to build them a new home, but Jack had a building crew, so that was no problem, a beautiful pole and dagga home could be finished in six weeks.

When they arrived in Nairobi, they drove to the local Hospital, there was the usual queues of sick, lame, and weary Africans, some in wheelchairs, some on crutches, others with bandages around their heads, all looking very sorry for themselves. Janet commented that it was the only time she hadn't seen Africans smiling.

"There is no more a sorry sight than a sick African," she said.

The men laughed, "You're right there, lassi," commented Jack, "half of them only have headaches."

They parked the Stud and walked into the large passageway, a sign with an arrow said: Office, this way. As they moved through the corridor, they passed several Indian and African doctors who all greeted them warmly and made them welcome. One Indian doctor stopped them and asked if they were the Munro family, they confirmed that they were and they shook hands, he introduced himself as Doctor IB Naidoo. He said that he knew why they were here and added that he would be sad to see Sam go as he had been at the hospital for five years and everyone would be sad to see him leave.

He led them down the corridor and into an office, sitting at a desk was a gentleman in a white coat with a stethoscope draped around his neck. IB introduced them and he stood and shook their hands. Lying on a stretcher was an African groaning and moaning, Sam spoke to him, "Come on now, Cyris, it's only an ingrown toenail, you will survive."

He turned to IB, "Will you take over, please? I want to chat to my new friends." IB nodded and took over. Sam ushered the Munro's into an adjoining room, and they all sat.

Frank began the conversation. "Well, Doctor Enfield, you know why we are here."

Sam responded "Ok, yes, you gave me all the details in your letter, I thought them very generous to say the least."

As they were talking the door opened and a tall woman with long, wavy, honey-coloured hair entered. She was quite beautiful.

"Ah," exclaimed Sam, "let me introduce my wife, Adeena."

The Munros all rose and shook her hand, she seemed relaxed and confident.

"Well, it's nice to meet you all, I hope my husband isn't boring you all to death," she giggled, and everyone joined in. She continued, "I must say, thank you very much for your offer, we accept it. It will suit us just fine."

Sam interrupted "Oh, my wife has a wicked sense of humour, she is the head nurse here at the hospital, this is where she trained."

Janet spoke, "Well, I know she will fit in well with this lot" and glanced at Frank and Jack.

Frank asked if it would be possible for the two to start at the end of the month, and they both nodded.

"Yes, that will be fine, we have already tendered our resignations," then Sam continued, "Now let's go and have some lunch."

They sat in the cafeteria, and though they all commented on how good the food was, it was hospital food, and they were just being nice. Jack asked if they had furniture and belongings that needed to be moved, and they said they had. So, Jack agreed to send a truck and some boys to help move. They thanked him and continued to eat. When everyone had finished, Jack stood and said, "Well, Mister and Misses Enfield, welcome to the Munro family, we look forward to your company at Honeydew."

The Enfield's smiled, they could see it was genuine, then Jack began again.

"Well, we must be off, we want to be back before midnight."

They said their goodbyes as they made their way to the stud. The Munros arrived home that evening just after ten. Rita saw the lights from far off and was waiting on the verandah, all the dogs were lined up as they pulled up at Jack's place, the russell family in the middle, Billie on the right, Rosie on the left. What a welcome. They all ran forward, barking and tails wagging, glad that their family were home. Rosie went to Frank, crawling on her belly, barking, with her tail beating against him like a drumstick.

"Alright," shouted Frank, "that's enough, everybody inside."

They mounted the stairs, and everybody gave Rita a hug. Frank noticed Jack giving his mum an extra hug, come to think of it, he thought, his mum had been spending a lot of time at Jack's place. Could it be? Nothing, he thought, would make him happier, so he would keep his eye on them for other telltale signs.

It was a perfect African night, the crickets were making their usual din, on the other side of the fence, a baboon barked a warning, "probably a leopard out for a feed," remarked Jack. There was a lovely breeze blowing through the passageway as they made their way inside.

Rita said, "I have prepared a nice meal. I knew you would be hungry; you all sit, and I'll serve."

Janet said she would help but Rita said, "sit down, you're eating for two now,"

"Thanks mum, I am starving and dog tired."

They made their way to the dining room tripping over the dogs now and again. A russell yelped because it had been stood on. The African staff had all gone home, so Rita went to the kitchen, everything was in the oven ready to serve, Jack made his way to the drinks cabinet and poured three whiskeys, he knew Janet wouldn't drink while expecting. Then another clue, "I poured you a dram sweet...." He shouted to Rita but checked himself at the "heart". Frank looked over at Janet, she wore a wry smile then winked a naughty wink as if to say, "you are the last to know". Frank brushed it off and started patting the dogs furiously, but Rosie wasn't having that, she pushed her way between him and the others as if to say, "leave them alone".

"You jealous old thing," he said, and she just looked up at him.

Rita started to bring through the food, "Here," she said, "I'll put it on the sideboard, you can help yourself."

It looked and smelled great, there was chicken, with a large platter of vegetables, and gravy. They sat eating and drinking till late in the night, then Rita finally said, "Well, I have school in the morning, so let's all think about turning in."

"You're right, mum," yawned Frank, "let's go, folks," and they rose from the table. They said goodnight to Jack and made their way down to the Stud, the russells and Rosie close on their heels. All had bones and there was much growling and snarling as they jumped into the back of the Stud. Rosie in pride of place next to Frank and Janet, as usual. A light rain began to fall as they drove off, lightning and thunder clouds could be seen out on the horizon. Everyone took a shower and fell into bed. It was good to be home, thought Janet. She was looking forward to the birth of her child and fell asleep within minutes, exhausted, as she was now eight months into her pregnancy.

***

Chapter 10

The old lion limped towards the river, he was tired, hungry, and thirsty. He hadn't eaten in five days. He made his way slowly down the bank of the river, lay flat, and began licking at the water. He was looking for an easy meal, he had been with his pride of five lionesses for twelve years and had sired many cubs. He had fought many battles over the years and managed to win them all except the last. A young lion challenged him for the pride and won, now he was alone and in pain. He rose painfully to his feet and made his way over the river and through the fence. Now he was on Honeydew land. He could smell the cattle. He had been badly mauled, so his progress was slow, and he had to stop often to regain his strength. As he topped a rise, he looked down at the lights twinkling in the distance, the smell was stronger now and he could hear voices and could smell smoke from cooking fires. It was the African compound.

It was late in the evening, he moved closer to one hundred yards away, but then the breeze carried his scent to the cattle and goats corralled behind the wooden fence. The animals became frightened and began to rise and bellow as he drew closer. They began to mill around as the old lion circled the enclosure. He grunted, then a cough to panic the beasts. He ran towards the fence and roared. All at once, they charged the fence and broke out, all escaping, except one. He charged in and caught the young steer by the neck, killing it instantly, he held it by the throat until it moved no more, then began to tear at its belly. The Africans were quickly on the scene but retreated and ran to the homestead for help. Tony Johnson was already awake when he heard the commotion and knew exactly what was happening. He had no firearms, so he quickly jumped on the phone to Frank.

Frank answered almost immediately, "What the hell's going on down there, Tony?"

"It's a Lion in the cattle corral. Can you come down?"

"Be there in five," replied Frank.

He ran to the gun cabinet and pulled out a pump action Winchester, twelve gauge shot gun, along with a Bandoleer of solid shot ssg. As he made his way to the verandah, Janet and Rita were in the passageway, both asked at the same time, "What's happening?"

"Lion in amongst the cattle," Frank replied, as he ran.

Janet called to him, "Be careful, darling."

He jumped into the Stud, the russell family piled in behind him. "Rosie, you stay here," but she jumped into her pride of place, and they took off towards the compound. The headlights were on, and they had a large swivel spotlight that could be operated from the passenger side. Picking up Tony on the way, it was three hundred yards to where the cattle had been corralled. It was empty. As Frank pulled up, Africans began to appear and pointed in the direction in which the lion lay. They needn't have bothered, the russell family caught the scent of the big cat and were immediately out of the Stud in hot pursuit. Frank tried to call them back, but it was no use, their blood was up, they would have to take their chances. Tony swung the spotlight from side to side, they could hear the dogs up ahead, then suddenly two bright green eyes, flashed in the beam, Frank slammed on the brake, "There it is," he shouted, as the beam fell on him, he was lying flat and made no effort to run off, he was too old, too sore, and too hungry. At that moment the russells spotted him and went straight in for the attack, no hesitation from any of them. They barked and snapped, the big lion swung a huge paw and caught two of the youngsters to Frank's surprise. They were not harmed, they just bounced along the ground, regained themselves and went back in. Frank jumped out, told Tony to hold onto Rosie.

"Be careful, for Christ's sake, the bloody thing is huge."

Frank got to within twenty yards but couldn't get a shot because of the dogs. He wouldn't risk hitting them, Janet would never forgive him, then the Lion roared in agony, one of the russels must have found a tender spot, it jumped up off the carcass, scattering the dogs, now Frank could get a clear shot, he put the Winchester to his shoulder and fired the heavy lead shot, hitting the cat square in the shoulder and knocking him over but it didn't kill him, he rose, and charged towards Frank. Frank went down on one knee and fired two more shots into the charging lion. At five yards the lion dropped, its last breath gurgling as blood flowed from its mouth. The russells climbed in, tearing at its huge black mane and ears. The old lion lay dead at Frank's feet, he had been badly wounded in the fight for his pride and his wounds had festered and oozed pus, it stunk. He must have been in terrible pain.

Tony walked over, "well done, Frank, it was touch and go there for a while."

Moths and other bugs began to fly into the light and the Africans began to gather and chatter loudly.

"He will make a nice trophy," said Tony, "I'll get the boys to skin him and salt the hide. I'll send him into Nairobi they will cure him and do a nice job of mounting him."

"Thanks, Tony," said Frank, "he certainly is a big one."

Just then headlights appeared, it was Jack and the ladies. Jack walked over with them, they all looked at the lion and admired him, they could see the young steer lying a short distance off, its belly had been ripped open and the Africans were already tying it to a pole, they would take it to the compound and butcher the rest of it. Tony told two of his boys to skin the beast.

Jack was the first to speak, "Well, lad. Well done. You are one up on me, I have never bagged a lion."

The two women looked at Frank proudly, Rita thought what a great son he was, and Janet was proud of her husband for being the man he was. Rosie was, as always, at Frank's feet and Rufus Milo, Tony's dog, had appeared, paying much attention to Rosie.

Then Frank spoke, "well, folks, that's all the excitement over for the night, let's all head home". They left a kerosene lamp for the boys who had started to skin the lion.

"Make sure the tail stays where it is."

The boys mumbled a reply as the group made their way back to the vehicles. Janet jumped in beside Frank, Rita with Jack, and they drove off. They dropped Tony at his home and said goodnight. As they pulled up at home, Janet said to Frank, "Well, Frank, we would never have had this in Scotland, you being a banker and all."

Frank grinned and broke into a fit of laughter. "Well, you're right there, sweetheart, now let's turn in."

The jack russells piled out and onto the verandah, did a quick, three hundred and sixty degrees to see if any invaders were about, and satisfied there was not, all climbed into their beds.

***

Chapter 11

The Enfields had moved into their new home, built only one hundred yards from the clinic, and both were very pleased with their new luxurious accommodation. Janet threw them a welcoming party, and all were invited. Adeena and Janet had gotten on well since their first meeting and were becoming close friends. Frank was really pleased she had someone her own age to keep her company. They had only been at Honeydew for a short while when Janet went into labour. It was late in the evening and Frank phoned Sam Enfield, asking if he could come at once, Janet was having the baby. He and Adeena drove to their house and found Frank running about frantically with both Janet and Rita trying to calm him. They eventually settled him down and he joined Jack on the verandah with a whisky.

"Well, laddie," said Jack "This is it, your big moment. What do you think, it will be, boy or girl?"

Frank downed his drink and poured another.

"Just take it easy now," said Jack "We've got all night."

Rosie was at Frank's feet as were the jack russells, all laid out in a row, not knowing what was going on. It was late the following morning when Janet gave birth and the sound of a baby crying from in the bedroom pierced the air. Frank woke, stood up and walked to the bedroom door, he opened it and glanced in. Adeena held a baby in her arms, it was crying.

Sam turned to Frank, "Well, Frank, well done, it's a boy, but give us a little while. There's another one here."

Frank was in a daze, he backed out and closed the door and rejoined Jack.

"Well?" asked Jack, "Boy or girl?"

"A boy, Uncle Jack, but there's another."

"Twins!" exclaimed Jack, "well, well, that will go down well."

It wasn't long before more cries could be heard from within and Frank couldn't contain himself, he had to go in, he again opened the door.

"Two boys." said Adeena.

Frank looked at Janet, she had both the babies snuggled in her arms, lying in the bed. Rita was smiling from ear to ear, and she sat close to Janet with her arm around her.

It took Janet four days to regain most of her strength and Rita was such a big help, she fussed about like an old hen. Of course, they discussed names for the boys and Frank and Jack were asked to participate and all agreed that Frank and Brian were the most appropriate as it would be a fitting tribute to Frank's younger brother, Brian, lost back when he and Frank were youngsters back in Scotland.

Rita became very emotional and wiped away a tear, then Jack walked over towards her, put his arm around her and spoke, "while we're all here, I have an announcement to make on behalf of us both. He hesitated then began, "Rita and I have both become very fond of each other and I am sure this will come as a shock to you both, Frank and Janet," Janet burst into laughter followed by Frank.

Frank spoke, "we wondered when you were going to get around to telling us."

Jack was taken aback. "You know?"

"Yes, and we couldn't be happier. Both of you have been on your own for too long."

"Alright," said Jack, "the cat's out of the bag," he said bluntly, "I have asked Rita to marry me, and she has agreed."

"Well," asked Frank, "When's it going to happen?"

Rita answered, "well, Jack says in September and that will suit us both."

Adeena and Sam were regular visitors, and everyone took turns at inviting each other over on Saturday nights around sundown. Everyone looked forward to this, especially at Adeena and Sam's place as Adeena was a wizard in the kitchen especially with Indian cuisine.

Now Adeena attended to the two boys every morning and checked on Janet. Two weeks passed, and Frank and Jack drove to Nairobi. Jack to speak to the government officials, and Frank to pick up a second cot. Jack referred to them as the 'pompous bastards' behind desks but Frank would remind him.

"Well, Uncle Jack, when all is said and done, they have been more than generous with the payments for the school and the clinic."

Jack grunted a reply, "Yes, I suppose so, laddie."

Frank went out and bought the new cot and some presents for the ladies, including Adeena. They spent the night at the Norfolk and left early the next morning. They would be home by the early afternoon.

The three women started their day at six with breakfast on Janet's verandah, Adeena had acquired a small Lambretta scooter, and she zipped about the farm like a true motorcyclist professional. Everyone had a giggle when they saw her approaching in a cloud of dust. She wore a hard hat and goggles, and when she removed the goggles, she had large white patches around her eyes where the dust hadn't settled. Jessee, the elephant, and Rosie with the jack russels also joined them. Jessee stretching her trunk over the verandah for a carrot. She was becoming a handful and very demanding. Cleaning up after her was quite a chore, dog poo was one thing but elephants, that was something else. They had spoken about when she would be released. They knew they would be sorry to see her go, but she must get back to the herd if they could find one that would accept her. Janet asked Adeena if her and Sam had thought about starting a family, but Adeena changed the subject on a couple of occasions, until one evening, she explained with a tear in her eye about the prejudice they had encountered when they married, her being coloured and Sam white. Most of Sam's so-called friends had turned their backs on him. It got so bad they wanted to leave Kenya for the United Kingdom, but it was going to be difficult for her to accompany him. They loved Africa and were so happy when they received this offer from Honeydew, but having children was a no, because there was no place for mixed race children, and no future. The white community could be quite cruel in this regard.

Frank and Jack arrived back mid-afternoon and settled down for a beer, the ladies hadn't arrived home yet, but it wasn't long before Janet and Rita pulled up in the Landrover. They climbed out, big grins on their faces because they knew there would be presents. Minnie brought the twins out and they lay quietly in their cot while the adults spoke. Frank had put the new cot next to the twins and Minnie made up the bedding and transferred one of the boys.

Frank went to the Stud and brought out six boxes, the ladies beamed, "Alright," he said and laid out three boxes each in front of Rita and Janet. They didn't hesitate, tearing open the boxes, both going for the biggest first. These contained a beautiful house coat, tailored by the Indian dressmakers back in Nairobi. They were silk with beautiful floral designs. In the next, Janet found a Kodak camera which she had been pestering Frank to buy for months. Rita's second present was a beautiful Mahogony Jewellery box, inlaid with mother of pearl, and with beautiful ornate brass corners. Jack said it had been made especially for Rita in Zanzibar by Indian craftsman. She opened it, inside was two strings of beautiful pearls, one was for Janet, the other for Rita.

"Good Lord," said Rita, "Jack, they must have cost a fortune," as they helped each other try them on. They ran to the lounge room mirror, giggling with delight, then returned to the verandah. Rita reached back into the box, there was another surprise, she pulled out a black- box about two inches square, she looked at it, then flipped open the top, inside was a gold ring with a diamond in the centre, flanked by two sapphires.

The women let out a gasp, "Good Lord," she uttered again. Before she could say another word, Jack stepped in.

"Well, it's a bit late, as you have already said you will marry me but it's your engagement ring."

"Oh, thank you so much, Jack, you are a sweetheart."

Janet gave it the once over when Jack placed it on her mother-in-law's finger. "Well, mum," she said, "Aren't you the lucky girl."

It was time for sundowners, and everyone laughed and giggled and drank too much.

The next morning was clinic and school day. They sat on the verandah, waiting for Adeena to appear, sure enough the telltale putt-putt-putt of the Lambretta could be heard not far off, then she appeared and pulled up in a cloud of dust. She made her way to the verandah and said her good mornings.

"Ah!" said Rita and Janet together, "there's something there for you on the table."

There were two packages. "Oh?" she asked, "what's that?" She opened the largest one first, it was one of the beautiful house coats that Janet and Rita had. She slipped it on and went inside to the mirror, she stared for a few seconds and began to sob. Rita and Janet heard her and went inside.

Janet asked, "What's wrong, don't you like it?"

"Oh, no," she replied, "it's lovely, it's just nobody, except my husband, has ever bought me a present. You are all so kind." She then gave Rita and Janet a kiss on the cheek, "Thank you all so much."

She opened the second package, it was a box of Cadbury Dairy Chocolates "This is nice too, but I will have to hide them from Sam, these are his favourite."

Frank was taking the Landrover into Tony at the workshop, so Janet took a lift from Adeena. Adeena climbed onto the Lambretta, gave it a kick start and Janet sat on the back and off they went, putt-putt-putt and disappeared in a cloud of dust, the jack russells in close pursuit. Rita and the men had a good laugh, then rose and went about their business, it was handy to have Minnie around, as she was a great nanny and loved the boys.

***

The army had had limited success in curbing the Mau-Mau threat. They had begun to round up whole villages and putting them into internment camps. A few stories were filtering back about atrocities and murders by the security forces, but these were always denied. They were British, they didn't behave like that, they were just ugly rumours. Jack discussed it with Frank over a drink. Jack told him that rumours had to start somewhere.

Big Boy and Dedan Omondi had been holed up deep in the forest, they had had some close shaves with the army and police, but their lookouts worked well, and they managed to evade capture. Big Boy had been informed of the birth of the boys at Honeydew, and now he was planning an attack on the farm. He had recruited eight young Africans who were dedicated to ridding their land of the whites and all had proven to be totally ruthless on attacks in the area. The rains had finished, so now he would make his move and have his revenge.

Big Boy, Dedan, and his eight recruits made their way out of the forest and began their trek to Honeydew. They would only move during darkness and would travel from village to village where they would receive food and shelter. The lookouts would keep them informed of the whereabouts of the security forces. It was going to take them probably ten nights' march to reach Honeydew and they carried an assortment of weapons between them. They had three 9mm Sten guns and assorted rifles and handguns, the villagers kept them well fed and they were all young and strong even though Big Boy's left arm and shoulder still gave him trouble. As they moved through the night, they could see the odd lights twinkling from isolated farm homesteads off in the distance now and again. The occasional dog could be heard barking. Big Boy dreamed that one day he would own a farm, maybe one of these he had just passed.

Their guides were good, and they made good time and reached the Honeydew boundary sooner than expected. The Mau-Mau guides took them to a village where they were given a hero's welcome, everyone had heard of Big Boy and Dedan Omondi, and they were most feared. The Mau-Mau ate and drank and slept until mid-morning when they arose.

Big Boy arranged with the village elders to have a meeting. They hid the weapons and would return the day before the attack to retrieve them, but for now, they must find out the routine of the whites. They must know what weapons they had and about the guard dogs and any alarm systems that might give away their attack. Big Boy and Dedan said that they needed to get into the farm compound and speak with the house staff, but the only one that lived in the compound was Minnie with her son and mother, the others all lived within the homesteads' areas, which were well secured. Benjamin, his wife and children, and the kitchen staff were untouchable. So, they entered the compound late at night and were led to Minnie's door. They knocked. Minnie cried out "who is there?"

"It is a friend," was the reply as she unlocked the door. Big Boy burst in and threw her to the ground. Big Boy growled at her, and then he spoke softly, "Do you know who I am, little one?"

She was terrified, "No, Master, I do not know you."

"Well, little one, I am lord of the Mau-Mau, now do you know me?"

She could see his face and blood shot eyes in the candlelight. "Yes, Yes, Master, I know you now."

"Well, little one, there are some questions I have for you, and some things you must do for me. If these things I speak of are not done, we will kill your child and your mother and then their bodies will be left for the hyena's. Do you understand?"

"Yes," Minnie replied, so terrified that she wet herself.

"Do you know why we are here?"

"No, Master"

"We are here to kill the whites." Now, tell me, where does the white man keep his guns?"

"They are locked in the main room," replied Minnie.

"And do they keep any where they sleep?"

Minnie gave the information, "Yes, one. The Madam keeps a small one locked in a drawer beside the bed."

"What does it look like?" asked Big Boy

"Like the one you carry in your belt," said Minnie.

Big Boy pulled out the .38 Webley, "Like this?" he asked.

"Yes, the same," she replied.

Bog Boy went on with his instructions, "this is what you will do." He held the Webley and opened the cylinder, holding the bullets, he removed the cartridges and closed it again, "now take it, do the same".

She took the revolver in her hand.

"Here" said Big Boy "press the lock and it will open."

Minnie did as she was told, fumbling at first, but after a few moments had mastered the opening of the cylinder.

"Now," said Big Boy "this is what you will do. Get the gun, take the bullets, bring them to me and put the gun back in the drawer. Do you understand?"

"Yes, Lord," replied Minnie "but the madam keeps the key with her."

"Then you must wait for your chance when she leaves it. She must leave it sometime."

"Only when she bathes, master."

"Then that will be your chance. If you do not do this, the hyena's will eat your son and mother.

Now the old man and his woman, where do they keep their guns?

The same answer, "in the main room, but they are not here. They are in the big town, gone to buy a wedding dress. They will be gone for four days."

"Ah!" said Big Boy, "this is good! Now the dogs?"

"Only the black one is in the house. The others are locked in the back, so madam can rest."

"Good, now the old man's dog, the devil dog. Where is he?"

"Yes, Master, Billie. He is with Benjamin at night."

Big Boy stared at Minnie "this is what you will do", He reached into his pocket and pulled out a small glass tube, from his other pocket he pulled out a rag. He put it on the table and opened it. It was a piece of raw meat.

"You will take this with you when next you go to the old one's home, open the tube, and rub it into this meat and give it to the dog. It will kill him, do you understand?"

"Yes, Lord," replied Minnie trembling with fear. "This I will do."

"Now that you know what you have to do, we shall leave, but we will take you son with us."

Minnie cried out, "No, Master, please!"

Big Boy hit her in the face, "Listen to me, no harm will come to him if you do what I have asked."

Minnie fell back on the floor. Big Boy rose, walked to where the child lay and picked him up, the youngster cried out for his mother, but there was no one to hear him. Big Boy opened the door and the Mau-Mau disappeared into the blackness.

***

Minnie was at the house early the next morning. Rosie and the jack russells were at the gate waiting to go and see Jessee and take her to the dam for her morning swim. Janet was on the verandah having breakfast and greeted Minnie with "Good morning", and "you're here early this morning, Minnie."

She noticed some swelling around her cheek and mouth. "Minnie," she asked, "what happened to your face?"

Minnie replied "Oh, I fell on the step, madam. There was no light."

"Come here, let me look."

Minnie drew back, "No, madam, I am alright."

Janet sensed something was wrong, "Alright, if you're sure," said Janet, but she made a mental note to mention it to Frank.

It was Saturday morning and Adeena was on duty, so she took the dogs and the young elephant for their morning swim. When she returned, she would bathe and take a drive out to where Frank was working. He was at the dairy making sure all the milk cows were being looked after properly. A lot had calves at foot, and it was time to separate the boys from the girls. They only kept the girls and dispensed of the male calves. Janet asked Frank what they did with them, but Frank wouldn't tell her the truth. He told her that they were sent to other farms, some were, but the majority were slaughtered. This is the only aspect of farming she hated. Janet began to walk back to the homestead; it was a bright morning, and she watched the dogs playing, even Billlie joined in. The little elephant and Rosie were together, the elephant's trunk resting on Rosie shoulder and Janet began to think how different their life had turned out since she was a schoolgirl back in Scotland. She loved her new life, she had everything she wanted, her own family and a great future, but she worried about the troubles with the Africans. Would the army and the police be able to contain it? She reached the verandah steps; Benjamin was there and greeted her with a huge African smile. "Good morning, Madam."

 "Good morning," she replied, "Ben, will you take Jessee to her shed please?"

Benjamin replied, "Of course, Madam. Come, Jessee," and off he went with Rosie close behind. Janet watched them for a few seconds then thought 'Jessee is getting too big, it was time she was released back into the wild'. She made her way to the bathroom and turned on the water, the hot water was steaming from the forty-four-gallon boiler at the back. It was heated by logs and Janet often wondered at the inventiveness and the things people came up with. She began to undress in the bedroom and laid her clothes on the bed, then went back into the bathroom and closed the door.

Minnie saw her chance and moved to the bed. The key to the drawer was in the pocket of her dress, she took it out and went to the side cabinet, slipped the key in the lock, and opened it. The gun was there, where it always was, she took it out and opened the cylinder and slid out the bullets, the way Big Boy had shown her. One of the boys began to cry, then the other. Janet heard them and rose from the bath. Wrapping a towel around her naked body, she called out, "Coming boys," and opened the door.

There was Minnie, standing by the door, "It's alright madam, I heard them. I am here," she hadn't shut the drawer properly, but Janet didn't notice and asked Minnie to tend to the boys. They wanted their breakfast, she returned to the bathroom and shut the door. Minnie quickly locked the drawer and returned the key.

It was late in the evening when Big Boy knocked on Minnie's door. She opened the door only one inch and peered out.

Big Boy pushed the door and burst inside, "Well, little one, did you do as you were told?"

Minnie trembled and answered "Yes, my Lord, I have the things you want."

Big Boy put out his hand, Minnie put her hand inside her pocket and pulled out the six shiny brass bullets and gave them to Big Boy, "and the devil dog, what of it?"

"Tomorrow, I promise. How is my son and mother?" Big Boy stared at her then answered, "they are both well, they have a roof over their head and food."

"Thank you, Lord," said Minnie.

"Now," Big Boy instructed, "take off your clothes and lie on the bed."

"No, Master, I cannot."

Big Boy struck her with the back of his hand striking her a hard blow on the left eye. She screamed in pain but did as she was instructed. After Big Boy was finished with her, he dressed and left without a word. The next morning Minnie left for work. With her, she carried the poison and the piece of meat. The meat had, by now, turned rancid and stunk. She would do Billie first, before everyone was awake. She opened the gate but instead of going into Janet and Frank's house, she made her way to the boundary fence. No one was awake, she moved to the fence and took the meat from her pocket, it was wrapped in a piece of rag. She had had it for two days now, she took the poison and poured it on the rotten meat, then threw the meat far into the old man's property where she knew Billie would find it, then turned and made her way back to the house. She went to the back room and washed her hands, but the stench stuck to her and her clothes. She was about to leave when all of a sudden Janet appeared, carrying one of the twins.

"My God," she exclaimed, "Minnie, what is that terrible smell. It smells like something has died."

Minnie thought quickly, "Yes, madam, a bird has died at the back, I took it and threw it away over the fence."

"Well, Minnie, you had better go and change," then noticing her eye, she exclaimed, "what on earth has happened to your eye, Minnie?"

Minnie did not reply and turned away.

"Minnie," said Janet, "get changed now! I am taking you to the clinic."

"No. Madam, I am alright."

Rosie had joined the pair and sniffed at Minnie, then her pocket. Now Janet was sure something serious was going on.

***

Billie was up doing his rounds, when he got the scent of something, he sniffed the ground and found where Minnie had come to the fence, he looked around and sniffed the air. It came from over there in the trees, he made his way over to where the rotten meat lay on the ground. He looked; he hadn't eaten yet as it was still early morning. He sniffed, but the meat was so spoiled that he could not eat it and turned away, as he did so, a resident hawk swooped in and picked it up and flew off over the boundary fence.

Benjamin had let the jack russells out and they all ran towards Billie. Then Rosie had also joined them, and they made their way to the shed, where the little elephant was waiting.

Big Boy had briefed his men and he had planned the attack on the homestead for that night, they would move in around midnight when all should be asleep. Janet spoke to Frank about Minnie and her injuries, and he promised he would

149

look into it at the weekend. It was still early and time to take Jessee for her swim, when they returned, Adeena was sitting waiting on the verandah drinking coffee, "Good morning," she shouted, "all is well, I hope."

The Jack russells made a fuss for a few minutes, then took off after a scolding from Janet. As they sat on the verandah, Frank appeared, gave Janet a kiss and said good morning to Adeena, then, "sorry girls, in a bit of a rush this morning". He put his coffee cup, still half full, on the table and bounded down the steps closely followed by Rosie. Frank was carrying his 12-gauge shotgun and as he jumped in the Stud, he shouted back, "guinea fowl for supper, darling," and took off with Rosie by his side. It was a long day; he went to the workshop and spent the morning with Tony Johnson. His old guide, Elijah, was there, so Frank told him to jump into the Stud, the next stop was the dairy. As they drove, Frank asked Elijah where the guinea fowl were and he answered in broken English, "Ah! Down by the river, Boss."

"Ok," said Frank, "When we finish at the dairy we shall see if we can shoot some."

Elijah smiled, he knew he would get some birds for he and his family.

It was late afternoon as they drove to the river. It was a short drive, only twelve miles, and they made good time. Not far from the river, Elijah spotted a herd of Impala, he pointed them out to Frank, "Look, Boss," he shouted, "Kill one for tonight," but Frank only had buckshot.

"Sorry, Elijah," he said, "another time,"

It was a large herd, probably thirty or forty animals, and Frank smiled to himself, it was nice to see them free, rather than in a zoo, like in Edinburgh. They reached the river with about two hours of daylight left and Elijah immediately spotted a large flock of guinea fowl, but they were on the other side of the river.

Frank spoke to Elijah, "well, that's bad luck, I don't fancy crossing the river, let's drive on and take a walk".

They drove another mile, stopped and got out, and walked towards the river, Rosie closely following. They walked along the bank. At this time of day all the birds came to drink and sure enough, around the next bend, they came across about twenty. The shotgun was already cocked, and they made no noise, Frank in his feltskins and barefoot Elijah. They moved to about fifty yards away when the alarm was sounded, the distinct KA! KA! KA! And they flew straight towards Frank. He aimed and fired, hitting one bird, killing it instantly, and wounding another, it fell to the ground and ran and flapped its way to cover. Rosie took off after it, her natural instinct was to catch and retrieve. Frank cocked the shot gun and fired again and again until the flock were off in the distance. In all, he had bagged six birds, if Rosie found the other, and sure enough, she appeared at his side with the bird flapping in her mouth. Elijah had picked up the rest and brought them to Frank with a huge smile showing pearl white teeth. Frank bent and gave Rosie a clap and said, "good girl, Rosie," and tried to take her prize but she resisted until Frank scolded her.

Elijah took the bird and quickly dispatched it. "This is good, boss."

"Yes," answered Frank, "take three, Elijah, and I will take the rest."

It was late when Frank got home and the sun was just setting. Life couldn't be better, everything was green after the rains, the farm was going well, and the boys were healthy.

Jack and his mum would soon be man and wife, and he looked forward to them coming home in a few days. As he drove over the crest of the hill, he looked down at the homesteads, how beautiful it looked with the dam in the background. As he drove in, he could see Adeena and Janet drinking tea. He dismounted and told Elijah to give three guinea fowl to Benjamin so he could clean them. Elijah disappeared with the birds and said goodnight. Frank climbed the steps and walked over to Janet and kissed her cheek and said hello to Adeena.

"Well," he said, "it's a bit late for Guinea fowl, maybe tomorrow."

Rosie made a fuss of the two women then moved to the cots and checked on the twins. Frank went inside with the shotgun; he took it into their bedroom and stood it against the wall next to his side of the bed. Normally he would lock it away, but he was dog tired, he then went back out and joined the women.

"Well," he said, Who's for a cold beer?"

Adeena apologised and said she must run, "maybe tomorrow, Frank, but thank you." She rose, said goodnight, and went to her scooter, "see the four of you later," she shouted as she putt-putted away.

Frank called to Minnie to bring two beers, which she did immediately, Frank thanked her then asked her what was going on with the bruises on her face, but she turned away and scrambled back to the kitchen. Then Frank turned to

Janet and said, "Well, sweetheart, not much we can do if she doesn't want to tell us." Janet agreed with him.

Big Boy and his gang set off at last light, they were going to attack the farmhouses in two groups, Big Boy and two of his best men would attack Frank and Janet's homestead. He wanted the children alive; he had been told they were male twins and would bring much strong medicine and courage to his followers. The rest would take the workshop and the doctor's house. They carried an assortment of weapons, three 9mm Sten guns, four .303 Enfield rifles and two hunting rifles. It was four hours journey to the farmhouses, and it was close to midnight when they arrived, they split into the two groups but before they split, Big Boy gave instructions to the second group not to attack until they heard shots from Big Boy. As Big Boy reached the perimeter fence, he thought back to the instructions he had given the girl: unload the handgun and poison the devil dog. He knew the other dogs would be locked away, and he smiled with confidence. He knelt at the fence and gave instructions to his men to be silent and dig under the fence. As they began, Big Boy looked at the homestead, it was in darkness, but the moon was bright, and they cast a shadow on the ground. It took nearly an hour to scrape away enough earth so they could pull themselves through on their backs, not one made a sound. It was just over two hundred yards to the front verandah, with small trees giving cover. All that could be heard were the crickets and the night noises, the fireflies hung in the air, looking like fairground lights.

They crept silently towards the front verandah of the house. As they got closer, one of the boys kicked his boot against a rock. They stopped. Rosie was asleep in her bed, but she opened her eyes and pricked her ears up. She growled; the boys were asleep in their cots. Frank heard her growl, strange, he thought and put a hand out toward her, "What's wrong, girl?" Then she gave a low bark and another growl and rose from her bed. Frank sat up and looked at the window, a shadow passed by, he reached over and silently grabbed the shotgun. It was already cocked, so he released the safety, shook Janet awake, and told her to be silent, instinctively she opened the drawer and removed the Webley revolver. Frank had told her to always be at the ready. Now Rosie was really agitated, he whispered to her to be quiet, but she growled and the hair on her back stood up, now Frank was certain it could not be any of the staff. As he waited, a shadowy figure moved across the window, the Mau-Mau stopped and listened, Frank and Janet were at the ready, the boys were safe in their cots at the side of the dresser, well shielded from the doorway. Just as Rosie was about to move, the bedroom door swung open, and two Mau-Mau appeared in the doorway. One raised an old .303 rifle and fired but the shot went high, and Frank fired the shotgun and hit him on the side of the head, tearing off his right cheek and ear, flesh and hair splattered over the wall. Janet aimed and fired at the same time, but the hammer fell on an empty chamber, she pulled the trigger again and again, but nothing happened. The second Mau-Mau turned and fled. Big boy was crouched under the window as his companion raced past. Big Boy was carrying a 9mm Sten gun and he let loose on automatic, his companion knocked the Sten off target and the bullets flew harmlessly into the air. Now Frank was after them, both the Mau-Mau fled into the dark and Frank fired wildly. Over at Jack's house, Benjamin heard the shots and released Billie, the young African looking after Jessee woke with a fright, the jack russells were going mad and scraping at the door. The young African pushed the door slightly open to gaze out and the russells were off. Now, Benjamin had opened the main gate and let Billie outside the perimeter fence, the jack russells were on the inner side.

Frank fired in the direction the Africans had fled and heard a scream. Big Boy made it to the hole under the fence and went under on his back, head first, but his injured arm slowed him down. Frank had hit the other African in the back and knocked him over, while not seriously wounded, he struggled to regain his footing. Screaming in agony, he tried to escape but now the jack russells were here and went in to the attack, they had never attacked a human before, but instinctively they knew he was a threat to their masters, all of them took hold and the African fell again, they bit into flesh and skin, he screamed, but it was no good, Frank was now there. He put the gun right against the African's stomach and pulled the trigger, the shotgun gave a thud, the muzzle noise barely audible. The Mau Mau writhed for a few seconds, then died.

Big Boy was next, as Frank closed in on the fence, Janet had lit lamps on the verandah and the light carried into the night. Big Boy's shirt had snagged, he was half under the fence, on his back. Billie rounded the corner of the fence and could smell the blood, he was out of control, this was the second time these black people had tried to hurt his masters and there was the scent of the big black man etched forever in his brain. He took Big Boy by the face and ripped at it, skin and hair came away in his jaws. Big Boy was begging for him to stop. He attacked again, taking Big Boy by the throat, now Frank was on the scene, he was about to dispatch this African but decided to let Billie finish his work. Billie punctured the jugular and the blood shot ten feet in the air, but Billie held on, and tore out his throat. Big Boy's legs and body began to quiver in its death spasms, and after a short while, stopped, and Big Boy lay still.

Tony Johnson had heard the commotion and Rufus Milo had been agitated for nearly an hour, the other six Mau-Mau had made it to the perimeter fence of Tony, and Adeena and Sam's place, they also heard the shots and the screams, but they were young, and they all turned and ran off into the night, not having the stomach for a stand-up fight. Tony ran to the Landrover, opened the gates to the compound, and drove as quickly as he could to Frank and Janet's.

As he arrived, he saw Benjamin in the headlights unlocking the homestead gates and he drove straight in. He jumped out and ran to where Janet was holding the two boys on the verandah.

"Are you alright, Jan?" he shouted.

She replied that she was, and could he please help Frank and she pointed in his direction. Tony ran to where Frank was and saw what had happened, lying in the torch light were two Africans inside the perimeter, the jack russells were standing guard over one and Frank had the other by the feet, trying to drag him back under the fence. Tony knelt and gave him a hand, each took a leg and heaved, he slid under easily and Billie followed. Billie again took a grip and Frank told him, "Alright, boy, He's dead," and Billie made his way to Frank's side and lay at his feet.

"Christ, Frank, you've had one hell of a night. Is everyone ok?"

"Yes, lucky we are, Tony,"

Frank could hear Janet calling as he made her way towards them, over her arm she was carrying the twins. When she got to him, she was out of breath and asked if he was ok.

"I'm fine, darling, the dogs did a fine job".

As she looked at the carnage, Frank knelt and began going through Big Boy's pockets. In one breast pocket he pulled out six shining .38 calibre ammunition rounds, he looked at Janet and said, "Big Boy was carrying a 9mm Sten gun, where do you think these came from?"

Janet answered, "That must be why my revolver wouldn't fire, those are the bullets. Minnie must have removed them." Minnie had heard the shooting and knew they had been discovered. The six young Mau-Mau had panicked and run through the compound, but Minnie dared not open her door. She hid in the corner of her hut until morning. There was a loud knock on the door, and still, she did not move. The door was broken down by the police. She was dragged outside by two African constables and thrown in the dirt, she was punched and kicked, until a white officer stepped in. He shouted at her, "Well, my girl, what have you been up to?"

Her face was bruised and bloody, her lips swollen, as she started to answer, she knew she had been discovered. Frank was there, also having briefed the police.

When they arrived, he looked down at her and held out the six cartridges. "Look", he shouted, "You did this, didn't you?"

She looked up and spoke, blood spurting from her mouth, "Yes, boss. I am sorry."

"Sorry?" Frank shouted, "they could have murdered our entire family."

"Yes, I am sorry. They took my son and my mother. They will kill them."

"But we have been good to you, Minnie, you should have come to us, we would have helped."

Minnie looked at Frank, "Boss, you cannot help, now they will be dead."

Minnie was dragged to the police truck and roughly thrown into the back and handcuffed to the floor. The Police recovered the bodies of the dead Mau-Mau and threw them in the back of the truck with Minnie. Tony Johnson joined Frank, they looked at each other, Rufus Milo was by Tony's side, Tony looked down and gave him a pat. "Good boy," he said, and Rufus wagged his tail.

"Well," said Tony, "quite a night, Frank."

"Yes, it certainly was, Jack's not going to be happy, we'd better contact him."

"Do you think that's wise, Frank, rather let him get back, the roads are bad and if he rushes back anything could happen."

"Yes," replied Frank, "on second thoughts, you're right, and the wedding's only two weeks away. I will wait until he gets back on Thursday. Let's go back to my place. I think we both need a drink."

They drove up to towards Frank's, the lights were on, and Janet was standing on the verandah holding the twins. Benjamin and the house staff were busy cleaning up the mess. Rosie ran towards Frank wagging her tail and sniffed at Rufus Milo. They climbed the stairs and before Janet could speak Frank told her, "Yes, it was Minnie, she admitted it to my face." And Frank explained about her son and mother.

Frank went into the lounge and opened the drink cabinet, took out three classes and poured whisky into two, he handed one to Tony and poured Janet a bitter Lemon. She walked over, cradling the twins, one in each arm, they had been crying but now had gone almost quiet. She looked at Frank and said, "darling, let me put these two down to sleep. It's been a hell of a night."

Frank acknowledged her and turned to Tony. They spoke for half an hour, drank another whisky then Tony said he had better make a move, thanked Frank and Janet, and said goodnight.

Janet walked over to Frank and gave him a kiss, he was looking at the pictures Janet had hung on the walls, his favourite was the one with he and Ian smith standing next to Ian's spitfire. Frank had his hand on Ian's shoulder, and both had broad smiles. Frank stared at the picture for some time, every now and again Janet spoke but he said nothing, he was wondering to himself if he had done the right thing bringing his family to Kenya. Tonight, he, Janet, and the twins could have been slaughtered. He thought of Ian and the letters he received from Rhodesia, all was going well down there and Ian was full of confidence and very optimistic about his country's future. Mining and agriculture had taken off and he had also gone into tobacco.

Janet gave him a shake and said, "Darling, I'm off to bed", they kissed, and she went to the bedroom, still Frank said nothing. He finished his whisky and followed her. They sank under the covers, said goodnight to Rosie, and fell asleep.

The next morning as they sat on the verandah they watched the sun rise, it was very quiet, not even the dogs were awake. Blood was still smeared on the verandah walls and floor. As they spoke to each other, they saw Adeena's scooter putt-putt-putting over the hill. On the rear seat, tightly holding on to his wife, was Sam Enfield. They pulled up at the front steps, and Sam looked white faced as he disembarked.

They called out, "Good morning, do you mind if we join you?"

Janet shouted down, "come up, both of you."

The jack russells were awake and out of control. Frank soon put them in their place, and they all slinked back to their beds. Rosie was never a problem, she just wanted a pat and followed them to the table, flopping down next to Frank, tail sweeping the floor.

Sam began the conversation, "Frank, sorry we couldn't get through last night, the lines were cut and when we tried to get up here, the police stopped us and wouldn't let us through. They said there could have been more about, so they sent us home with an escort. They stayed all night."

Frank was the first to reply, "We thought that might have been the case, Sam, anyway at least you are both ok. Grab some tea, I will order you some breakfast."

Benjamin and his sister were both in the kitchen and Frank shouted through that they had company. Just as he did, Tony Johnson pulled up and joined them on the verandah. Again, Frank shouted to Benjamin – "Ben, that's an extra three please."

Benjamin appeared at the end of the verandah with a white tea towel draped over his right arm, looking every bit the professional waiter.

"Very good, Boss, twenty minutes."

They discussed the last night's incident, and how lucky Sam and Adeena had been as Sam was not keen on guns and probably had not been targeted because he was a doctor and ran the clinic with Adeena. Tony dismissed that theory and chipped in, "I doubt that was the reason, these bloody Kaffirs don't care about their people and the clinic, you were probably next on the list."

At that moment breakfast began to arrive. It was set up on a long table so they could all help themselves. There was fresh ham, scrambled eggs, French toast, and small grilled steaks. Janet and Adeena went to the table and started to dish up for the men. Janet turned to Tony, "bit of everything for you?"

"Of course, Jan, thanks."

The jack russells were, again, out of control, so Frank gave them a telling off and took them out back and gave them each a bone. At first there was much snarling and biting, but eventually, they settled down.

Frank returned to his guests and breakfast. They made light conversation as they ate, then Frank spoke up and said, "I think we had all better take the day off, it's been one hell of a night." They all agreed, except Adeena, she said she would work until noon and Sam said he should be there just to get through the most serious casualties, the police and army had left a few bruised heads. Then Frank told them that they were not going to tell Jack and Rita what had happened until they returned just in case Jack panicked and tried to speed home on the bad roads. The others agreed.

"Anyway," said Frank, "in two weeks we have the wedding, so let's all look ahead."

***

It was eight am when they finished, and Benjamin was busy clearing away. Janet stood up first and went to tend to the twins, when she returned, everyone was standing on the verandah waiting to say goodbye to her, then off they went, Adeena and Sam first. She kick-started the scooter, Sam climbed aboard, and they were gone, putt-putt-putt. Then off went Tony. Janet turned to Frank and said, "Darling, I'm going to take Jessee to the dam, would you like to come along?"

Frank said, "Yes," and asked if she was ready.

Billie had joined them and was over by Rosie, flirting. Last night's events not even a memory. He was still blood stained and Frank bent down and gave him a pat on the head, he looked at Frank, wagged his tail and licked Frank's hand. Frank said to him, "You need a swim, Billie, clean you up a bit, then shouted to Rosie, "Come on, girl,"

Rosie was already up and ready, her tail slashing the air. As they walked towards the shed, Frank put his arm around his wife and leant over and gave her a kiss. She looked at him and asked what was that for? Just for being you and being here with me. They walked on, the jack russells running up and falling in behind them. As they neared the shed, Jessee saw them, she raised her trunk and screamed a greeting, flapping her ears, the fold in the left ear clearly visible, even at this distance. Rosie moved forward and Jessee ran to meet her. She lowered her trunk and sniffed at Rosie then gripped her gently around the neck.

Now all the dogs had joined in, and Janet shouted, "all right, you lot, let's go." Janet and Frank turned around and headed in the direction of the dam. Then Jessee smelt the dried blood

162

on Billie, raised her trunk and gave a loud squeal and took off. She ran towards the dam but must have got a terrible fright and crashed through the fence, tearing down the wire and ripping out four posts. Everyone took off after her, when they reached the dam, she had settled in the water. Rosie had run behind her and now sat on the bank watching her. When everyone else arrived, Billie was the first in and off chasing the ducks, swimming as close as he could before they ducked below the surface. This went on until Billie was exhausted, when he swam to shore, all the blood had been washed from his coat.

Janet and Frank sat for a while on the edge of the dam taking in the morning sun and laughing at Billie and the jack russells. Rosie was stretched out at Frank's feet as usual, her pride of place, her eyes fixed on him. Then Frank said to Janet, "Well, old girl, time we got back." They got up and shouted to the menagerie and after a few moments all heads turned to their masters. Jessee let out a loud squeal and made her way to Rosie, she wrapped her truck around her neck and the whole group took off towards home.

It wasn't long before they broke into a conversation, Frank began, "You know, sweetheart, I think it's time Jessee went back to a herd, what are your thoughts?"

"Well, after the fence," she laughed, "I think you're right, we don't need any more of that."

"Well," Frank went on, "perhaps before the wedding, that's only two weeks away, anyway. I'll organise that for next week. The boys say there's a lot of elephants moving across the river, so we can take her out and see if we can find her a new home and some new friends, but I know she and Rosie will miss each other."

When they arrived home, the jack russells disappeared to retrieve their old bones. Then Janet said to Frank, "Darling, I'm going to check on the boys. Then I'll go to the clinic for an hour and be back for lunch and the rest of the day is ours."

"Sounds good," replied Frank.

Janet returned as promised, but didn't bother with lunch, instead, she made a suggestion and Frank couldn't turn it down. It was early evening when Frank awoke, he could hear Janet with the twins. It had been a great day after all and they both needed the release that the afternoon had given them. He called to Janet, who answered, and appeared in the doorway completely naked. It was too much for Frank, so he made a suggestion and Janet and he dived under the covers once again. They rose early the next day and were both ravenous. They hadn't eaten since the previous morning and of course Benjamin and his wife were busy in the kitchen. They all ate well, Rosie, the jack russells, and the Monros. They sat and talked, mostly about the trouble with the Mau-Mau and also about the future and whether they realistically thought the country was going to be a viable proposition for whites. Frank said he would give it a couple of years as all was going well, the farm was prospering, and they were becoming quite well off financially. They spoke about Rhodesia and Ian Smith and how confident he was about the white's future in his country and that he planned to enter politics. It was just after three in the afternoon when they saw Jack's truck come into view. He was travelling at speed and pulled up with a screech of brakes in front of Frank and Janet's house. Both he and Rita got out and walked up the steps.

Jack spoke first, "Well, you two, a spot of bother the other night, I hear."

"Yes, indeed, Uncle Jack. How did you hear?"

"No secrets amongst the farmers here, laddie, everyone was on about it in Nairobi."

Rita went on, "Thank God, the lot of you are safe and ok. How are the twins?"

Janet reassured her and said, "Everyone is ok".

"Well," said Jack, "I need a dram. Let's sit down and you can run through the whole goings on."

Frank fetched a decanter of Johnny Walker and four glasses. Frank told him about Big Boy and the two dead Mau-Mau and how Billie had dispatched the big black man.

Jack Interrupted with "Good value, that dog."

Billie was sitting not far off and wagged his tail furiously when he heard his name. They drank more whisky and talked about the wedding. Frank had arranged for two huge marques to be delivered. Everyone in the neighbourhood was invited and all the African staff on the farm which numbered at least one hundred and fifty. They would have a marque one hundred metres from the whites, they had to organise beer for the Africans, as they preferred their own brew made from maize, like a watery porridge and quite potent. Tony Johnson was in charge of all that. Pork, beef, and lamb had to be supplied and they had it all at hand on the farm. They spoke about Jessee and told Jack and Rita about the fence and that they had decided to find her a new home with new friends. They both agreed that it was a good idea. She must go now, while she was still young, she already stood five feet tall at the shoulder.

When it was time to eat, both the men were a little unsteady on their feet. So, they ate, said their good nights, and made their way to their beds. Now that that they had been discovered, Jack and Rita had decided to sleep in the spare room at Frank and Janet's place as their home was still shut down since they had been away. The next morning, Frank asked Benjamin to send word to Elijah to come to the house. Elijah arrived at ten o'clock and Frank and Benjamin explained what they had planned.

Elijah broke into a huge smile. "Ah! Boss," he said, "plenty elephant crossing the river now, the little one will find a new family."

"Right," said Frank, "tomorrow morning, first light, be here with three other boys. We will do it then."

"Right, Boss," replied Elijah, "this is a good thing for the little one."

Jack and Rita had risen and were listening in, Janet had already eaten and gone to the clinic. Elijah took off at a run and soon disappeared over the rise.

"Well," said Jack, "all organised, will it be alright if Rita and I join you tomorrow, laddie?"

"Of course, Uncle Jack, I was going to invite you anyway. It's not something we do every day."

"Right, lad, well me and Rita are off to our place, we will be here tomorrow, bright and early."

Frank said goodbye to his mother and Jack as they stepped off the verandah, closely followed by Billie.

***

The next morning after breakfast, the family had assembled ready for the day ahead. The trailer was hitched and ready to go, and Frank, Rosie, the jack russells, and the boys made their way to the barn to get Jessee. When they arrived, the little elephant was outside grazing on some green grass. She heard them coming and raised her trunk, smelling the air, then let out a screech when she saw Rosie and ran forward with outstretched trunk and wrapped it around Rosie's neck.

"Right, Rosie", called Frank, "bring her around."

The little elephant followed on, still clutching Rosie. As they got to the trailer, Frank could see the tailgate was down and everyone was assembled and ready to lend a hand. They stopped at the back of the trailer and Frank ordered Rosie in. She went in and Jessee followed. Two Africans on each side, Frank and Jack closed the tailgate and they were ready to go. Frank and Janet were in the front, Jack and Rita in the rear with Benjamin in the hunting seats. He had packed a picnic hamper as they would probably be away most of the day. It was fifty miles to the river, and it would take at least three hours to get there so, as they set off, everyone was chattering excitedly and looking forward to the rest of the day. In the back, Jessee gave a loud squeal and Rosie replied with a loud bark. The attack on the farm was out of every one's minds.

It was a beautiful morning, the Africans in the back began to sing as only Africans can sing, as they bumped along the road. As they left the main buildings, about ten miles out, game began to appear, first impala then some Tsebe which was unusual for this time of year, Kudu leapt across the road, Frank thought he saw a bushbuck, and turned to Janet and said, "look, sweetheart," but when they turned back to look, it had gone, disappeared into the thick bush that they loved.

As they approached the river, the Africans stopped singing, they looked at the road and they could see the deep tracks of the elephant moving through the area, huge heaps of dung littered the ground, dung beetles could be seen with golf ball size dung balls clasped behind their back legs, running off into the distance. Frank pulled up and turned to Benjamin.

"Right, Benjamin, we will stop here, let Jessee out, she can graze for a while, send the boys out, two upriver, two down river, to see if they can locate the herds."

Benjamin jumped out and spoke in Swahili to the boys, they obeyed and dropped the ramp and backed Jessee out. Rosie was there to meet her, and she immediately wrapped her trunk around her neck. Benjamin gave the instructions to the boys and off they went down towards the river in that long-legged run that Africans are good at.

On the far side of the river, the thick forest reached to within one hundred yards of the riverbank. On the farm side, the trees had been cleared to make way for grazing cattle. Jack had given up trying to fence this side of the farm as the elephants and buffalo just trashed it. Broken bits of fence and posts littered the river boundary. Now he employed herd boys to keep watch over his livestock.

Benjamin broke out the picnic hamper and the family began to enjoy some lunch, but it was only about thirty minutes later when two of the scouts returned, both grinning from ear to ear and showing their white teeth. Even though they spoke in Swahili, Jack could understand, and Frank most of it. Apparently, a herd of about thirty elephants were drinking, and the boys pointed in their direction. As far as Frank could make out, it was close to where he had shot Jessee's mother. "Alright," said Jack, "we can walk from here, it's only about a mile, just leave everything as it is," he called to Frank to tell Rosie to bring the elephant along, she barked at Jessee and turned towards Frank, then set off. Jessee quickly caught up and took hold of Rosie. The women were at the rear, chattering away as only women can. They walked for about twenty minutes until they came to a bend in the river, another half a mile and that's where Jessee lost her mother, they walked on and there was the tree where Jessee's mother had leant on in agony and the small thicket where Jessee had hidden. It had been over a year and no trace could be seen, but Jessee released her grip on Rosie and sniffed at the air, raising her trunk, something was here but she knew not what. Something was in her memory, and she looked at Frank and walked towards him, they both stopped, facing each other, her ears flapped, the fold in her ear noticeable then she extended her trunk and smelled his face and nuzzled his shoulder as if to thank him.

They continued along the riverbank and climbed a small rise. They looked down and there they were, half the herd were drinking, the other half scattered for about one hundred yards at the forest edge, breaking off branches with their trunks and stuffing them into their mouths. Jessee got their scent and raised her trunk to smell them, she recognised the smell and let out a loud scream. They were only about one hundred yards away, and all the adults turned towards her, sniffing the air. The elephants at the water's edge turned away and walked back to the edge of the forest, the largest of the herd bringing up the rear and moving backwards into the trees but remaining visible.

Jack spoke to Frank, "Right, lad, let's get her down there before they wander off," then turned to the ladies and said, "girls, you had better stay here just in case. Right, let's go."

They moved down to the river and picked a spot to cross, it wasn't deep, and they were soon across. Rosie and Jessee were in the lead. As they stumbled up the riverbank, they could see a change in Jessee and she released her grip on Rosie and made her way towards the herd, then she stopped halfway and looked back at Rosie and the humans who had cared for her so well.

Just then two young elephants broke out of the forest and rushed towards her, they were bigger than Jessee, but she stood still. Frank called to Rosie to come back, and she turned and ran towards his side. The two young elephants moved closer to Jessee, looked at her, then began to headbutt her, trying to drive her away back to the river. Jessee let out a squeal, then fought back but it was no good, they were too strong for her. It didn't look good.

Jack turned to Frank and said, "Not going to be as easy as we thought, laddie,"

"Doesn't look like it." Replied Frank.

The two youngsters began bullying Jessee again. Frank was just about to call her back when a huge elephant appeared out of the forest, trumpeting loudly. It pushed into the trio.

"This must be the matriarch," shouted Jack.

When she got to Jessee, she lashed the two smaller elephants with her trunk. This sent them scurrying back to the forest edge, then she gently took Jessee by the trunk, sniffed at her, took her again by the trunk and led her towards the forest. When they reached the edge, they both stopped and turned towards the Monros. Rosie let out a loud bark, then the elephants turned and disappeared into the dark undergrowth. Jessee was gone.

Jack turned to Frank, "Well, Frank, that's good, you know who the big girl is."

"I have an idea, Uncle Jack, that was the most important one in the herd."

"Aye," said Jack. "Jessee will be fine, the matriarch will teach her everything she needs to know and look after her."

They turned back towards the river, looked up at the women and waved, the women waved back, then Frank said, "I suppose those two will be upset, I can see from here."

They crossed back over the river with Rosie in tow, and walked up towards Rita and Janet, then Janet asked, "Do you think she will be alright? She looked so small next to the others."

"She'll be fine" said Jack, "you saw who came to look after her. The big one, probably seventy years old, has all the smarts any elephant will need. No doubt we will cross paths again."

They walked back to the stud but were silent all the way, except for the boys, they were proud of what they had done.

When they reached the Stud, Benjamin laid out the lunch again and they sat on the grass chatting, the boys were on the other side, they had cold meats and corn. As the ladies ate, they looked out over the river. On the far side, a small herd of Impala emerged from the forest and began grazing, then a Kudu came into view, a female and she had a youngster following close behind.

It was a beautiful afternoon and Janet's gaze turned towards Frank. How lucky I am, she thought, having met such a wonderful man who has given me and the two boys such a wonderful life. Then she thought about how such a wonderful country, and such nice people could be so violent. She remembered talking to Jack about how, no matter what colour the skin or which country you live in, all their history was violent. He had explained that, before the British arrived, the Africans had many problems: disease, starvation, tribal wars, short life expectancy. He explained the two main reasons the Africans will never advance on their own was tribalism and that while the male sees himself as a warrior and a hunter, the women do all the work. Only after the intervention did they get off their arses and do some work. They needed white supervision for that, they got clothes, medicine, a wage, and regular food. Janet had to agree with him, she saw the injuries and the disease that came through the clinic and how eager they were to see their children getting a basic education from Rita's school.

It all came to an end too soon. Jack broke the silence, he stood up and shouted at the boys to load up, then Frank said to the ladies, "Ok, girls, let's go."

In a couple of minutes everything was loaded. Rosie hadn't moved, she was staring back along the track watching for Jessee, but she never came.

Frank called to her, "come on girl," and she turned and ran towards the truck and jumped up and sat between Frank and Jack.

Jack gave her a pat and spoke to her "It's ok, girl, she will be ok. She's with her own kind now."

Rosie turned her head and licked his hand.

***

It was late afternoon when they arrived back at the farm. Janet and Rita went straight in to visit the twins, they looked fine, both lying on their backs in their cots. The new house girl, Constance, a family member of Benjamin's, was very good. It had been a long day, so, they ate and went straight to bed. Rita and Jack said they would be back in the morning to discuss the wedding plans, it was only five days away, planned for Saturday the coming weekend. While he and Rita were in Nairobi, Jack had organised Indian traders to do the catering, they would arrive on Thursday with the marques, tables, and chairs. They would supply all the tableware, cakes, alcohol, and other beverages. Tony Johnson had organised three beasts to be slaughtered, along with six sheep and some goats for the boys, they would go on the spit Friday morning, where they would cook all day and night, ready for Saturday. Jack had spared no expense. Of course, Frank would be his best man.

Thursday arrived and the Indian caterers turned up mid-morning. Jack and Frank took them to the site, the African's tent was set a good two hundred metres away from the guest's and Jack had organised an African combo for them. He was expecting around one hundred Africans at least. The caterers began their work erecting the tent. It was larger than Jack had imagined. The weather forecast was good, so they didn't expect any rain, and most of the tables had been set up in the small grove of trees about one hundred metres from Jack and Rita's house. It was a beautiful setting. Coloured lights had been strung up in the trees as they expected the celebrations to go on well into the night especially with the Africans, who, if there was meat available, would fill their guts until they burst.

Saturday arrived and everyone was still busy, both households had risen early, and Tony Johnson soon arrived to lend a hand. The wedding ceremony was to be at midday and Jack had organised for the Presbyterian minister to marry them. The minister was also a Scotsman, a large highlander with a booming voice. He had served with the British Army in the second world war and moved to Kenya as a battalion chaplain, just after the war had finished. He knew the people well and loved working with the Africans. To anyone who complained about the bloody Kaffirs, he would reply, "They're all God's children."

He was a regular visitor to Jack's place and could finish a bottle of whisky in a couple of hours and still drive home, but Jack would insist he sleep it off and give him a bed for the night. He arrived about ten in the morning, shook hands with everyone then gave Jack a long stare, Jack knew what it meant, off went the four of them, Jack, Frank, Tony, and the Reverend into the front room. The celebrations were about to begin. It was only another hour before the ladies would appear, and it wouldn't be long before the Enfield's arrived, Adeena was so looking forward to the day.

The men enjoyed a large whisky, then they left to get ready for what was ahead. Jack, of course, would be dressed in the Munro tartan along with Frank. They left the honourable minister to look after himself. Frank made his way back to his home. The ladies were there getting ready, he could hear them halfway down the path leading to his house. At his side, as always, was Rosie, Frank looked down at her, she was beginning to grey around the muzzle. Frank commented on it, and she looked up and wagged her tail.

Frank climbed the steps and made his way to his bedroom. The ladies were in the sitting room with the door shut.

Frank's kilt and tunic were laid out on the bed, the last time he had worn it was at his own wedding and he smiled to himself. He took a shower and began to dress. It didn't take him long and when he finished, he stood in front of the full-length mirror and admired himself. It was a smart outfit, he thought, and he smiled again. He looked at the time, this was it, time to get the ladies. He opened his door and made his way to the sitting room, he stopped outside and knocked, a voice on the other side said, "Please come in." It was Janet. He opened the door and went in, all the women were standing in a row, then Janet said, "Well, what do you think?"

Frank was quite stunned for a second, they looked beautiful. Adeena looked like a movie star with her hair all blown out and her tanned skin, and wearing a beautiful crème coloured tight fitting skirt. His mother, though not a young woman anymore, still held herself high, and was also stunning. She hadn't gained a pound since she was a young girl, she was dressed in an off-white suit, and wearing a wide brimmed hat, but the most beautiful of all was his wife. He just stood for a moment and stared at her. She was also wearing an off-white suit, very tight, it showed off her long legs and fantastic figure. Then Janet interrupted his thoughts and said, "Well, put your eyes back in, Munro, they have popped out onto the end of your big nose."

"Oh!", he said, "sorry, sweetheart, I was just wondering how you got into such a tight-fitting dress with that big bum of yours." She glared at him, then they all burst out laughing.

Frank interrupted, "Well, ladies it's time to go. You all right, mum?"

"Yes, son" and off they went towards Jack's place, Rosie bringing up the rear. They entered by the rear door and made their way to the front room, then Frank said he would go and join Jack, if he could find him. He gave them instructions that, when the music started, it would be their cue. He went down the stairs and in amongst the guests. There was Jack, over by the bar, he was busy chastising Benjamin who was off his face and had fallen on the red-hot barbeque plate. He was in agony and holding his burnt hand.

Jack was giving it to him, "You see you, stupid bugger, you have been into my whisky again."

"Ah! No boss. Not me. I'm sick, my hand is burnt." Jack replied, "well, that's your fault. Do I come and bother you when I'm injured."

"Ah! No, boss" was the reply.

"Right. Go inside and let the ladies look at it."

In tears and agony, he went inside and spoke to Janet, she took one look and said, "Well, we haven't really got time to look at it now, come with me."

She took him to the kitchen, filled a bucket with water and stuck his hand in it. This eased the pain immediately.

"Keep the air away until it blisters," she instructed.

He said it was better and took his hand out. Immediately, the pain returned, so she stuck his hand back in, but he was so drunk he fell over, then she heard the music begin and the guests went silent.

"Well, Benjamin, you know what to do, get on with it."

With that she turned and ran. Adeena and Rita were just on their way to fetch her.

"Ok," they said, "it's time," and they walked down the front steps, where the guests had lined up on each side, leaving a path down the middle. At the end stood Jack and Frank and Rosie, the men looked quite dashing in their Munro tartan kilts.

The Minister had his back to them, talking to the groom and best man. Rita saw he was a bit unsteady on his feet but didn't give it a second thought, he was a Scot, after all. Sam Enfield fell in beside Rita and took her arm, she looked at him and smiled. Now the minister turned towards them and staggered a bit, regained his composure, and summoned them forward. The ceremony was somewhat hurried, and it was all over in less than ten minutes, then it was back to the celebrations.

As the afternoon wore on, the noise grew louder. The Africans had their drum band, and as it grew dark, the lights turned on, it was wonderful, and everyone was having a great time. The Indians caterers had organized music, some wonderful new songs coming out of America and people were drinking and dancing, all enjoying themselves. Jack and Rita had organised to spend the two weeks of their honeymoon in Mombasa, they would leave in the morning, stay overnight in Nairobi, then on to Mombasa the next day, they were both looking forward to the break.

The party went on into the small hours, then gradually, the numbers began to dwindle, until only a few diehards remained. The Africans had all left and each guest bid the Munros farewell and wished Jack and Rita all the best and thanked them for a wonderful time. Rita and Jack decided enough was enough and sneaked away, they wanted to leave early the next morning. As they made their way to the house, they passed the minister, he was unconscious, lying in the garden at the edge of the steps. They decided to leave him and made their way inside. They undressed and got into bed, and it wasn't long before they were both fast asleep, Billie curled up next to the bed on Jack's side.

As far as an early start, that didn't happen. It was ten in the morning before anyone stirred, even the African house staff. There was no sign of Benjamin, Jack knew he would still be off his face, and would be for a couple of days. As they lay in bed, they heard some noise coming from the kitchen followed by a knock on the door. It was Janet. Rita told her to come in, and she did, holding a tray of mugs steaming with hot coffee and followed by Adeena, carry a breakfast tray. It had eggs, bacon, beans, and toast. They put it on the table next to the bed then Janet asked if they could join them and of course, Rita was the first to say yes. Adeena dished up for four then they started talking about the previous night's events and what a great party it was and what a wonderful time everyone had. They had been talking for nearly an hour when Janet said, "Well, it's time you two got up, we should leave you to it," and the two ladies cleared away and took everything to the kitchen.

It was only minutes before Jack and Rita heard them leave by the front steps. Billie was busy finishing the breakfast scraps. Jack turned to Rita and said, "Well, my lady, doesn't look like we will get to Nairobi tonight, maybe we can stop at the Settler's Inn bed and breakfast and stay overnight, that's halfway, what do you think? There's a nice little bar there, and we can catch up with some of the locals."

"Sounds great, sweetheart."

"We need to get away around one o'clock if we are to make it before nightfall."

Rita phoned Frank to let him know their plan and he agreed it was a sound option and they would all be over to see them off. Rita finished packing and told Jack to load up the Landrover. Jack had been busy trying to track down Benjamin but had come up negative. Wait till I get back, he thought to himself. Jack had just finished loading as everybody began to arrive to say goodbye. They all gave Rita a hug, but Jack wasn't a hugger. Then into the Landrover and off they went. It was about four hours' drive to the Settler's and the roads were good.

As they drove, they spoke about Jack's brother and how happy he had been when he married Rita, their childhood in East Lothian, Scotland, and all the people and friends they had left behind and the hardships the working people had endured under a conservative government. Then the war and how everything changed. Four years of bitter fighting in Europe left the population decimated. When it was all over Jack and his brother, Tom, had returned to the village, but half the young men never came home and others did but with terrible injuries, not only physical but mentally scarred for the rest of their days. Rita didn't say much, she just listened, and she remembered the change in her husband. Sometimes he would just sit in front of the fire, smoking his pipe, and drinking a whisky, sometimes he would have a little too much and he would take his medals and throw them into the fire. The next morning, she would pull them out of the ashes, clean them, and send off to the war office for new ribbons. Then they lost Brian and he changed for ever, but she had still loved him dearly and stuck by him.

It was just after five when they pulled into the Settler's. There were half a dozen different types of vehicles parked outside. The bar opened out onto a wide verandah, and it was full. The owner, Paul Henry, saw them pull into the drive and waved to his wife, Sonia, and they came out to welcome them. Paul extended his hand to Jack. They shook hands, "Nice to see the both of you," said Jack, then turned to Rita and introduced his new wife.

"Well," said Paul, "before we do anything, Jack and Rita, I must buy you both a drink to celebrate." He beaconed to the boys to take care of the luggage, "Now come with me."

Jack thought this was unusual for an Englishman because the English have the deepest pockets, and he was a Yorkshireman, which was even worse, but they made their way into the bar. Jack knew everyone there and they all said hullo and came to shake his hand, give him a pat on the back, and look Rita up and down. Jack was a bit of a legend in his own right, Rita was very aware of this and proud to be his wife.

After an hour, Jack could see his wife was beginning to tire, so he gave her a wink and glanced towards the door, then leant over and said, "Come on, let's sneak away, lassie."

Jack hadn't paid for a drink since they entered the bar, and being a Scotsman, this suited him down to the ground. Now it was time to sneak away which he did. It had been a busy two days and they looked forward to a hot bath and a good night's sleep.

Early the next morning there was a knock on the door, it was Sonia and Paul, they had brought breakfast and a huge bunch of fresh flowers just picked from the garden.

"We didn't get a chance to say goodnight last night," said Paul, "so we thought we would give you special treatment. Eat your breakfast, and good luck to both of you. Now we'll be off, you make sure to say goodbye before you leave." And they shut the door behind them.

Rita commented on what nice people they were.

It was just after eight when they left, they said their goodbyes and promised to stop in on the way home. It was a beautiful morning, not a cloud in the sky.

Jack said to Rita, "Well, sweetheart, we should be in Nairobi by mid-afternoon."

She turned to him and said, "I am so looking forward to it, this is the first time we have really been alone together." And she reached over and took his hand.

As they drove on, they passed an army convoy going in the opposite direction. About thirty trucks and Landrovers, all crammed full of young army and police lads.

 "Must be something going on dear." Jack commented. They saw the usual game on the way, mostly Impala, Kudu, and off in the distance at one point, half a dozen giraffe with a newborn at foot. They didn't stop and it was nearly three in the afternoon when they reached the outskirts of Nairobi. It was about a thirty-minute drive to the centre of the city and Jack drove on towards the hotel they were booked into, the Norfolk, as usual. Jack turned into the long driveway that led to reception, Rita commented on how beautiful the gardens were as they pulled up.

The usual hotel staff were there to welcome them, Jack and Rita sat for a while, chatting, while the boys took out their luggage.

Rita said to Jack, "It's such a wonderful life here, Jack, I haven't thanked you yet for taking us all in," and leant over and kissed his cheek.

Jack put his arm around her, "Rita, sweetheart, I'm the one who should be thankful, now I have you, Jan and Frank, and two lovely grandsons. I honestly thought I would die a lonely old man. Now I have so much to look forward to. Come on, let's get cleaned up and get something to eat."

They walked to their chalet, opened the door, and went inside, all their cases were there and one of the house girls was busy unpacking, but Rita stepped in. The girl's name was Eunice, according to the gold tag on her smock.

"No that's all-right, Eunice, we are only here for one night."

She looked at Rita and said, "Oh! Ok, Madam."

Rita handed her a silver shilling which she clutched with both hands. She curtsied, said "thank you, madam", turned and left the room, closing the door quietly behind her.

Jack and Rita agreed a drink in the bar would be a good idea, so they made their way there first. It wasn't crowded, and at the far end, stood that big-nosed chinless wonder, Lord 'Muck', waffling on about how the British army were going to sort out this Mau-Mau threat and return Kenya to the way she used to be. Jack pointed him out to Rita; she had heard him talk about him…. And knew his feelings. She felt him tense up when Lord 'Muck' spotted him. She knew how much he disliked the so-called English Aristocracy.

"Ah!" he shouted from the far end of the bar, "Jack Munro, please come join us."

He was standing with three others, sipping pink gins, "Well, Jack, goodness me, who is this fair lady?"

Jack introduced Rita, "This is my wife".

Lord 'Muck's' jaw dropped then he started, "Good lord, Jack, I had no idea," he extended his hand, Rita hers, and he kissed it gently. "So nice to meet you, my dear."

Jack noticed he never offered to buy a drink.

"Well," He asked, "when did this happen?"

Jack answered gruffly, "two days ago. Well, we are off to get something to eat," Jack grabbed Rita by the arm, "come, dear, we're both hungry" and left the group. Jack wasn't even in the dining room before he started, Rita didn't interrupt him, she just let him rant on about bloody English 'Toffs'.

"They have their fingers in every pie, stealing and exploiting the working man as soon as they're born, not one of them's ever done a day's work, did you know, sweetheart, that English officers are forbidden to do manual labour?"

Rita Replied, "I didn't, dear, but I do now."

Jack went on, "I'm surprised they manage to wipe their own backsides."

Rita smiled and managed to supress a giggle.

He went on, "You know we had them in Aberlady, Gullane, and Longniddry, bloody Englishmen with great estates, twelve-foot stone walls all around. What are they doing in Scotland? Let them go back to England where they come from."

Rita took his hand and spoke quietly to him, "You know, Jack, if you want to eat you have to stop talking."

Jack looked at her and laughed, he saw the funny side of it, "Yes, you're right, I have met a lot of good lads, especially in the war, even they were ready to turn on them, only the fear of being shot kept them in check".

They made their way to their table, and each ordered a steak with vegies of the day, had a beer, and talked about Mombasa and how they were looking forward to seeing the ocean again. They had both been brought up next to the coast in the Firth of Forth.

Jack finished his meal and started again, "the best thing that happened in British politics was when Labour swept to victory after the second world war, brought the unions in, negotiated a fair working wage, gave the country free health service, saved tens of thousands of lives, lives that would have been lost under a conservative government. It's a pity we couldn't get rid of that House of Lords, they're not only a drain on finances but on society, bunch of big-nosed chinless halfwits, then we could start on the palace with all the bum lickers they have there, generals, admirals, air force, all stabbing each other in the back to get the swords on the shoulder. The knighthood should stick it in their hearts. Bloody infants the lot of them".

Jack stopped to catch his breath, so Rita jumped in, "Well, Jack, darling, you haven't done so badly for yourself, you would be considered a bit of a 'Toff' back home."

Jack looked at her for a second, said nothing, then started to laugh, "Yes," he said, "Rita, I do go on a bit, don't I? Thanks anyway for listening."

They went to bed and soon fell asleep; they had an early start the next day.

They woke early, cleaned up, and ate breakfast. By the time they had finished, the waiter came to them and told them the Landrover was packed and waiting for them at the front entrance. They said their goodbyes, settled the bill, and were on their way. Jack continued to ramble on, but Rita was too interested in the beautiful country that was passing, it was a terrific morning, the sun was just above the horizon and the city was just coming to life, they drove into the outskirts of the city and were soon on the main road to Mombasa. Jack had said it would take about four hours, as long as the roads were good. Rita turned to Jack and asked if he could put the canvas down, so they could enjoy the cool air, Jack pulled over and folded down the roof and they were off again.

As they bumped along, Rita began to doze off, every now and again she would be jolted awake as jack hit a pothole, so she missed most of the conversation, but she picked up a few names, General bloody Haige, Churchill, Welsh miners, but she didn't pay much attention.

The hotel had packed a lunch or mid-morning snack, and they had made it about halfway, Rita estimated, when she turned to Jack, "Sweetheart, would you like a bit to eat?"

He nodded enthusiastically, "Yes, but I don't want to stop, can you do the honours. I could do with one of those sandwiches."

Rita took one out and handed it to him with a smile. It would be the only time he would shut up if he had his face around something to eat. After they ate, Rita dozed again, she'd grown tired of spotting game, there was so much of it. Jack gave her a nudge and she sat up, they were climbing a slight rise, and at the top was a sign, it read 'Mombasa, 15 miles'. As they reached the top and drove down the other side, the view of Mombasa in the distance and the ocean was spectacular, a light blue at the shoreline with white sandy beaches, lined by what looked like palm groves.

"Oh, Jack," said Rita, "it takes your breath away."

As they looked out onto the ocean, they could see many Arab Dhows with their distinctive white sails coming and going, some were heading out to sea, some were making their way to anchor in the harbour. They hit the city and Jack turned north. "Another twenty minutes, sweetheart, and we will be there. We're booked at the White Sands Hotel."

"Jack, I'm so looking forward to it. Two weeks of doing nothing."

"Well," replied Jack, "not exactly 'nothing', dear. It is our honeymoon."

Rita blushed.

***

Chapter 12

Janet and Frank did their best to see that Rosie was locked up when she was in season but the inevitable happened, she managed to escape late one evening and waiting at the bottom of the fence was Rufus Milo. He had managed to tunnel under the fence, and they cavorted until the early hours. Rufus's offspring were scattered about the native compounds and the Africans had nicknamed him the scourge of the neighbourhood, but his pups were still prized for their hunting abilities. Now Rosie had fallen victim. Frank knew something was up when he woke, Rosie was there in her bed at his side, she looked up at him with her ears back, "Rosie, what's been going on?" Her ears were still back and her tail beat like a drumstick against her bed. Frank rose from his bed, slipped on his shirt and shorts, and went outside to inspect the perimeter fence, sure enough there it was a hole under the wire, great footprints could be seen in the freshly dug soil, too big for Billie the staffy. Definitely Rufus, he thought, oh well, too late now. He walked back to the house, Rosie at his side.

"You're a bad girl," he said to Rosie, her tail wagged, and she looked up, ears still down. He went inside, Janet was sitting up in bed with the twins, they were walking now and trying to run but were still clumsy.

"Well," Frank said, "good morning, sweetheart, I have a surprise for you."

"Oh, yes", she said, "and what's that?"
"Rosie's been had, I suspect Rufus Milo."
"Jesus," exclaimed Janet, "not more pups."
"It looks that way. We'll know in a couple of months."
***

Chapter 13

Dedan Omondi was well hidden away, deep in the think forests surrounding Nairobi. The area was huge, but the British army and police had been having a lot of success tracking and killing his Mau-Mau friends. He had assembled seventy-seven hard recruits and they had been together now and training for nearly six months. A lot of his people had taken up with the white man, so now, he had decided to make an example out of his own people. He had decided to target the village of 'Lari' as most of the men there had joined the police reserve. Traitors he called them, and he swore to make them pay. They were all were armed, and supervised by four white officers, two of whom had their families housed just outside the village in a secure compound, surrounded by a ten-foot security fence. His plan was to wait until they went out on patrol, then attack the village and, hopefully, gain entry to the white's compound. He had arranged for some of his men to travel nearly fifty miles and create a diversion that would tie up the security forces and give him time to carry out his plan.

The diversion was to be the burning of a mission and the killing of the occupants: black nuns, and orphans, also the burning of one of the farms nearby and the slaughter of stock. Dedan's new headman was a slightly built Kikuyu of about thirty years, his name was Boniface Magube and he had proved to be absolutely brutal and loyal to the cause. He had been tasked to lead the diversion attack on the mission, he would attack the mission the day before Dedan attacked the village of Lari. The army would hear of the attack and follow up at first light, drawing them away from the Lari district.

Boniface left late on the Sunday night, it would take him and his Mau-Mau men at least two days to reach striking distance of the mission. He had with him fifteen good men; all were well armed. Dedan had planned to attack the village on Wednesday night at last light. If all went to plan, it would be a great success and victory for the Mau-Mau. Boniface's men made good time, they had spies and guides in every village, one guide would take them to the next village where they were fed and rested until, at last, they were in sight of the mission.

They were still some way off, and they had stuck to the heavy cover of the forest. Boniface moved forward to view his target, it was about three miles distant. It was early in the afternoon, so he sat and watched. He could see the children running about and the nuns in their black frocks and headdresses, with white bands across their foreheads. As it grew dark, he watched the nuns call the children to assemble for prayers and then their evening meal. Boniface counted twenty-eight children ranging from about six to fourteen he estimated.

It was getting dark now and hard to see, lights were beginning to flicker on, so he summoned his men to make ready and they moved off. It was Boniface's intention to kill and mutilate everyone at the mission. The white-owned farm came into view, its lights also burning. The farm was owned by an Irishman by the name of Paddy Giblin, he was a big man of sixty-two, he had served in the Irish Guards in the last war and was considered a tough customer. He drank like a fish and could fight like a threshing machine. He'd earned a medal and mention in dispatches for his bravery, but now he was aging, and it had calmed him a bit.

He and his family had just sat down to their evening meal, he was married to a coloured girl, and they had two children. One son aged eighteen and one girl aged fifteen. His home was very modest, but they were a happy family, and they grew the usual crops and kept cattle and ten dairy cows on their twelve-hundred acres and did quite well. They often worried about the situation in the country, he had taken precautions, however, and he had heavy timbers in place around the home's verandah and the doorways, with heavy timbered doors. He had also obtained a Bren gun and one thousand rounds of ammunition from a good friend in the police and the three dogs of mixed breed were a good early warning system.

He had cut slits in the verandah timbers so that, in the event of being attacked, he could fire on the security fence. He had also trained his family in weapons handling and his son was a particularly good shot. He'd been down earlier in the evening, and locked the security gate, and now had all settled down for the night.

Boniface and his men entered the mission, all the children were in the main building which acted as a church, dining hall, and classroom. It was a large building with high windows covered by curtains that stretched from the ceiling to the floor and a thick thatch roof. There was only the one entrance, with heavy timber doors that could be locked from either side but now one side of the doors was open, and he and his men stepped inside. The children and the nuns were all taken by surprise. All the nuns stood; they knew who these men were. Boniface ordered the nuns and the children outside and assembled everyone in a semicircle, the nuns were told to stand in the centre with their backs to the children. Boniface had ordered his men not to open fire, so as not to alert the white pigs at the farm. They would pay later.

Boniface walked towards the nuns and stopped, three were trembling but one, the senior of the four stood her ground. She must have been in her mid-fifties.

Boniface began, "so, you are the white man's disciples?"

"No," said the nun, "we are God's disciples. He is our savour."

"Ah," said Boniface, "but you wear his clothes, you eat his food, you teach his language."

The nun looked at him and said, "Look at your feet, do you not wear his shoes? Look at your trousers and shirt, are they not from the white man?"

Boniface looked at her, she had embarrassed him in front of his men. He flew into a rage and smashed the nun in the face with his rifle butt, the nun fell to the ground, her teeth had been smashed but she did not utter a sound. The blood ran down her chin onto her dress, some of the children began to cry. Then Boniface ordered his men to strip the four nuns and said, "It is your turn," and he ordered them to lie on the ground and directed his men to take them one at a time as the children looked on.

Some of the older children had heard of this act but had never witnessed it. They noticed the black sticks that stood out from between the legs of the men, and they wondered at the different sizes. Some were huge, others not so. The nuns made no noise just allowed the Mau-Mau to finish. Boniface ordered the four women to kneel on the ground in front of him, "this will send a lesson to all the others who live for the Whites".

The eldest nun spoke up, "The whites look after us, they tend us when we are sick", her words were garbled as she spoke through blood and broken teeth. "They teach us to read and write, they feed us well. What is it you do for us, this?"

With that Boniface struck her unconscious, he ordered his men to do the same to the other three, and in seconds, all were unconscious, he then ordered his men to cut the heads, hands, and feet from each. Some of the children were in shock and collapsed.

Boniface shouted at them, "Let this be a lesson to all, if you support the Whites, this is what will happen. I will let you all live".

He ordered his men to put the children in the church and lock the door from the outside. The security forces would release them. They were bundled inside, and the doors slammed shut and the lock closed from outside. Inside the kerosene lamps lit the church. Now it was secure, they could concentrate on the farmhouse and the family.

Boniface and his men moved off; it would take only thirty minutes to reach where they would launch the attack. Inside the church, one of the children came to with a start, one of the kerosene lamps spilled over and broke on the stone floor, instantly the flames spread, first across the floor, then to the long curtains that reached the thatch roof. Within seconds the church was ablaze, there was no way out for the children, many collapsed from the smoke and lack of oxygen. They screamed, so loud it carried to the farmhouse and Boniface's men. Boniface looked back, smoke was billowing into the night sky and the flames rose out of the walls, the screams began to wane as the children died, the roof collapsed onto the ones left alive, then all went silent as the last child died.

Boniface's men made their way towards the farm buildings where the dairy cows were housed. As they opened the barn door the animals began to bellow, it was too early for milking, but they made their way towards the Mau-Mau. Each animal was caught, and Boniface ordered his men to slash open the udders and hamstring each beast, the poor animals were stricken with pain as they hobbled about on their broken back limbs only able to drag themselves about by their front legs.

When they were done, they made their way towards the security fence and the homestead, but the family dogs had begun to bark at the noise and ran to the verandah. They couldn't get outside because of the barriers, but Paddy had a generator on the back verandah which fed the security lights on the fence. He had expected an attack and had prepared himself. He told his son to switch it on while he made ready with the Bren Gun. As soon as the generator fired up the lights began to flicker on. There they were, three were at the main gate, Paddy opened fire, the Mau-Mau were taken by surprise by the lights. Paddy killed two and wounded the third, His son was at the rear of the house and his daughter and wife were on each side, his son opened fire at more on the rear fence, Paddy ran to the back, his son had hit one and the others were making a run for it. Paddy opened fire again, hit another two, then they were gone. He heard his daughter on the phone to the operator and telling her what had happened. "Please contact security forces, farm is under attack." As Paddy looked out towards the mission, he could see the smoke. He could also hear the bellowing of his poor animals in pain.

At first light, Paddy, his son, and the family dogs drove towards the barn. As he opened the gates, the wounded Mau-

Mau tried to rise and escape but was set upon by the three dogs. He screamed in agony. As Paddy walked towards him, he drew his pistol and dispatched him with a shot to the head.

***

At the first shots during the night, Boniface had seen his comrades fall, he gave the order to withdraw, the element of surprise had been lost. He and his men had achieved their objective, the farmer would call the security forces and they would be on their way. Now they had to put as much distance between themselves and the mission as possible, and quickly, leaving their wounded comrades behind. They took off at a trot. They must make the forest by daybreak.

***

Paddy and his son pulled up outside the barn that housed his dairy cows, the agonising noise from the animals was almost deafening. As he entered, the morning light illuminated the inside of the barn. Paddy's son began to vomit as the scene before them unfolded. The cows were all beautiful black and white milk cows, Paddy's wife had given them all names and she knew each one. They followed her about, like children, now they dragged themselves about on their forelegs, their hind legs flopping behind them. Some had been disembowelled, their udders had been slashed open and their intestines lay next to them. Flies had begun to gather. Paddy took his revolver and his son's, told his son to go outside, then dispatched each animal one by one. He said nothing as he climbed back into the vehicle. He could hear another wounded Mau-Mau screaming and begging for help, he drove towards the noise, he could see him now and pulled up a short distance from the wounded African, then ordered his dogs to get him. They immediately leapt from the truck and raced towards him. The Mau-Mau saw them coming and raised his arm to protect himself. Paddy just sat and watched as his dogs ripped him apart. After they finished, Paddy walked over just to make sure he was dead, and shot him for good measure.

Dedan Omondi and his men had made the journey to their target and Dedan had hidden his men well. He now lay on the edge of a hill with three of his leading men. It was late afternoon and all the herd boys had taken the cattle to their Kraals. He could see the Police guards moving around in their navy-blue uniforms. None were carrying their weapons. He had not seen any white officers so far; they must be in the company offices not far behind the compound. He could see the white families' homes; he saw two white women and three children. He was so looking forward to letting his men have their way.

The two women were the wives of two of the white officers, one was Debra Thorne, she had two daughters, Fiona, fourteen, and Grace, sixteen. Her husband was the Police Inspector in the area, His name was Jack and they had moved to Kenya from Belfast. He had been with the Royal Ulster Constabulary but had been selected for his new post in Africa, a chance he and his family had jumped at. The other wife was Livy, she was married to the Station Sergeant, a big Englishman from Cornwall named Peter Gray. They had a twelve-year old daughter named Tracy.

All the girls were playing on the front verandah of the Gray family home. The homes were government built, both identical in construction, solid cement block walls with corrugated iron roofs and very comfortable inside. The two wives always commented on how lovely it was to hear the rain falling on the steel roof. The four white officers were in conference in the front office, discussing the following day's patrol and which villages they were going to visit. They planned to load up at nine the next morning, two three-ton trucks with twenty Askari, ten to each truck that would leave ten black reserve officers at the village. Dedan knew that the Police went out on patrol twice a week, overnight, so that would leave him time to put his attack in the late afternoon of the next day. The white officers finished the briefing, and as they walked out of the office, two black sergeant majors snapped to attention, Peter Gray, the big Englishman gave the orders for the following morning, the sergeant majors replied with a "yes sir", saluted, turned, and walked towards the compound. The shift officers said goodnight and walked off home. The two single men had quarters behind the police office.

Peter Gray walked to his house, his wife saw him coming and poured him a beer and handed it to him as he climbed onto the verandah. he thanked her and she kissed him on the cheek. He sat in his usual chair and started muttering about the bloody Kaffirs and how cruel they were most to their own people. He had little respect for them, but his wife intervened, "now dear, don't talk like that, we have committed far worse atrocities than the Africans, not only here, but all over the empire, besides, we came here uninvited and took the land". That shut him up and he fell silent. It was much the same routine at the Thorne house, his two daughters and Peter's daughter, Tracey, had been playing together. Now it was time to go home for supper. She said goodnight, but instead of Jack's wife joining him, he was joined by the family dog, a huge Alsatian called Voo-Doo. Voo-Doo flopped himself down next to Jack and lay next to his master with his head on his paws. Jack could hear his wife and the girls busy in the kitchen, school holidays would soon be over, and the girls would return to boarding school in Nairobi. He always missed them, and they always looked bigger and brighter each time they came home. He often thought about what kind of future they would have here in Kenya, especially if the blacks took over.

All four of the Officers had been in Kenya since the trouble with the Mau-Mau had started and they knew of the horrors committed by both sides, one was as bad as the other in lots of ways. The British had brought stability to the land, but a lot of the more radicals didn't want to be ruled by the Whites.

It grew late and both families started to turn in, the lights began to flicker out and the main generator was turned off and all went silent. The next morning everyone was up early and at seven, the white men made their way to the police office. The Askari were being assembled in three ranks by their sergeant majors ready for inspection. Both trucks were packed not far off. The inspection finished and the Askari were ordered into the trucks. As they left, they waved goodbye to their wives and daughters. Dedan Omondi watched from his hiding place; he would start his attack at three in the afternoon. The day dragged on, and Dedan and his men watched the main compound that held the African families. It could not be seen by the whites; it was hidden by high ground and trees but the ten Askari were going to be a problem. They would have to attack with weapons so this would alert the white women and they would be straight on the radio, but hopefully, the white officers and Askari would be at least seven hours away, so he gave himself and his men five hours for the attack. This should be plenty of time.

Dedan Omondi was indeed a wanted man; the whites had placed a bounty on his head. This he was proud of. At three in the afternoon, he gave the order to move, there were two groups, one group of twenty were to attack the Askari, the other to round up the villagers. As he moved to the village, locals began to scatter, but most were rounded up or shot. At the first sound of shooting, the Askari ran from the station, straight into a hail of gunfire, three were killed instantly and two wounded but they soon ran out of ammunition and were forced to surrender, death would have been better.

As the noise in the village continued, it carried to the whites. Debra Thorne ordered one of the Africans to lock the gate, but it was too late, he was shot dead at the entrance, the Mau-Mau stormed in, but the women had been well trained. Debbie was joined by Peter's wife, Lilly, they began to return fire and ordered their daughter inside with Voo-Doo. The three girls knew what to do, they ran to the back of the house and locked themselves in the back bedroom with Voo-Doo. The women both had Sten Guns, 9mm automatics, they backed up into the house, they had killed one and wounded four but were running out of ammunition. They locked the front door knowing this was to be the fight of their life.

The girls locked themselves in the back bedroom, the two youngest hid in a cupboard but Grace, the eldest, had armed herself with a 45-calibre naval revolver, a huge handgun, gradually the firing begun to wane as the two women ran out of ammunition. This was what the Mau-Mau had been waiting for. They hammered at the thick timber door until, eventually, it gave way and crashed open. Four of the Mau-Mau rushed in. The two women screamed as they were thrown on the floor but Debra managed to struggle upright and ran to try and protect the girls but it was no good, she was grabbed by the hair and thrown down again, he Mau-Mau ripped her dress, she screamed in fear as the Mau-Mau revealed his genitals and he climbed onto her. Grace was on the other side of the bedroom door; she could take no more and she threw open the door. She was wearing a flowing dress that concealed the revolver, keeping it hidden from view as she walked into the entrance. She could hear her mother screaming. The Mau-Mau looked up at Grace and uttered "you next, little whitey," He looked her straight in the eye, his eyes were bloodshot from the alcohol he'd been drinking. She stared back at him, pulled the revolver from under her dress and pointed it at the Mau-Mau, for a second he froze but it was too late, she pulled the trigger, the bullet hit him in the left eye, blowing out the back of his head and clear of her mother. The recoil knocked her back against the wall, but she immediately regained herself. Her mother jumped to her feet just as two of the other Mau-Mau who heard the shot ran into the room but Voo-Doo had broken free of the two girls and raced into the fight. He attacked the nearest African, he stood taller than the Mau-Mau now that he was on his back legs and seized him by the face, the other went for Voo-Doo with a huge Panga but was blown clean off his feet as Grace shot him dead. She left Voo-Doo to finish up. She ran after the fourth and final black man. He had left Mrs Gray half naked whimpering on the floor; she took two shots at him but missed and he disappeared into the darkness. But it wasn't over, Voo-Doo ran to the door and Grace gave him the command, "Go, Voo-Doo, kill him." Voo-Doo leapt forward and it wasn't long before they could hear the screams coming from the darkness and he soon returned covered in blood and wagging his huge tail.

The two younger girls were shut back in the bedroom while the two women bludgeoned the first Mau-Mau just to make sure he was dead. As Voo-Doo walked back inside he sniffed at each dead African and lifted his leg on each one. The ladies locked themselves back in the house and waited for the men to arrive.

It was growing late, and Dedan could spend no more time in the village, he gave orders to finish off any of the locals and then follow him away towards the forest. It was twenty miles and eight hours before the sun rose. The army would begin to track them. The whole village was ablaze, and the villagers could be heard screaming as Dedan and his men disappeared into the night.

At first light, the Army arrived at the scene of the attack at the mission, they couldn't believe what they were witnessing. Some of the younger members were physically sick. The white ones, but it didn't seem to affect the Africans the same way, they just stared at the dismembered bodies of the nuns, now swarming with flies that could be heard fifty yards away. Then they moved to the smouldering remains of the church, small bodies could be seen, clothes all tattered on tiny bodies so badly burnt you could smell them as if they had been roasted.

The commanding officer called for his tracking team and ordered them to leave immediately in pursuit. The trackers, there were six in all, three whites and three African, the Africans were all Maasai led by Harry 'Tin' Cann, Tommy Keaton had also joined, he was out for vengeance for his family. The third white was a young army lad, extremely fit and strong, a volunteer. All the men were lightly armed, carrying one hundred and fifty rounds, a gun, and a sten. The Army lad was Roy Pennington, from Manchester. He carried the radio.

Now it was light enough to see, and they took off at a run. A fixed wing aircraft would join them mid-morning. Boniface knew he would be hotly pursued and employed the same tactics. He must put as much distance between himself and the mission as possible before dawn. Now the sun was up, and he, and what was left of his men, were growing tired. He stopped and listened, sure enough, he could hear the noise of an aircraft in the distance. As he listened, the small aircraft came into view, it was weaving left to right, he knew the trackers had given them their direction and it was too late to make the safety of the forests. There was only three of them left and he ordered his men to split up. He ordered the remaining two to move off to the east and still make for the forest, he would continue north. He knew the trackers would follow the two while he discarded his weapons and made for the nearest village. The villagers would help him because he was Mau-Mau.

Boniface could see smoke rising in the distance, it had to be a village. He started off at a run, but he was tired and decided to walk the rest of the way. It wasn't far now, he would get food and drink and a bed for the night, maybe even a woman, as soon as the villagers knew he was Mau-Mau.

He made it to the thornbush fence surrounding the village. A handful of villagers were there to greet him.

He called to them, "I am Boniface of the Mau-Mau. Slayer of the white man," but instead of being welcomed, he was set upon and beaten to the ground and tied with rope. News had already spread to the locals about the mission, and many locals had children there. A similar fate had befallen the other two and runners were set off to alert the army.

Tin Cann and his trackers received the news over the radio as the light aircraft flew overhead. They were given a direction and a rendezvous point. The army would be there to pick them up. Tough luck, he thought, there would be no bounty this time. They reached the RV and climbed aboard the first truck. They drank their fill of water and sat back. They were headed back to the mission, and as they arrived, they could see a group of people in a circle. Tin Cann and his men dismounted and made their way to the group. It was just in front of the church. He pushed his way through, and there, lying on the ground, were the three remaining Mau-Mau. Paddy Giblin and his son were there, the Mau-Mau moaning in agony. The commanding officer stood over them and he spoke through an interpreter. Because of the atrocities they had committed, he had ordered the right ear be cut off each of the Africans, and the left ear pierced and a rope strung through between all three so they could not run, and they were handcuffed. Because of their work, they would be tried and sentenced to death.

As they were pulled up and loaded into the vehicles, the rope pulled on their ears, and they screamed in pain. Tin Cann looked on but felt no sympathy for them, he looked into the church at the burnt young bodies, the locals had begun to bury the youngsters and the nuns, a few still remained but that was enough. He decided that he would quit the army and return to hunting full time.

***

Chapter 14

Jack and Rita had returned from their honeymoon, they had both gained a little weight, and when Frank made a comment, Jack just grunted. Jack settled back down to the running of the farm and Rita to her school. She had over one hundred and fifty children now, and it was getting difficult to give them all the attention they each deserved, so she had divided them into three classes, each class had two hours of teaching each and this was working. The children loved it, she couldn't get over all the happy smiling faces.

***

The weeks passed and it was now only days before Rosie was expected to give birth. Frank and Janet fussed over her as did the jack russells and she lapped it up, rolling on her back and shaking her front paws, her tail never stopped. Then one morning, Frank woke to a squealing noise at the side of his bed, it was Rosie and she had given birth to a pup.

Janet also woke, "what's that?" she asked.

"It's Rosie, she's having the pups."

Janet got out of bed, sure enough, there was Rosie fussing and licking a little four-legged bundle. She looked up at Frank and Janet with her tail wagging as if to say 'look'. The jack russells heard the commotion and came rushing in, but Rosie growled defensively. Janet ordered them outside, but they took no notice, so they were manhandled and plonked unceremoniously on the verandah and shut out.

Janet brought in an old blanket and moved the pup into the large basket they had prepared for this event. Rosie followed on, licking, and nudging the pup. By the time the sun came up, she had given birth to six pups. It was obvious who the father was, it was the scourge of the compound, Rufus Milo. The pups had his colouring, all except one, the runt of the litter, it was a girl, and she was pitch black, like her mother, she might have been little, but she pushed and roughly shoved her brothers and sisters out of the way to get at her mother's milk. Janet had already claimed her and named her Sophie. Frank was the first to congratulate Rosie with a pat and a good girl and Janet did the same. Rosie curled her top lip as if in a smile, then settled down to tend her new family.

***

Jack and Rita had brought Frank and Janet a present back from Mombasa, and it became Janet's most treasured item. It was a beautiful new radio, and it could pick up so many different stations. She played it night and day, there was so much fantastic music coming out of different countries, especially the USA. She knew them all by heart, the Everly Brothers, The Platters, Johnny Mathis, The Coasters, Toni Bennet, Johnny Rae, Frankie Lane, and Dean Martin, but there was one that was her definite favourite, and as she danced and sang around the house, Frank thought the sun had got to her but said nothing. Quite often the twins would join in, shouting, "Dance with me mummy, dance with me".

Of course, the jack russells had to get in on the act as well. Rita would call in, in the mornings, and pick up the boys and take them to school and after a while they waited for her to take them home. They would go to the compound and play with the African children. Rita wondered at the tolerance of the children, she had heard the whites talking about the bloody Kaffirs and the bloody Africans being good for nothing, but she did not agree. She found them to be mostly kind and respectful, especially to their older people. As she watched the children, she could see no sign of discrimination, just playing and having fun, then when she called out to them that it was time to go, they would shout, "Oh grandma, just a little while longer". And she would always relent. By the time they got home, they were so exhausted they could barely bathe and eat, then they would go straight to bed, ready for the following day.

At weekends, twice a month, the Enfield's would drive up with Tony Johnson, Rita and Jack would join them, the twins were sent to bed and the party would begin. The three women would dance and ask the men to join in, but they got grumpier as they drank more beer and Johnny Walker. Sometimes it went on until three in the morning. Everyone had drunk too much, and the ladies were exhausted with legs like jelly after dancing for hours, so they just slept where they could until the staff shook them awake and offered hot tea or coffee.

Every second weekend Jack ordered films from Nairobi, these were delivered on a Thursday or Friday ready for *The Saturday Picture Show*, it was held at the workshop, Tony Johnson was an expert projectionist and organised a large screen, it was a plaster wall on the side of the workshop and Jack had acquired a top-of-the-range projector, just like the cinemas. The show was open to all comers, black or white, the white's sitting up front and to one side. Sometimes families from the surrounding farms would come along with their children. Janet had given up counting the Africans that appeared, it seemed to double every show. Jack laid on the drink free for the Africans, their local beer and maybe a Kudu or Impala on the spit. They started with Benjamin as supervisor in charge, but he would be off his face by interval.

The movies were mostly Roy Rogers, Hop Along Cassidy, Tom Mix, and of course, everyone's favourite, The Three Stooges. The Africans loved them and rolled about laughing. Sometimes they would get John Wayne or a war movie with aeroplanes, some of the Africans had never seen a plane before and looked on in disbelief. Sometimes there was musicals, The Wizard of Oz, or Oklahoma, great songs, but there was one singer who stood out amongst the rest, and everyone loved him.

Frank and Janet sat up front with the twins, Rosie at his right side, Sophie between Frank and Janet. It would have been difficult to tell them apart except Rosie was now very grey around the face and she limped a bit when she walked. Rufus Milo was there as well, all his offspring had been given to good homes in the area, the farmers needed good dogs and his pups fitted the bill.

Interval lasted thirty minutes and everyone got around the barbeque for a steak sandwich or a hamburger. Tonight, they had been watching Abbot and Costello and everyone were still chuckling about their antics. Laurel and Hardy also proved very popular but all too soon it was over, and everyone started their goodnights and their journey home. Janet and Frank said good night and took the twins home, Rosie and Sophie jumped in beside Frank, but Rosie got up very close, and there was no room for Sophie next to Frank. The twins were put to bed, then Janet and Frank did the same, they talked for a while about the movies and laughed a little. Janet talked a bit more then realised she was talking to herself; Frank had fallen asleep. She looked at him then leant over and kissed him, he grunted and rolled over. She thought about what a wonderful man he was and how lucky she had been to run into him again that day in Edinburgh, it seemed so long ago.

She whispered, "I love you so much, Frankie, darling."

Rosie looked up at her in disgust, Janet thought, as she looked down at her, "yes, you're a good girl, Rosie, but he is mine forever."

***

Life on the farm was good, Jack had taken a bit of a back seat and left most of the work to Frank. Jack and Rita spent most of their off time driving around the farm and visiting neighbours with the twins, Janet spent her days off and free time dancing around the house fantasising about that outstanding singer from America, she loved him.

Some papers had to be signed in Nairobi, so Frank mounted up in the Stud and set off early one morning, he kissed Janet goodbye, then stopped at Jack's and did the same to his mother. He would be back in three days as there were other things that needed his attention. As he drove off, the sun was already above the horizon, the top was down, the wind was blowing in his hair, and he would make good time. He passed the odd Kudu, Impala, all the usual, and he only stopped once to relieve himself by the side of the road and stretch his legs, he opened the hamper, pulled out a sandwich and poured a cup of tea, it was still quite warm, then remounted and took off. He thought about stopping at the inn but decided not to, rather to get the business done and get back home. It was early afternoon when he arrived at the Norfolk Hotel, he pulled up, and the Africans recognised him straight away and said they would park the truck and take care of everything. He handed them each a bright shilling and they smiled and cupped their hands in thanks. He decided that he would clean up, take care of the matters at hand, then have an early night. Frank rose the next morning, shaved, had breakfast, then drove into Nairobi, it was still early with only the Africans making their way to work. He stopped and bought a newspaper and read the headlines, 'Army kills 48 Mau-Mau and detains hundreds.' Christ, he thought, it's not getting any better. As he read on, he came across a story of another two white farmers that had been butchered, that brought the total, so far, of whites killed to twenty-six. He didn't know how many Africans had been killed but he knew it was in the thousands. Will it ever stop? he thought.

Things went well and by late afternoon he had completed all his and the farm's business. As he drove back to the Norfolk, he thought he would phone Janet and let her know he would be home tomorrow, a day early. On his way, he stopped at one of the local watering holes, and spoke to a few of the faces he knew. The conversation was always the same, "Damn blacks want to take over, no chance," said one elderly farmer. He finished a cold beer, ordered one for the road, and as he was drinking, he listened to music over the bar speaker and the latest hits from America. He recognised a few simply because Janet played them from morning until night and he had to admit they were kind of good but there was one who stood out amongst the rest, Frank never cared about who it was, he just sang along.

That was enough, he was off. He jumped into the stud and found himself whistling to the music. It put him in a great mood, and he couldn't remember being happier. He drove into the Norfolk, through the beautiful gardens, parked and handed the keys to the boys at reception. He went straight to his room, whistling all the while. He would phone Janet straight away. He dialled reception and they put him through within one minute.

The phone rang, it was answered by the new girl.

"Ah", said Frank "is the Madam home yet?" He could hear the music and all the dogs were barking.

"Yes, sir, I will call her." There was silence for a moment, then, "Madam, it is boss Frank," then the pitter patter of feet as Janet skipped to the phone.

"Hello darling," she said.

Frank said, "I'm fine, I can hear the music." They spoke for a while then Janet changed the subject, she just blurted it out, "I'm sorry to tell you, darling, but there is another man in my life that I'm in love with."

Frank never let her finish; he slammed down the phone in such a rage that it fell off the bedside table. Bloody hell, he thought, what now? Janet tried to desperately to call Frank back, but he had left a message at reception, no calls under any circumstances. Frank didn't eat or sleep, he left at first light, still in a rage. She had said his name, Frank promised himself when he got hold of this bloke, he would give him a good hiding, one he would not forget. Janet would also be in the firing line, but the name didn't ring a bell, he certainly wasn't a local, what kind of name was that anyway? Elvis, bloody Presley.

It started to rain hard, and it made the roads very difficult, but he drove on still in a terrible rage. Janet tried frantically to contact Frank to finish the story, but he was taking no calls. She knew he had a terrible jealous streak in him, her only criticism of her husband. She hoped his drive home would be a safe one as the skies had opened up and visibility was poor. Frank was halfway home, as he rounded a bend, he looked down into the valley below, he could see the motel in the distance and decided to stop and have a drink and try and think things through. As he pulled in, he bumped into some old friends but was not in the right state of mind for niceties and brushed them off. He entered the reception, and he heard one remark, "What's wrong with old Frank then? that's not like him".

He walked into the bar, sat down, and ordered a beer, the radio was playing loudly, he had to admit the songs sounded pretty good, The Platters were singing their latest hit as Frank sipped his cold beer, then the song finished, and the announcer came over the radio, "All right, all you people out there. This is the latest song from that man that all the ladies are in love with, the one they have christened the King of Rock and Roll, Mr Elvis Presley".

Frank almost choked, his jaw dropped, almost hitting the top of the bar. What a bloody fool I am, he thought, looking in the bar mirror, his face was red, how am I going to get away with this? So, he sat and had another beer and began to hatch a plan, it was complicated, but he decided he would deny everything and say nothing. Brilliant, he thought. He resumed his journey after saying hello to his friends, one said to him, "that's a bit better, Frankie, we thought you were cranky."

"No, just a touch of weariness, lads".

***

In the distance, Honeydew came into sight. As he drove up the drive, Janet was there to say hello, the dogs were there also, tails all sweeping the verandah. Frank jumped out and went to Janet and gave her a kiss and hug. "Hi darling, everything okay?" Then turned to the boys, "look what dad's got!" and gave them each a box of Cadbury's chocolate and they were off.

"And what do I get?" asked Janet.

"Oh, you'll see in about an hour, once I clean up."

"I was worried Frank when I couldn't get hold of you. The line went dead."

"Yes, darling, they told me an elephant ripped down the lines."

"Really," she said, "that's unusual, that would never happen in Scotland." She smiled naughtily to herself.

"Anyway, that's enough about that, I'm home now."

"No, Frank, I want to hear about the elephant,"

"Let's not dwell on that."

"No, but I want to Frank."

The more Frank tried to dismiss it, the more determined she became to pursue the matter until they went to bed. Frank did a good job on her and that finally shut her up. Both fell asleep exhausted. Telling lies always made Frank tired and listening to them did the same for Janet. They woke the next morning and as they were eating breakfast, Jack and Rita arrived and joined them, they sat down and poured coffee then Janet got up and dished them up a nice breakfast.

One of Frank's jobs, while in Nairobi, was to go and see the land commissioner, he and Jack had heard that the British were offering generous sums of money to farmers who wished to leave Kenya because of security concerns. A number of whites had taken up the offer and left, surprisingly enough, for southern Rhodesia. The British Government had guaranteed that anything south of the Zambezi would remain in white hands.

***

They had a week off, the school was closed, and Adeena and her husband would take care of the sick, lame, and weary Africans that lined up for treatment. So, the following day they decided that they would load up and take the twins to the river for a picnic lunch. Janet decided to take a drive to the clinic and say hello to Adeena and Sam. As she arrived at the clinic, she could see the line of Africans, mostly women with their children waiting for treatment. She recalled how, when they had first arrived on the farm, she and Rita had wondered how the Africans kept themselves so well dressed and clean, there was no electricity and their clothes were always immaculately pressed, not a wrinkle, especially the children, so she asked Benjamin and he took her to the laundry and showed her a heavy iron with a wooden handle, "You see madam, you do like this," he flipped a catch on the side and the top hinged open, "then you fill with hot coals, close again and the coals heat the iron."

How wonderful, she thought. When the children attended school, Rita always commented on how the children looked fantastic, never misbehaved, just listened, and took everything in.

The next day they loaded up, Frank took his 30.06 and Jack a Sten 9mm. Frank noticed Rosie was hanging back a bit and had to be lifted into the stud next to him, she gave a bit of a whimper as she settled in. She was looking very grey around the muzzle but gave her master a lick just the same. Benjamin had been given the job of organising everything and of course he came too, he was also part of the family. Janet sat up front with Rosie, Sophie, and Frank driving. Rita and Jack in the back seat and Benjamin with the boys in the tray in the hunting seats; the top was down, and the wind was blowing their hair about.

While jack and Rita were on honeymoon, they had bought a very expensive transistor radio and it played along. Everyone was either singing or humming to the tunes when the announcer came on again. 'And here he is the King of Rock and Roll, Elvis Presley," Frank made a slight glance towards Janet, but he could detect nothing, just that slightly wicked smile. He thought to himself, I wonder, then forgot about it and drove on. He looked over again at his wife, just as the wind blew her dress way above where it should be, yes, he thought, she has great legs, and he wished they were alone, he would have pulled over, dragged her out then and there and given her a quick one, then thrown her back in, well, maybe not so quick. She caught him looking and pointed to the road ahead as if to say, keep your eyes on the road, and they smiled at each other.

They covered the fifteen miles to the river quickly, and it was still only mid-morning as they pulled up under a grove of trees just fifty yards from the river. Benjamin started unloading and setting up the tables and chairs, Rosie managed to get out of the stud by herself but had a noticeable limp, "bit of arthritis setting in, old girl?" said Frank, she turned, put her ears down and wagged her tail. The boys were off and running and Janet shouted after them, "Not too far, you two."

They both shouted back, "ok, Mum."

The family all sat around the table drinking hot tea and coffee, Benjamin had done a wonderful job as always. He wore a smart white shirt and Khaki shorts, and over his left arm he hung a white towel like a waiter he had seen. This was in one of the movies and now it was part of his dress code, but he was happy as they drank and listened to the music.

Jack interrupted, "look over there, on the other side of the river at the edge of the forest."

It was a herd of elephants that had wandered out and were making their way to the water. The river wasn't wide or deep, so Janet called the boys back. Frank went to the stud and brought back the 30.06, cocked it, and put the safety on just in case. The elephants reached the edge of the river. Tick birds flitted from one to other pecking off parasites. They all looked peaceful and began to drink, all except one. It raised its trunk and gave out a deafening trumpet, the dogs, Rosie and Sophie, stood up. Sophie crept up to Janet and lay down next to her. "This one looks like trouble," said Jack. The elephant was quite large with good tusks, Rosie ran forward as if to defend her family, and Frank called her back, she stopped, but the elephant plunged into the river and raced toward Rosie.

Frank stood up with the 30.06.

"Not unless it's really necessary", shouted Janet.

The elephant's ears were flat against its body, a danger sign to any hunter of elephant, then it stopped twenty yards from Rosie and flapped its ears and raised its trunk to sniff the air. Frank raised the 30.06 to his shoulder and flicked off the safety, he had not seen the fold in the young elephant's ear. He began to squeeze the trigger when Janet shouted, "Stop, Frank! It's Jessee."

Just then, Rosie and Jessee came together, Jessee extended her trunk, yes, it was her old friend, Rosie, and now Sophie was by her mother's side and Jessee sniffed her and looked down at Rosie as if to say, yes, old girl, I know who this is. Rosie turned towards the stud and Jessee followed on like she used to, her trunk gently resting on Rosie's shoulder. Rita and Janet went forward and put out their arms, Jessee gently sniffed the two women and then the men. Yes, this was her human family. She also recognised Benjamin, but not the two little ones. The boys were not afraid, they put out their arms for Jessee to sniff, then she turned to Janet and Frank and looked at them both, first one, then the other, as if to say, yes, I also know who these are. Jessee grazed around the family. Frank and the ladies offered her buttered bread which she accepted and extended her trunk and fed it into her mouth. She must have stayed for nearly two hours, then a loud trumpet from a large cow on the other side of the river, the matriarch of the herd, startled everyone, Jessee trumpeted in reply and accepted a last piece of bread.

Frank looked at her and spoke, "I knew your mother, Jessee, I had to take her life, it was the kindest thing to do". Jessee curled her trunk gently around Frank's neck and looked in his eyes as if to say, I know. Frank was thinking about when he and his brother Brian, together with their father, visited Edinburgh Zoo to feed the elephants, Janet could see a tear in his eye and the slight cough he made gave him away. Then Jessee turned and walked to the river, she crossed, then halfway to the forest she stopped and turned to look at her human family one last time. She gave a trumpet, Rosie barked, she trumpeted again, then turned and disappeared into the forest. Everyone just stood and looked for several minutes, but she was gone.

Jack broke the silence, "all right, everyone, let's pack our bags and head home."

The journey home was a quiet one, not even the radio was on. The family pulled up at the steps to Frank and Janet's, and Jack asked if he could take the stud. He said he and Rita were both worn out and they would see them the next morning, as he had something important to talk about.

Frank had to help Rosie down, her back legs were stiff, "bit of arthritis setting in, old girl," he said again.

She looked at him and wagged her tail, she climbed the steps and went straight to her bed. Sophie bit her playfully on the ear but Rosie snapped at her. Frank had never seen her do that before.

"Must be tired," he said to Janet "and missing Jessee, they were the best of friends."

***

Jack came over early the next morning and sat down for breakfast. Frank asked him what was troubling him.

"Well," replied Jack, "l received this letter the other day from the government land office. Apparently, the cost of maintaining security in Kenya is beginning to worry Westminster. The bean counters have come up with a number they say it's costing to kill the Mau-Mau gang members. You won't believe this; they say it's ten thousand pounds per head. They just can't afford it any longer. So, they are pushing for an African led government, they have someone in mind by the name of Jomo-Kenyatta".

They looked at each other for a moment, then Frank replied, "but everything was going so well. The farm's doing well, everyone seems happy."

"Yes," said Jack, "everyone here. The government are prepared to make an offer to all the whites who have farms. I am led to believe they are being quite generous. I'm going to be blunt, Frank, ladies, I think we should take the offer, if it's a worthwhile one. A lot of the farmers are heading to

Southern Rhodesia, and I would like you, Frank, to come with me to take a look."

"Ok, Uncle Jack. Just let me catch my breath here. This is a lot to take in."

"I understand, laddie, but it's urgent."

"Ok," replied Frank, "I am in touch with Ian smith, I'll contact him and get the run down. I would certainly like to meet up with him again, you know he's gone into politics."

They ate breakfast then made ready for the day. Sophie was out playing with the jack russells, but Rosie was still in her bed, unusual, thought Frank, so he gave her a shout and she came hobbling through and lay down next to her master's feet. She looked up and wagged her tail, she was so grey around the muzzle and her eyes were sad. Janet knew but said nothing. Billie was there and he lay next to her, and when the jack russells came near, he growled and kept them away. They knew better than to get on the wrong side of Billie, so they ran down the steps with Sophie and down to the dam for a swim, maybe even catch a duck, even though they'd had no success in the past.

***

One morning the following week, Frank woke with a start, something wasn't right, he sat up and looked at the floor next to the bed, it was Rosie, she was lying there, still, her eyes closed, she had died during the night, her right paw was stretched out as if to touch her master for the last time but the effort had been too much and she had died.

Sophie lay next to her mother, then Frank shouted her name, "Rosie, my Rosie."

Janet woke and looked at Frank, he had picked Rosie up and was holding her to his chest, "No, No, No. Rosie my girl."

Janet went around to Frank's side and put her arm around him "Oh, sweetheart, she's gone," but Frank was in tears and couldn't speak.

"Frank, darling, she was old, she had her time, we don't have them forever. They are just on loan."

Sophie looked at Frank and licked his hand. Janet said, "look at Sophie, this is part of her, she will take over now."

The twins heard the noise and came running in, "What's wrong, Mum?"

"It's Rosie, she's died, and dad's very upset."

They looked at each other and burst into tears. They had known Rosie all their life and now she was gone. Frank walked outside with her and sat on the verandah and waited for the sun to rise, it would be about an hour before it began to get light. Then Frank made his way, still carrying Rosie, down the steps and outside the security fence, to a small grove of trees. This was Rosie's favourite place, she would just lie there on her back or playing with Sophie or the jack russells, and often Billie would come and join in. Frank put her down on the grass, then went to fetch a shovel. When he returned, he dug a hole about three feet deep, and when he finished, he placed Rosie in it and gently began to shovel the soil over his old friend. With each shovelful, she began to disappear, and his thoughts kept coming back, she had always been there, when he lost Brian, she was there and knew he was unhappy, when he came home from school, she was waiting on the corner, and his mother used to tell him that when he was away in the war, she would sit and wait until after dark to see if he was coming home every night.

And when he did appear, she knew! She would bark, just once, and race to meet her master and Frank would brace for impact. Now she was gone. Janet and the boys had brought Frank coffee, but he hadn't touched it, he just sat on the grass next to his Rosie's grave, choking back tears.

As the days passed, Frank began to slowly get over Rosie's death, he did realise she was old, and it was her time, and she had travelled to Africa as part of the family. Now he had Sophie, who was there at his side, she was the same nature as her mother and was Frank's shadow. She had taken pride of place next to Frank in the Stud, it was as if Rosie had never left.

***

One day, completely out of the blue, the phone rang; Janet was home and picked up the receiver, it was a women's voice, and she had a distinct accent.

It was Ingrid Benz, "Hello, is that Janet Munro?"

"Yes," replied Janet "and I know who you are."

"So, you remember me, Janet?"

"Yes, its Ingrid," Janet was so pleased, "where are you?" she asked.

Ingrid replied, "The three of us are in Nairobi,"

"The three?" Janet asked.

"Yes, I have a little boy, his name is Gunter."

Then Janet asked, "How is Klaus?"

"Yes, he is fine, he says hello."

Then Klaus came on the line, "Hello, Janet, I hope we find you all well, we have just arrived in Nairobi and as you know, Ingrid is a keen photographer, we have an Australian hunter here called Harry Caan, Tin Cann they call him, he says he knows your family."

"Yes," replied Janet, "my Uncle Jack knows him well."

"Well, he is taking us to the Massai-Mara so Ingrid can photograph the herds migrating. Apparently, it is quite a sight. Ingrid is doing it for, we hope, National Geographic Magazine and Harry says we drive very close to where you are at Honeydew, can we stop and visit?"

"Of course, you can," replied Janet "and we would be upset if we knew you were in the area and didn't. We have plenty of room so, please come and stay as long as you wish."

"That's very kind, Janet," replied Klaus, "Now here is Ingrid again."

"Thank you, Janet. The last time we spoke you were expecting."

"Yes," said Janet, "we have twin boys."

"Oh! I can't wait to see them. Ok," said Ingrid, "I will hang up now, Klaus wants to do it," they both laughed.

"You haven't changed, Ingrid,"

"No, I do it just to upset him, but he still wants to do it no matter how upset. We should be there in three days."

When Frank returned, Janet gave him the news, "Oh, that's nice. Do a bit of catch up, see what they have been up to. It'll be nice to have some different company and find out what's going on in the outside world."

For the next three days, Janet and Rita spent their spare time getting the guest rooms ready. The Benz's had a lovely room, with a bath and shower but would have to use the thunder box outside for the other, she hoped Ingrid would be ok with it. Tin Cann was at the other end of the house. They hoped they would stay for a least two nights, maybe three. They had a party planned for the second evening and a movie show for the first night.

It was Thursday afternoon when Janet spotted the dust, quite far off, this would be them, she thought. The whole family were there, waiting, and as they came into view, they counted three vehicles. Then they spotted Tin Cann in the lead truck, it was an old Thames he had fitted out for his Safari business, and it was quite comfortable, Janet noticed, as they pulled up in a cloud of dust. His three Moran, as always, in the rear, dressed in their Moran dress. Each holding two long shafted spears, the next two vehicles were both German Mercedes, brand new by the look of them. The unmistakable three-pronged star within a silver circle visible on the fronts. Ingrid and Klaus were in the first Mercedes, Klaus was driving, Ingrid next to him wearing a head scarf and covered in dust. Between the two sat a young boy, maybe seven or eight years of age. He had blonde hair and blue eyes, just like his mother and father, a very handsome young man. Everybody began to wave and moved to the transport, soon everyone was shaking hands and the women hugging each other. Janet and Rita ushered everyone onto the verandah, and they sat down, Benjamin and the maid brought tea and coffee, but nobody drank much because they couldn't stop talking. Eventually, Janet said, "Ingrid, I am sure you would like to clean up."

Ingrid had already introduced Gunter to the family and he and the twins were out front playing with the jack russells, who had been divided into two groups for the twins, half for Frank and the others for Brian.

Ingrid said to Janet, "Your boys are lovely" and Janet returned the compliment. Janet ushered Ingrid and Gunter through to their room, Ingrid walked in and looked around, then turned to Janet and said, "this is exactly how I imagined it, it's lovely, Jan." The French doors opened out onto the verandah and a cool breeze blew throughout the whole house. Janet began to tell Ingrid what was on for this evening, about sundowners, then down to the workshop to watch the films, she asked Ingrid if it would be ok with Klaus, and she clapped her hands.

"Oh! Yes, Janet, both the boys love movies," she was referring to Klaus and Gunter as the boys.

Janet said, "You'll love it, half the African population come from all around".

***

The Indian traders had delivered the movies earlier that week and everyone was excited to see what had arrived. There were great movies coming from America and they were always favourites. At five in the evening, everyone met on Janet and Frank's verandah, they sat for a while talking and drinking beer and whisky. Ingrid loved her beer, and it made her even more of a chatterbox than usual. The Enfields were there too, they drove up in their farm vehicle. Everyone got on so well, laughing and chattering. When Frank interrupted, "All right, ladies, let's mount up, ready for the movie show."

Everyone made their way to the transport, the ladies all climbed into one vehicle and the men in the other. Sophie jumped in next to Frank, the jack russells stayed behind on guard duty, but Billie was next to Rita, he had taken a real liking to her, and she patted his head. They arrived at the workshop where the Africans were already assembled and sitting, waiting for the show to start. Tony had set everything up and was ready to go as soon as everyone was seated. Then the lights went out and the screen flickered into life, moths danced in the projector light, then it started. It was a couple of shorts, the first, a favourite with the Africans was The Three Stooges, Larry, Curly, and Moe, the Africans roared with laughter at the antics and so did everyone else. When that finished, the next was taken from the new TVs which were popular in the western countries but had not made their way to Kenya yet. It was a western, in black and white, another favourite, especially with the Africans. There was total silence as it started with the theme song, 'Rollin, Rollin, Rollin, keep those doggies moving, don't try to understand them, just rope, roll and brand them, Rawhide! Then a list of the actors and credits came on, one was called Clint Eastwood, all the ladies turned to each other and remarked how good looking he was, the men overheard them and Klaus turned to Frank and said, "now, there's a young man with a bright future, I wonder if he will amount to anything." The next film was called 'The Gunfighter' starring Gregory Peck, not a sound came from the Africans, this was the kind of western they loved. It all came to an end too early, and it was time to retire.

It had been a long day, Tin Cann and his Moran were all there, his Moran had never seen anything like this and moved forward to examine the screen, they looked behind but found nothing, they spoke amongst themselves and looked bewildered. How could this be, they wondered. Everyone arrived back at the house and settled down to a night cap, Frank was in the main lounge pouring a whisky, when Klaus walked in and asked Frank if he could please join him, Frank welcomed him, "Please, Klaus, come in."

"You have a wonderful life here, Frank, but are you not a little worried about the politics at the moment?"

Frank replied, "Yes. To be honest, we are keeping an eye on things, it would be a disaster if the blacks took over so, at the moment, Klaus, it is watch and see."

Klaus moved around the edge of the room talking as he went, "Ah! These are pictures of home, I imagine."

"Yes," replied Frank, then Klaus stopped talking, he looked quite shocked, Frank asked him if he was all right. Klaus did not speak for a minute; he was gazing at a picture of a spitfire with two men standing beside it. On the fuselage of the aircraft were the letters and numbers S.P.171, then he spoke, "Ah, Frank, this is you, of course, and who is the other gentleman with you? You are obviously both pilots."

"Yes," replied Frank, "that's my good friend, Ian smith, we are still in contact with each other."

"You did not tell me you were a flyer with the R.A.F. Frank. Would it shock you if I told you I was also a Pilot with the German AirForce?"

"It wouldn't shock me, Klaus," replied Frank, "but were you?"

"Yes, my friend, and was this your aircraft?

"No," said Frank, "that's Ian's."

"Well, do you know he shot me down on the final day of the war?"

Frank looked at Klaus in amazement, "That was you? Christ, Klaus, I was right behind Ian, he was just about to give you another burst, then it came over the radio to cease all hostilities, the war is over. We both gave you a wave when we turned around and headed home, that was your lucky day.”

“Yes, it was indeed,” replied Klaus, “I sincerely hope this will not affect our friendship.”

“Certainly not,” replied Frank, “we were both young men doing what we were ordered to do.”

Tin Cann had left the veranda and joined frank and Klaus.

Klaus thanked Frank and then changed the subject, “Well, Frank, tomorrow we make ready to travel to the Maasai-Mara, Tin-Cann has already organised most of what we will need, isn’t that so, Tin-Cann?”

“It is, indeed, Sir,” was the reply,

“Please, Tin-Cann, Klaus is fine, I keep telling you we are all on a first name basis now.”

Ingrid had now joined the trio and made a comment, “it’s all right, Tin Cann, you should hear what I call him sometimes.”

Klaus glanced in her direction but said nothing; it worked better that way.

“Right you are, sir.”

Klaus began again, “As you know, Frank, Ingrid has become quite well known for her photos and stories, quite a wildlife warrior I think you say. We were going to ask you and your family if you would like to join us.”

All four returned to the verandah, sat, and refilled their glasses.

“Yes,” Interrupted Ingrid, “we would love you to join us.”

Frank looked over at Janet and asked her what she thought.

She replied, "Can we afford to, Frank?"

Then Jack spoke, "Hey, you lot, go. I will stay here and mind the farm. It will probably only be a week, two at the most."

Rita agreed, "Yes, go, I will stay here and keep Mr Cranky company."

Jack smiled back at her, then Janet said the boys would love it.

"OK, done deal," said Frank.

Sophie sat wagging her tail as if she understood every word. Janet said, "Frank, we will load up the Stud, we have everything we need,"

"Oh!" said Jack, "you better take Benjamin, he knows the routine".

Benjamin was standing within earshot, and he beamed when he heard his name mentioned.

"All set then, preparation tomorrow, leave first light the next day, it's about two days drive, if the roads are good," interrupted Tin-Cann.

That evening, as the sun went down, the beer and the whisky made its appearance, and they were joined by the Enfields. Janet spoke to them and asked if they would like to join them "it's all last minute, I know, but all you will need is basic overnight gear."

Sam spoke quietly, "Well, I definitely can't go, I have surgery for the next two days, but Adeena can certainly go."

Adeena's eyes lit up. "Can I, darling? I would love to."

"Ok," said Janet, "all done, it'll be fantastic."

Then Klaus lit a fire under Jack's bum, "I believe, where we are going, was one of Lord Delamere's favourite places."

The whisky had loosened his tongue, and it was like a gun going off. "Lord Bloody Delamare? That witless scoundrel, he and his so called 'aristocratic friends' caused more trouble than you can imagine".

Rita came to the rescue, "Now, Jack, sweetheart, you really need to control that tongue."

Klaus looked at Jack, "I'm sorry, Jack."

Then Jack controlled himself, "No, No, No, not your fault, Klaus. Just when that lot come up, Lord and all, what a crew! Bloody Lords, indeed."

Then everyone began to laugh.

Frank spoke, "You see, Klaus, Uncle Jack is not a great lover of the so-called English Aristocracy."

Jack was about speak but Rita glared at him, and he thought better of it. Then the conversation turned to the situation in Kenya, security, and politics. The evening took on a party atmosphere, everyone drank too much, until eventually, first one, then another, and another, gave up and said goodnight and made their way, as best they could, to their beds.

The following morning, everyone was late to rise, and a couple were suffering from a hangover but the African staff and Tin-Cann had the stores and vehicles assembled by eight at Frank and Janet's main gate. Everyone ate a good breakfast, Adeena turned up on her scooter carrying an overnight bag, she looked quite beautiful in her Khaki shirt and tight blue jeans. All of the ladies really looked the part, but it was still Janet that caught Frank's eye. She bundled the three boys into the rear of the Stud, Frank and Klaus were up front, the women in the rear. Sophie was between Klaus and Frank. Klaus gave her a pat and placed his arm around her.

Then Tin-Cann shouted to Frank, "All ready, Frankers, you take the lead," and off they went, the Stud in the lead and Tin-Cann's two safari trucks following behind.

It was mid-afternoon before they reached the river, and this is where they had decided to set up camp. It was close to where Jessee, the elephant, had last been seen but there was no sign of elephants this time. In the morning, they would cross the river, just downstream, and make their way to the Maasai-Mara. On their way, Frank had stopped and bagged an Impala ram. The boys beamed, this meant fresh meat tonight. Tin-Cann had to keep his eye on his Maasai as they would not ride with Kikuyu, so they travelled in different trucks. Tribalism would be Kenya's downfall, he always said, and he was probably right, maybe even the whole of Africa.

As it began to get dark, Benjamin and the camp staff lit the hurricane lamps, and they began to hiss into life. A lamp was suspended outside each tent and the campfire illuminated the dining table and the campfire chairs. It grew darker, and the lights brought out the insects. Small insects by the thousands began to accumulate around the lights, huge moths, the size of small birds, that the bats would swoop in and carry away for an evening meal, praying mantis, six inches long, were perched on the tents, and geckos appeared from nowhere. Then it was time for sundowners, and everyone gathered around the campfire, the women on one side, the men on the other.

Klaus continued the conversation from the previous gathering, while taking sips of a whisky and water, "Well, Frank, you and your family certainly have a wonderful life, but honestly, don't you worry about the political situation?"

Frank answered, "Well, yes, of course, there are a lot of the whites leaving and Africans are moving onto their lands."

Then Janet raised her voice to the boys, "Right, you boys, get cleaned up and into bed".

None of them spoke back, they were all exhausted by the drive and disappeared behind the flaps of their tent, dodging the bugs as best they could.

Then Tin-Cann spoke, "Well, you know, you speak like the Safari business is finished. With this Mau-Mau crap, no one wants to come here, they all go to Rhodesia and South Africa. I have only survived because of the Army, so I have decided to move, myself. I'm off to Rhodesia. Place called Wankie, Western side, just north of the city of Bulawayo. Right next to Victoria Falls and I can fly people to the falls, put them up in the hotels there, and we can do game tours and hunt at the same time, right on the Botswana border. Plenty of game and no security problems, great potential."

Frank took up the conversation, "You know, my best friend from the war lives there, Tin-Cann?"

"Yes," replied Tin Cann, "hope I will bump into him sometime."

Then it was Klaus's turn "You know, when I was a pilot, it was he who shot me down in the channel," and he explained how it came about, the photo and Frank's confirmation, they all laughed and Tin-Cann finished with, "A lucky bugger, you are, Klaus."

The ladies were all chattering away amongst themselves until Frank stood and said, "Goodnight, everyone, I'm off, early start tomorrow."

He looked up, there was a full moon in the clear sky, and every now and then, a shooting star would streak across as it hurtled to earth. Everyone began to rise and started their goodnights, drained the remains of their glasses, and made their way to their tents. The Africans were silent, they had drunk their fill and filled their guts with fresh meat, ready for a fresh start. They planned to leave Benjamin to break camp and load everything onto the camp truck. Tin-Cann, Frank, and Klaus, along with the young boys and the ladies would leave straight after breakfast, Benjamin and the boys would follow on. As soon as heads hit the pillows, it was lights out, even the roar of a lion and the cackle of the hyenas didn't bother anyone.

The next morning, surprisingly, everyone was up at first light, some nursing sore heads, but alive. It was only thirty minutes until breakfast was served, steaming hot coffee and plates of scrambled eggs, beans, and bacon. The ladies were up late, they were all tittering about with important stuff, eye lashes, lipstick, and hair brushing, but eventually they made it. Everyone was excited about the journey to the Maasai-Mara, even Tin-Cann, and he had been there several times on Safari with rich clients. Everyone listened when he described it, a sight to behold, he would say, animals as far as the eyes could see. The boys bombarded him with questions until he could stand no more.

"All right, folks, let's load up."

He gave last orders to the African team and jumped into his truck. He drove off and the others fell in behind. They drove down to the river; it was shallow here and he had made the crossing several times. It wasn't long before they were on the other side and climbing the opposite bank. The trucks bumped and ground their way up the slope until they eventually reached the top, it was another four-hour drive to the Maasai, and as they trundled along, it was impossible for Frank and Klaus to hold a conversation. The bumps and the hum of the engines was very loud, and yet, somehow, no matter how loud the engine was, it never interrupted the ladies' conversations.

Frank was astounded, again, it was all the important stuff, lace, curtains, the latest knickers, high heel shoes, and handbags from Italy and France. Adeena and Janet listened to Ingrid as she had been shopping in Paris and Milan not six months ago. Even with changing gears, engaging four-wheel drive, bumping, and grinding, they never skipped a beat.

As they came towards the edge of the forest, it began to thin and the trees became sparser, and then just ahead, the open grasslands came into view. Tin-Cann raised his hand and stopped in front, the others followed suit, Tin-Cann made his way to Frank's truck, placed his foot on the running board and told Frank and Klaus that it wasn't far now, but he would like to wait for Benjamin and the camp staff to catch up, they all agreed and broke out the Safari box in the back of the stud.

The boys were the first to dive in, grabbing a handful of sandwiches then making off towards a beautiful umbrella shaped tree and gulping down their food. Not far off, in a neighbouring tree, a troop of Baboons watched on, now and again giving their distinctive bark, Bahoo! Bahoo! One of the boys threw a crust and a young baboon ventured over, grabbed it, and took off, racing up another tree. Three or four others went after him, keen to steal his prize, but it was gone, stuffed into his cheeks. An hour passed before the camp truck came into view. Frank said to Tin-Cann, "They made good time."

Tin-Cann agreed. He briefed everyone, "In about thirty minutes we will be on the slope ahead", he pointed in the direction, "on the other side is the Maasai-Mara, prepare yourself for a spectacle that has no equal".

As they drove on, a large Acacia tree came into view. At the base were five hyenas, looking up at the branches. As they drew nearer, they could make out the tell-tale sign of a leopard, its long tail hanging from the branches. It had made a kill and climbed the tree and secured it in the branches, it was a young Thomson Gazelle ram, easily distinguished by its horns. The vehicles pulled up and the Hyena's took off with their awkward gait and that Ho! Ha! Ho! Ha! That sound that gave them their name, laughing hyena. The leopard looked down at the people below and let out a growl. Ingrid had her camera at the ready but after a few moments, the Leopard decided they were a threat, bounded down the trunk of the tree and took off into the long grass, but she smiled and said to Janet and Adeena "I did get some very good shots."

They started up again and it wasn't long before they were at the base of the slope. The trees had become sparse, and as they edged closer to the top, they could hear sounds like a battle below, then they were at the summit, and they edged over just enough to take in the view. There was the Maasai-Mara, beyond was a sea of black wildebeest with the odd spattering of Zebra and Impala, Thomson Gazelles darted about, rams chasing the females. As far as the eye could see, there was wildlife, the greatest and largest migration of animals on the planet.

Frank was out of the Stud and spoke to Tin-Cann, "God, man, how many do you think are down there?"

"Difficult to say," was the reply.

Ingrid had her movie camera operating, Klaus tried to speak to her, but she wasn't listening. The three boys stood in front of the Stud, shouting to Janet, "Look, mum, there's a Tommy over there. Look, impala."

Tin-Cann had spotted the ideal camp site, a small grove of Acacia. He yelled to the boys in the camp truck to follow him and told Frank and Klaus to follow on when they were ready. It was only about half a mile in the distance. He told them it would rain again during the night, and he wanted to ensure everyone would be comfortable. Then he took off, the three-tonner following on with its huge trailer in tow. As they pulled up, the Africans began to jump out and immediately started unloading. The tents were large with upturned edges at the base, so water couldn't enter, the dining area was raised on wooden pallets, four inches above the ground and they laid these out to each tent so there would be no wet feet.

Everyone was very impressed with his camp and the way he set it up, it was very Safari like. It was amazing how comfortable it was; large rectangular canvas sheets were propped up with poles and angled to allow the rain to run off. The boys had it ready within two hours, with kerosene lamps hung every ten yards or so. The kitchen was set up and Benjamin and Tin-Cann's chef went to work. The water bowser had been filled at the last water crossing and water was on the boil, tea and coffee was ready as the rest of the group pulled into camp.

Klaus was the first to compliment Tin-Cann, "You know, Tin-Cann, I can see why the Safari industry has proved so popular. This is truly wonderful." And everyone agreed.

They made their way to the dining area and took their seats, Benjamin brought each, in turn, a cup of hot coffee. The three boys were off climbing in the trees. It wasn't long before it began to get dark. The day was coming to an end, the noise from the wildebeest also began to wane as they settled for the night, it wouldn't be long before the big cats stirred and began to hunt. Benjamin banged on the bottom of a pot; this was the signal that supper was up. Everyone freshened up, changed into clean clothes, and made their way back to the dining area. Sundowners first, Gin and Tonic, Whisky and water, but only beer for the Aussie. Everyone was seated around the table; it was dark now and the men were discussing the timetable and decided that three days was all they could allow. They asked Ingrid if that suited her, and she smiled and said that would be fine. Janet and Adeena also agreed. Everyone had a few drinks and tongues began to wag loosely. As they sat there, a huge moth flew from out of the darkness towards the Kerosene lamp. Tin-Cann was the nearest and he was quite startled, he shouted out in shock, "Look at the size of that fucking thing, it's the size of a fucking crow."

Straight away he realised his mistake, and was about to apologise, when young Brian popped up and asked his mother, "What's that, mum? What's fucking?"

Everyone had slight smiles on their faces except Janet, "Oh, it's nothing, darling, just what they call a verb."

But Brian continued, "so fucking is a verb? Grandma never taught us that. I'll ask her why not when we get home."

Everyone began to snigger, "No, no you'd better not, Brian."

"But it must be a funny word, Mum, everyone is laughing."

Ingrid and Adeena both had tears in their eyes.

"Alright, you three, eat and bed."

The boys finished up and made their way to their tent for the night. It was getting late, and it began to rain, so everyone began their goodnights and made their way to their tents. Janet and Frank's tent was very comfortable with a double bed and lovely soft mattress, Frank stumbled slightly as he bent to enter the tent.

"Had a little too much, darling?" Janet quipped, a wide grin on her face.

Frank looked at her, "I can see you smiling," he said "even in this light. I'll give you something to smile about."

He made a grab for her but tripped and went head long into the far end of the tent. Janet laughed loudly at Frank lying on the floor.

Then a voice came from outside, it was Adeena, "Now, now, you two, straight to bed."

Frank pulled himself onto the bed and fell sound asleep.

Klaus wasn't much better; with Ingrid's help, he made it to the tent entrance then collapsed. Ingrid just left him there and went to bed. She was awakened during the night by what sounded like grunts, it was Klaus, he had managed to find the entrance to the tent, went inside, and fell into bed next to her. She un-ceremoniously took both legs and shoved him out, he landed with a groan and a thud on the canvas floor.

When Frank and Janet woke the next morning, Frank was holding his head.

"Morning, Ace," said Janet, "flying by the seat of your pants last night then, flying officer Monroe?"

Then a voice came from outside, it was Benjamin, "Madam, Sir, I have coffee."

"Come in, Ben," said Janet "I think the boss here had too much to drink."

"Ah! Yes, Madam, it makes him crazy."

"I agree," said Janet, "let's get come coffee into him."

Ben set down the tray and left, as he did, he said, "Breakfast in thirty minutes, Madam. Mr Tin-Cann is already up and ready to go."

"Bloody Aussies," said Frank holding his head, "don't know how they do it."

The ladies made their way to the dining tent, Tin-Cann sat up "Well, good morning, where're the boys?"

Ingrid was the first to respond, "think mine will need a day off," and Janet shared the same thought, "Just leave them."

Everyone at the table ate a good breakfast while Tin-Cann spoke about his plans for the day. Ingrid asked if he could show her some lions and he said he knew of a pride not far off, their territory was close by, the pride was watched over by two huge male lions. Tin-Cann had named the largest one 'Black Douglas' because of his huge black mane. He told them that they were believed to be brothers, and the last time he saw them, the pride numbered fifteen. The ladies listened while Ingrid checked over her camera equipment, all the latest from Germany. Benjamin, and Tin-Cann's driver turned up, the boys in the back of the vehicle, they had all been up at sunrise, of course, and they all wanted to know where their fathers were, "Oh," came the reply, "they are very sick today."

"Both of them?" they asked.

Benjamin had loaded up the lunch box, and when everything was ready, off they went. Tin-Cann was driving, and as they bumped along over the grasslands, the game began to come into view. Huge herds of black wildebeest, zebra, Tommies, impala, all moving as one. The zebra pranced and gave out that whistling sound Twee-Twee-Twee and the wildebeest didn't seem to be at all fussed about these humans and their transport. They just gave way and allowed them to pass, then the formation began to change, they entered a huge patch, circular with no game, probably a mile across. Tin-Cann stopped and explained, this circle is the pride's hunting area. We should catch sight of some lions soon; the animals know to give it a wide berth, but the lions hunt mostly at night, as the herds sleep.

Sure enough, just ahead, lying under an Acacia Tree was a pride of lions. Two huge males lay on their sides, as they heard the truck approach, they stood and made no noise. They were fat and in excellent condition. The lionesses lay, not far off, and five cubs could be seen playing in the grass. Tin-Cann pulled up about seventy yards away and Ingrid was about to get out, but he held her arm, "I wouldn't do that if I were you. Stay in the vehicle and film from here."

"But they don't look dangerous," she said.

"Believe me, if they want to, they could cross that distance in seconds. You wouldn't know what hit you. It's not the males, it's the females with the cubs."

"Ok," she replied, "I understand."

It was just after midday, and it was hot. Ingrid filmed for about fifteen minutes, changing the film three times, then said to Tin-Cann, "Well, that should do. I would like to find some of the smaller animals."

So, they drove off, the twins and Gunter keeping watch for anything new that would impress their mothers.

Frank and Klaus had finally risen and were seated at the dining table when Klaus spoke to Frank. "Frank, what do you think will happen here when independence finally arrives?"

"To tell you the truth, I have discussed it with my uncle, and he is not at all optimistic, but we don't want to return to the U.K. So, we are looking at options, the most favourable is southern Rhodesia."

"Ah!" said Klaus, "Yes, of course, Ian Smith, your friend. Well, that would be a good place for you and your family. Independence in Africa is not going well. Look at the Congo, now a total basket case, I think you call it. Before we left South Africa, they were advertising in the newspapers for mercenary soldiers to go and fight there. Also, I heard in the U.K. about a man called Mike Hoare, an Irishman, and another black, Jack Shram, and it would appear they have many recruits. West Africa is the same, Black Rule is not working."

"No," agreed Frank, "they are just not ready yet. I have been in touch with Ian, he has been in politics now for a number of years and is looking forward to a prosperous future. The British government have indicated that anything south of the Zambezi will remain in White control. Besides, the English have too much to lose. Gold, diamonds, agriculture, so that is an option."

The rest of the family returned sometime later, Ingrid was smiling a broad smile, she ran to her husband and kissed him on the cheek, "What a wonderful day, darling, wait until I develop it. You will be impressed, I know."

"Well," replied Klaus, "I am so glad, and how did the youngsters fair?"

"Oh! They were great, but look at them, they are exhausted. I think the three of them need a clean-up and to be fed, then off to bed. What do you think, Janet?"

"I agree totally, it's been a long day."

Around the dinner table that evening, Ingrid asked Tin-Cann if one more day would be an option.

"Of course," he replied, "if you like, we can go and track down some rhino. We haven't seen any yet and I know a great little place."

"That sounds terrific," replied Ingrid, "then, I think if everyone is in agreement, that should do us, and we can return to Mombasa."

Everyone agreed and decided on an early night. It had been a long day. Janet and Frank turned in first, as they made their way to the tent, Sophie closely brought up the rear, she had become Frank's shadow and rarely left his side. She was the spitting image of her mother, Rosie.

They left early the next morning, and as they drove out it began to rain, not heavily, and Tin-Cann assured everyone it wouldn't last. Sure enough, in about thirty minutes, it stopped. Off on the horizon, a rainbow touched the earth, Adeena remarked that it was the brightest she'd ever seen. As they drove on, a pair of secretary birds came into view, tall blueish grey birds of prey, with their long spindly legs and quills hanging from their head. They were out feeding on insects, rodents, snakes, anything they could find in the grass. Ingrid asked Tin-Cann pull up so she could film them.

"What beautiful birds," she remarked, and after about five minutes she said, "That's fine," and they drove on. Up ahead, a grove of trees came into view.

Tin-Cann pointed and said, "Look up there, in those trees," everyone stared in the direction he had indicated, where they could see small figures bounding about in the branches.

"Ah! Yes," exclaimed Ingrid, "Look, baboons,"

"No," said Tin-Cann, "have a look again."

As they drew closer the colours of the monkeys gave them away, all the ladies shouted aloud, "by God, they are beautiful. What are they?"

"These are one of the most beautiful of all the monkeys."

As they pulled up, the troop glared down at the humans, their long black and white tails, and coats splendid in the sunshine. The males barked angrily and raised their eyebrows to look intimidating.

"These," said Tin-Cann, "are Colobus Monkeys."

Ingrid's camera was already rolling, "OH!" she said, "they are wonderful and so colourful."

The two men, Frank and Klaus, had decided to join the ladies for the final day and Klaus said he had never seen a Rhino in the wild. As they drove along, Frank could see Klaus was becoming bored and indeed he was. Klaus looked back at his wife and the other ladies and, of course, the boys. He thought to himself that they were all having a great time. Ingrid was indeed a beautiful woman and the best thing he had ever done was to marry her and she had given him a beautiful son. Everyone was happy and he could see Africa was in their blood. He had to admit that he had caught the bug, but he was a businessman, and a top representative of Mercedes Benz. He had been in South Africa negotiating with the South African government on opening factories in the country. He had suggested the South African Boer, difficult, to say the least, but he won through in the end. While there, he and Ingrid had fallen in love with Cape Town, it offered everything he wanted, a good place for the whole family. He had looked at buying a vineyard in a place called Stellenbosch, it was fifty acres of prime land, twenty with vines, and a wine distillery. He realised he knew nothing about the wine trade, but it had a good manager, so, he would put it to Ingrid at the first chance he got.

It wasn't long before Tin-Cann indicated that, just up ahead, two rhinos were coming into view. They were black rhino, the most cantankerous of the two, white and black. They pulled up, and Ingrid began her routine of filming, it was a mother and calf quietly browsing. Tin-Cann began to explain the difference, the black rhino is a browser, mainly with a pointed upper lip, normally very bad tempered, the white is a grazer, like a great big cow with the same nature. They finished filming, and as it was getting late, started the journey back to camp. This would be their last night together. Klaus had asked Tin-Cann if it would be possible to drive straight back to Mombasa, but he replied that was too much and they decided to make a stop at the half-way inn.

They arrived back just as the sun was setting, Klaus looked back over his shoulder at his family, yes, he thought, I have been bitten by the Africa bug. He could make this place his home, but he also thought, realistically, how long would it last? All the African colonies were clamouring for independence, but never-the-less, he would give it a chance.

It was soon time to get some sleep, everyone ate well, but were utterly exhausted, so they made their way to their tents.

It was an early-rise the following morning, they had breakfast as usual, then loaded up, Tin-Cann had been given instructions to make Honeydew Ranch by late evening. He gave the boys their orders, they knew the routine, they would break camp and follow on. It was midday when they reached the river, they had made good time, and they would make the farmhouse by four in the evening. Frank had noticed that everyone was silent, even the ladies, except for the occasional "look over there, giraffe," or some other wild animal.

It was, indeed, just after four when the farmhouse came into view. Everyone was looking forward to stretching their legs as it had been one hell of a ride bumping along, sometimes reaching speeds of forty-five miles per hour and hitting every bump in the road. Sophie was first out; the jack russells were all there to greet everyone. They always made such a fuss.

It was good to be home, Janet could see Rita making her way over and Jack just coming into view behind her. Frank had driven in through the north road and bypassed the workshops and compound. Adeena had phoned her husband from Janet's house to alert him that they had arrived home, and he said that Tony and he would be right over, fifteen minutes had passed when Sam's Landrover came into view, everyone greeted each other, and as they were doing so, Frank appeared on the verandah with the kitchen staff carrying the drink tray. They laid it on the long table and Frank told everyone to help themselves. They talked and laughed about the time they had spent at the Maasai Mara.

They had been there for two hours, the boys had finished refuelling the trucks, and just as they were about to pour another drink, the Safari truck came into view. So, it was time to mount up and hit the road again. Janet and Frank tried their best to get them to stay the night, but Klaus was adamant they must be gone, he explained his tight schedule and apologised, but thanked his hosts for a great time and assured the Munros that they would meet again and said, "Frank, please tell your friend, Ian Smith, that I look forward to meeting up with him", and that was it, as quick as that, they were gone.

As they drove out the gates, Ingrid turned, waved, and blew a kiss. Gunter had to be carried to the truck, he and the twins had become great friends. Janet and Frank were quite honestly glad to get back to normal.

***

Chapter 15

The following morning, Rita and Jack turned up for breakfast. As they settled down to eat, Jack began the conversation. "Frank, while you were away, a man from the lands department paid me a visit, accompanied by a representative from the embassy, the home office. It would appear Britian is going all the way for independence for Kenya and a lot of the other colonies, and they are making offers to all the white landowners to buy up the land and hand over to the Africans. The majority of the offers, I was told, have been taken up, as many are of the opinion they couldn't live under a black government. My personal view is that I agree, the offer we have been given is a generous one, but before a decision is made, we need to discuss it amongst ourselves."

"God, Uncle Jack," said Frank, "I would hate to give up all this, also there's the clinic and the school."

"I know, laddie," replied Jack, "but I want you to think about it. I, personally, want to go. The security situation is worsening, plus the home office rep gave me a briefing, apparently there is Russian involvement in freeing Africa from the white man."

They looked at each other, "and Russians, what are they?"

"They, as the home office put it, are the new shit-stirrers in the world, they have an office in Dar-E-Salam, headed by the KGB. They think we don't know, but the British Secret Service have known from the start, apparently, they are stockpiling weapons. This afternoon, I would like everyone to come over here and we can let them know what's happened, that's Tony, and Sam and Adeena.

That afternoon, everyone arrived at Frank and Janet's and took their places on the verandah. Benjamin and the kitchen staff served tea and coffee. Benjamin sensed something was up. When everyone settled down, Jack stood up and began to explain what had taken place. He told them about the offer and also the home office reps' rundown on the security situation, not just in Kenya but all over Africa. The Congo was turning into a blood bath; missions burnt, missionaries and nuns brutally murdered and mutilated, white mercenaries were being recruited quite openly, and being paid well for their services, even the British SAS regiment in London, twenty-one Squadron, were recruiting. There were rumblings in Tanganyika, Zambia, West Africa, Nigeria, and Biafra but it wasn't just against the whites, it was one tribe's dominance over the other, the most powerful would be the winner of the next government.

"From my point of view," said Jack, "I want to accept the offer."

Everyone was silent.

Finally, Tony spoke, "So, what will happen to us?"

"Well, Tony," replied Jack, "I personally don't wish to return to Britian, I am an African, my thoughts lie south of the Zambezi, Southern Rhodesia. You can all come, lock, stock, and barrel."

Then Sam spoke, "and what about the Clinic, and the patients?"

"That's a difficult one, Sam."

"Yes, it is," he replied. "There's no use in my wife and I moving there because of the apartheid."

Jack looked at them in silence for some time, then he spoke, "Sam, Adeena, I can only apologise for the behaviour of some whites, unfortunately it's their laws, it's not against the law in Rhodesia to be married to a person of colour, but it is frowned upon by many. I can only repeat that you are welcome to accompany us if you wish, or you can stay here at the clinic, but I don't know who will fund it. The British, after independence, won't. They have made that quite clear. Independence means independence. You have one other option".

Sam looked puzzled and asked, "and that option, Jack, what is it?"

"Botswana, they need doctors in Gaborone, the capital. Will you think it over?"

Sam looked at Adeena, "Well, darling, that might just suit us."

Tony interrupted again, "when do you see this happening, Jack?"

"I'm going to accept the offer, it's a very generous one, so I expect it to go ahead within a couple of months. Frank has a good wartime friend down there, Mr Ian Smith, he has just been elected the head of the Rhodesian Front, tipped to be the new government."

Jack turned to Frank, "Frank, I would like us to fly down in the next couple of weeks to take a look. You said your friend, Ian, has his eye on a place near Salisbury, I think you said, Marandellas. Tony, if you agree to come with us, I want you to make a list of equipment we can take. We will load everything on the trucks and take a freighter to the port of Biera in Mozambique. The Portuguese are very friendly, we can offload and drive through to Umtali on the Rhodesian border, it's only one hundred and thirty miles and the roads are good."

Then Tony replied, "Well ok, Jack, I'm in. They tell me it's a beautiful country, well organised, very happy."

That night, Frank and Janet lay in bed discussing what was about to happen, both were excited, Janet had only read about Rhodesia, and she looked forward to moving to a country with a larger white population, it sounded wonderful, and the boys could look forward to a bright future. They even had their own university for blacks and whites, although segregated.

Rita and Jack were there at breakfast the following morning, the topic, of course, was the move.

Rita said, "Well, at least, Jack, life is not boring with you around. When do you plan on flying down?"

Jack replied, "Next week. I will book this morning, soon as I can get through."

That night, Frank phoned his friend Ian Smith, to his amazement it was only a thirty-minute wait. Ian lived in Gwelo but was at his residence in Salisbury, the phone rang, an African picked it up and answered, "This is Mr Smith's house."

"Good evening, is Mr Smith available?" asked Frank.

"Yes, sir," was the reply, "who is calling?"

"Tell him it's the best pilot the RAF ever had."

In the background he heard a lady's voice call out "Sampson, who is it?"

"Madam, it's the best pilot the RAF ever had."

Then Frank heard Ian's unmistakable drawl, "Who is it, darling?"

She replied, "It's the best pilot the RAF ever had".

Then he heard Ian "Can't be. That was me, must be that Scotsman, he used to think he could fly."

Ian put the phone to his ear, yes, there was no mistaking the Scottish voice on the other end. "Ian, old friend it's good to hear you again".

"What's going on up there in Kenya, Frank?"

"Well," Frank replied, "as you probably know, the country is heading for independence and a lot of the whites are leaving, myself and my family wish to make the move to Southern Rhodesia".

"Yes, Frank, we have a lot of white Kenyans moving here. We welcome them with open arms. You and your family will be most welcome. What's your time frame?" Ian asked.

"Well, we have already started the ball rolling, I phoned also to ask about the farm in Marandellas, is it still available? If so, we would like to look."

"It is still on the market, a bit expensive for the average farmer, but well worth it and it is a going concern. It has a resident manager, I believe, he is doing a great job experimenting with new crops, asparagus for one, and also livestock, chickens, can't raise enough. When do you plan on coming down?"

"Well," said Frank, "how about next week?"

"Ok, Frank," said Ian, "you're a good man. I look forward to seeing you again, it's been too long." And they ended the call.

***

Chapter 16

Dedan Omondi had travelled to Tanganyika; it took him over a week. He walked across the border with his two trusted men, both veterans of the Mau-Mau war against the British, all three had been involved from the beginning. Their guide was a young Tanganyikian, no more than fourteen or fifteen years old. He had been paid by an Indian muslin trader, who hated the British, to meet Dedan and his men and guide them to the main road to meet the bus to bring them to Dar-Eslam. He had arranged a meeting with some new residents whom he knew would help in their fight for freedom.

Dedan and his men had eaten their rations and were hungry. They asked the boy where they could eat and he pointed, "This way, my lords, this way." He led them off the road and into a small clearing, there was a tin shack with open sides and a cooking fire smoking in the centre. Around it hung meat, blackened by the smoke. The boy moved forward, towards a group of men and women sitting at tables, they were mostly elderly Africans, their hair beginning to grey, and some carried sticks. Their fingers were stained by the coarse tobacco cigarettes that hung from their mouths.

The boy began, "Behold, Madalla, these men, they come from beyond the mountains. These men, they are freedom fighters."

Heads turned and stared but no one spoke.

The boy went on, "They have travelled far and are hungry."

An old woman came to her feet, "We have food," she said, "do they have money?"

The boy looked at the three, waiting for an answer. "We have money, silver shillings, but we want proper food, not these dried sticks you have hanging."

At the mention of silver shillings, the old woman's face opened up in a huge grin, showing broken and black teeth.

"Look," she said, and lifted the lid from a large pot steaming over the fire, "here," and she took three plates, "give me three silver shillings and take your fill."

Dedan stepped forward, followed by his men, they each accepted a plate and spoon, it was good food, plenty of meat and vegetables in a thick brown gravy. They ladled large helpings on to their plates and went to sit at the table, the others moved aside to make space for the freedom fighters. The old woman went to a cupboard and brought out a loaf of bread and cut it into three pieces.

Then Dedan gave the old woman an order, "Old woman, you will feed the boy also," and flicked another shilling at her. She missed it and it disappeared into the long grass, but before long, she had retrieved it.

The boy thanked Dedan, "Thank you, master, many thanks, I am very hungry also."

The three freedom fighters all ate twice, then the old woman gave them blankets and they went to sleep in the grass while they waited for the bus. When Dedan awoke it was from the young boy shaking his shoulder. It was dark.

The boy said, "Lord, the bus is here. We must go."

The three awoke and stood, they could hear a vehicle reviving its engine. They followed the boy to the edge of the trees, to where the bus stood. Dedan boarded first and paid the driver, his eyes shone when he saw the shiny shillings. As they moved down to the back, they passed several Africans, some with large sacks, some carried chickens, their legs trussed, which, although alive, made no sound, strapped to the outside of the roof. There were pigs and goats caged in cane baskets. Dedan thought it the same as in his homeland. They each picked a seat; the bus was not full so they could stretch out for the five-hundred-mile journey to Dar Es Salaam. The driver crunched the bus into first gear, and it lurched forward with a rumble. As he crashed through the gears, and moved down the dirt road, a huge cloud of black smoke trailed behind them. Dedan looked out the window into the dark. He could see green lights by the side of the road, the bus's lights illuminating the animals as they passed. The boy had told him they would not reach the city until mid-morning the next day. They stopped and started several times, passengers got off, more got on. It must have been half-way through the journey when the bus pulled into a small town, they stopped, and Dedan could see a fuel pump next to the bus.

The boy informed them, "we stop for thirty minutes for fuel, lords, if you want, you can drink at the canteen."

They made their way to the canteen, a ramshackle tin shack that smelt of urine. Outside were half a dozen African women and another coloured girl, all dressed in short skirts and wearing heavy makeup. They all wore wigs except for the coloured girl, she noticed Dedan staring at her, and waved him over, he obeyed and went to her side.

"For some money, we can go to the side over there".

Dedan agreed, and they disappeared into the darkness. After fifteen minutes, Dedan returned, tucking in his shirt, a broad smile on his face.

It was nine the following morning when they reached the outskirts of Dar Es Salaam, the buildings were a ramshackle mixture of brick and tin shacks. People moved along the road, some on foot, others on scotch carts towed by bullocks, some road bicycles, some waved as the bus passed them. As they reached the centre of town, the buildings become less crude, shops had goods displayed, traders watched as they drove past. Then they were in the open-air markets. The bus began to slow, and the stench of rotten meat became overwhelming. They stopped in front of a large open building with a steel roof. There were other buses there, some were off-loading passengers, they could hear animals squealing and dogs barking. People began to stand and make their way to the front of the bus; it was almost empty when the four rose and disembarked. The boy looked around; in the distance he saw a white minivan with a Muslim dressed in white standing beside it. The Muslim waved and the boy acknowledged him and led his three friends to where he stood.

The boy bowed and the man introduced himself, "My name is Mohamad Rashid, I am here to welcome you. I have people for you to meet, but you must be tired and hungry, so first, we will attend to your needs." They did not shake hands. Dedan was suspicious of the Muslim man but nodded in agreement. He opened the door of the van and the four piled in.

"First," said Mohamed, "we go to my home where you are most welcome."

It was a thirty-minute drive before they pulled into the driveway of a walled villa-style home. The gates swung open and on the other side stood a young African man. They drove through, and he closed the gates close behind them. They stopped in front of a large white house, open at the front.

Dedan and his men had been speaking in Swahili, which everyone understood, but now Dedan spoke in his own tongue, Kikuyu, "So, this is how the Muslim lives. What do you think he wants or needs from us?"

To the right, three small trucks were offloading goods, another was loading. Dedan and his men could see rows and rows of elephant tusks ranging from small to huge, on another were the horns of the rhino, too many to count at a glance. Zebra skins piled high, other skins as well.

"So," said Dedan, "this is how this one makes his money. He is a thief."

Dedan's men grunted in reply. That afternoon, Dedan and his men rested, it had been a long and tiring journey. At about six in the evening, the young boy came and knocked on their door, "Masters," he called, "it is time to eat, are you awake? The lord has prepared a great feast for you all, the freedom fighters from the north."

The men rose and followed the boy to the dining room. Mohamad Rashid greeted them, "Please! Please! Come and sit. We shall drink beer first, yes?"

Dedan nodded and his two accomplices also nodded in agreement.

Mohamad went on as he poured large mugs of beer, though he poured none for himself, "My people have prepared a great feast for you, so eat well, for tomorrow we meet the Russians."

At six the next morning, the young boy knocked on Dedan's door "Master," he shouted, "Are you ready?"

Dedan answered, "Yes, we will be there."

The Muslim was already at the dining table, he ate with his left hand only and looked up as the three Kikuyu walked in. The servant was already dishing up their food.

"As soon as you are finished, we will leave, my friends," said the Muslim. "We are going to the dock yard; you will be most impressed at what you see."

They drove through the city and made their way to the docks. When they entered the dockyard gates, an African guard snapped to attention and waved them through, they drove to the wharf area where they passed a dozen ships loading and unloading cargo, then they came to a long gap and at the end stood two cargo vessels next to a large warehouse. There was no signs or indication of who owned the warehouse. On the ships were three names with Panama under each name and beside one of the vessels stood a tractor with three large flatbed trailers attached. The two front trailers were fully loaded with wooden crates. The third was half loaded and they could see a net full of the wooden boxes being lowered onto the docks ready to be unloaded by a waiting forklift. Mohamad did not stop, he pulled up in front of a large door and tooted the horn.

After a short wait, the door began to slide open, they drove in, and the door slid closed behind them. At the far end of the shed there was an office block with stairs leading up to an office. At the top of the stairs, two armed guards sat smoking, each had a rifle slung over their shoulder. Dedan did not recognise the weapons; they were small compared to the .303 and the new SLR's the British used. They had curved magazines and it looked like the butt folded in. As they drove down towards them, the guards stood and took the guns from their shoulders, one turned and made a sign through the office window. Dedan could see many wooden crates stacked nearly to the roof, some were on the floor, open. Inside, he could see rifles, ammunition, and long tubular things with what he thought must be bombs sticking out from the front. As they pulled up, the office door opened and another white man stepped out on to the landing, he waved a greeting to the Muslim, and he waved back.

They climbed the steps and the man from the office spoke in broken English, "Please! Please! My friends, come in, sit."

All the white men were dirty looking and unshaven. On the office table stood an open bottle of Vodka, the ashtray was full of cigarette butts and the place smelled of urine. These must be the Russians, thought Dedan, and he grunted to his two men.

Then the Russian spoke. "Well, my friends, Mohamad has told me of you and that you are freedom fighters from the north. My name is Vladimir Rabinski and I represent the Russian Government here in Africa. My government has told me to extend their best wishes to you and all your comrades, we are here to offer you our help in gaining independence in all of Africa. We also had to fight for our own freedom and fairness for all our people. Now it is your turn."

Dedan responded, "Thank you and your country, but what do you want in return?"

The Russian answered "Only your freedom, only your freedom. We offer you weapons and sanctuary and training camps for all your followers who can cross the borders. They will be made most welcome, the ones who show real promise will go to Russia for political training. We already have many from the African National Congress with us now."

Dedan looked at his comrades and spoke in Kikuyu, "This white man is not telling us the truth but maybe we can use him."

The Russian turned to the table, took four glasses, and poured Vodka in each one, he knew the Muslim did not drink, he raised his glass, "To my new friends and friends of the USSR. To freedom for Africa!"

****

Chapter 17

Janet and Rita had decided to join Jack and Frank on the trip to Rhodesia, so they were making themselves busy packing. They were excited. Adeena and Sam had agreed to look after the boys while they were gone, they did not expect to be away for more than a week.

The trip to Nairobi was uneventful, they drove into the airport, and Frank couldn't help but notice how shabby and unkept the place looked. The roads were badly maintained, and litter lay in the streets, the Brits were gradually pulling out, and with them went the funding and the white supervision. A great number of ex-pats had left and returned to the U.K. or moved south to the white-run countries. Frank parked the Stud, and everyone got out, two African staff came over pushing a four-wheeled cart. Benjamin was in the back, he jumped out and gave instructions to the airport porters. They loaded the cart and made off towards the airport terminal.

Jack called him over, "Right, Benjamin, take the stud back to the Norfolk, park it up, and you stay there until we return."

"Yes, Sir." He knew something was going on but was not sure what. He had heard that a lot of the whites were leaving, was his boss doing the same? And if so, what would happen to him?

The family made their way to the check-in counter and confirmed their bookings. All was well and the staff informed them that their flight was due to leave in two hours, and if they would like to wait in the lounge, they would be called to board. They made their way to the lounge and up to the bar. Jack and Frank ordered beers while the ladies settled for coffee.

It was nearly an hour before the Tannoy broke its silence, 'Attention - Attention. All passengers booked for flight number CEAA 312 to Salisbury, Rhodesia, now boarding at main gate.

Frank was the first to stand, "Right! Come on girls, let's go." He was excited to see his old friend, Ian Smith again. They made their way downstairs from the lounge and were ushered to the edge of the tarmac. On the runway stood a new four-engine Viscount Aircraft. Printed on the fuselage were the words, *Central and East African Airways*, as they boarded an attractive air hostess showed them to their seats. The loudspeaker crackled into life, "Hello everyone, this is your captain, Neil Smuts." He had a heavy south African accent, "welcome aboard. Our flight to Salisbury will take approximately eight hours with one stop in Lusaka, Northern Rhodesia, where you will be able to stretch your legs."

The engines roared into life, Frank was the only one to have flown before, and as the plane lurched forward, he could see a look of desperation on his wife's face. He took her hand gently and whispered, "It's ok, old girl."

She looked at him, "less of the 'old girl' from you, thank you very much!"

They smiled at each other and looked across at Jack and Rita. Jack looked as if he'd messed in his pants. As they taxied on to the runway and gathered speed, the undercarriage rattled underneath.

"It's ok," said Frank, "all normal."

Then they were in the air. Looking out the window, they could see Nairobi disappearing in the distance. Then they were gone, whipping through some fluffy clouds, they levelled out and soon the hostesses were up and offering tea or coffee. It was a four-hour flight time to Lusaka. Jack and Rita had dozed off but were startled awake by the captain when he came on the intercom again, "Well, ladies and gentlemen, we will be landing in twenty minutes at Lusaka airport."

Minutes passed, then the rumbling of the undercarriage could be heard throughout the plane, it began to descend, and it wasn't long before they hit the ground with a slight bump, and they were down. They taxied towards the airport building and they could see faces looking out of the windows and people waving, then the plane came to a halt, and the captain cut the engines.

"When you are ready, ladies and gentlemen, make your way towards the front of the aircraft and to the lounge area. We shall be here for approximately two hours".

As the Munros entered the terminal they could see it was extremely busy. Northern Rhodesia was part of the federation which included Nyasaland, Northern Rhodesia, and Southern Rhodesia. The federation was divided by the Zambesi River and the north was rich in copper. Miners from around the globe came to take advantage of the generous salaries and the huge copper bonuses on offer. They took a seat, and before long, they were asked to reboard the aircraft for their final flight to Salisbury. None of them knew much about Southern Rhodesia and they were all excited for the coming weeks. The aircraft gained height and levelled out at fifteen thousand feet, they flew just below the clouds, and they could see the African landscape below, now and again they crossed a river.

After an hour, the captain spoke over the intercom, "Ladies and Gentlemen, if you look out of your windows you will see that we are flying over the Zambesi River. The river was dammed in the early fifties and is now the largest man-made lake in the world. The water is still rising, and it has created many small islands. This has caused a problem for a lot of the game animals, but the Rhodesian government has put a plan in place to rescue the stranded animals. It is still in operation as we speak. It is called operation Noah."

Necks craned to get a better view and the plane became very noisy with people chattering, "Oh! Look, there and there."

Then the Zambesi disappeared behind them. As they all settled again, Janet reached over and took Frank's hand, he turned his head and looked into her eyes.

"Frank, darling, I am so looking forward to moving to our new home. No more security worries, we have a future. The boys will have a future. We will know peace in our lives once more."

"All passengers, please fasten your seat belts," it was the captain, and a red light came on at the front of the aircraft with the same direction. The stewardesses walked the aisle checking that everyone was secure and assisting some of the elderly passengers where needed. Another rumble came from beneath their feet as the undercarriage was lowered.

The captain was back on the speaker, "Ladies and Gentlemen, in twenty minutes we will be landing at Salisbury airport. I hope you have had a pleasant journey."

Janet's ears popped as they descended, Frank told her to hold her nose and close her mouth and blow, she thought he was joking, but tried it anyway, it worked, her ears popped again, and she was back to normal. Frank looked out the window, watching trees whip past, then the plane slowed as it came in sight of the runway. When they reached the tarmac, Frank could see black and white stork-like birds walking in the short grass, then with a thud and a jolt, the plane was down. They slowed to a walking pace and taxied to the airport building, stopped, and cut the engines.

The hostesses were on their feet giving instructions. "All right, ladies and gentlemen, we hope you have enjoyed your flight and thank you for flying with us, please collect your luggage and have your passports ready."

The doors opened and Frank could see Africans wheeling boarding ladders towards the aircraft. He was the first of the Munro family to exit the aircraft and as he stepped onto the ladder, he felt a cool fresh breeze. He looked towards the terminal building, it wasn't far, only forty, maybe, fifty yards and there, standing on the first-floor landing, was the unmistakable figure of his good friend, Ian Smith. Frank was the first to wave, then Ian saw the raised arm and recognised him among the other passengers. He waved back, turned, and made his way into the terminal. In the lounge area, there was a waist high barrier dividing the passengers from the waiting families and friends.   The Munros entered the terminal and Frank spotted his friend immediately. The tall slim figure of Ian unmistakeable, the burn scars on his face still visible from the crash landing in the desert during the war, where his Hurricane had caught fire, and he was badly burned before he could be rescued. He had spent six months in hospital; upon release he joined Frank's squadron and that's when they became the best of friends. At Ian's side was a lovely well-dressed lady, Frank knew, of course, that this was Ian's wife, he had seen photos of her. Her name was also Janet. Ian pointed to a side entrance and as the Munros approached, the door opened, and they were invited through straight to immigration.

The immigration officer looked at them and took each passport in turn and stamped them, then said, "Welcome to Southern Rhodesia. Mr Smith is waiting on the other side."

Jack looked at Frank, "Well, lad, special treatment, eh?"

"Not what you know, it's who you know, Uncle Jack". he replied, laughing.

Frank was the first to leave immigration and rushed through the main gate, Ian and his wife were waiting, they walked towards each other and extended their hands.

"God, Ian, it's good to see you again, you haven't changed a bit."

Ian introduced Frank to his wife, Janet, she leant forward and kissed him on the cheek, "Heard so much about you, Frank, it's nice to finally meet up."

Now the rest of the Munros had caught up and introductions were made all round. People were staring and pointing towards Ian.

Then Frank spoke, "Well, we'd better pick up our baggage."

As they walked towards the baggage trolleys, Ian gave them their accommodation details.

"You are booked in at the Meikles Hotel, an old colonial place in the centre of Salisbury, you'll love it. Oh, and it's all taken care of, courtesy of the Rhodesian Government."

"Are you sure, Ian? We don't want to drop you in it."

"It's all done and dusted."

Frank replied, "Thanks, old friend."

The rest of the Munros agreed, "It's very good of you, Ian and Janet."

Ian said, "I'll drop you off, then tonight around eight, we can all meet up for supper. How does that sound? I have a little business to take care of, and it will give you time to get settled in."

"Sounds great, Ian."

The drive into Salisbury didn't take long. The Munros sat, chattering among themselves, and commenting on how clean and neat the place was, and the transport Ian was using - a huge black Bentley Limousine that seated them all comfortably, the driver and his assistant both dressed in immaculate grey uniforms with peak caps.

They drove into Salisbury, and Rita commented that they had not seen so many white people since they left the UK.

They drove into the city, it was beautiful, the streets were wide and lovely blue Jacaranda trees lined each side of the streets. They turned a corner and the car slowed, Frank looked out his window, there was a sign above the entrance, it read, 'Meikles Hotel'. On the opposite side was a park.

"Well, we're here, over there is the park, Cecil Square," said Ian.

The driver and his assistant got out of the Limousine and opened the door. The Monros climbed out first, when Ian and his wife moved on to the footpath, people began to wave and call to them, "Hello, Mr Smith. Well done, Mr Smith."

Ian and his wife waved back, then they all disappeared into the hotel.

Ian spoke to Frank, "Don't worry about your baggage, the staff will take care of everything."

It was a beautiful old place, on the left was a hair salon, Janet and Rita remarked, "We'll have to give them a visit." Then there were some shops, and beyond them, the most beautiful gardens and, finally, reception.

Ian walked up to the desk and all the staff came running, "Mr and Mrs Smith, if there is anything we can do, anything you and your guests need, please do not hesitate to call."

The rooms were beautiful, large, and airy. Ceiling fans cooled the whole area, including the balconies. They were on the first floor, the french doors opened out onto the balconies which overlooked the gardens. They were just above the tree line. They had interconnected suites and before long there was a knock on the door and a voice, "Room Service."

Frank opened the door and the staff entered carrying silver trays, they made their way to the balcony and began to set the tables. It was late afternoon, time for a light tea.

Ian interrupted Frank, "We must go. Tonight, eight o'clock, dinner, ok?"

Frank replied with an "Ok, old mate, thanks for all of this."

Ian and Janet left, closing the door behind them. The table was set, and the Munros sat down and looked at what was in front of them. A large, three-level revolving tray, crammed with cakes of all colours and description, along with silver tea and coffee sets. The African staff were fantastic, they were dressed in immaculate white uniforms with maroon cuffs, and white towels over their left arms. Benjamin would be impressed, thought Frank, and he opened his wallet and gave each of them a tip, he only had Kenyan currency, but they accepted it with a smile, bowed, and left the room.

"Well," said Janet, "let's have a quick snack, then mum and I are off to the hairdressers."

Ian and Janet turned up that evening on time, the Munro family were already in the dining room, a beautiful Mahogony table had been set to one side and the Munros sat around it, with various drinks. When the Smiths walked in, Ian was dressed in a dark suit with a bow tie and Janet in a beautiful long silver gown, they made their way to the table, Frank and Jack stood and they all shook hands.

Ian was carrying a folder in his left hand, on the cover were the words, 'Sabi River Farm'. He handed it to Frank.

"Frank, this will give you and Jack the rundown on the farm you will be looking at tomorrow. It's the department of Agriculture report on the size and exactly what is produced."

Frank and Jack thanked him, then Ian continued.

"Before we start the evening, tomorrow at eight, a Landrover with a driver will meet you outside as your personal transport. He knows exactly where to go. I hope everything meets with your approval."

"Well," said Frank, "up till now, old friend, everything has been one hundred percent. We can't thank you enough. One thing I have to tell you, Ian, do you remember the last day of the war when you accidently shot down that German pilot?" Everyone laughed, even Ian.

"Well, his name is Klaus Benz."

Then Frank related the story, "He has promised to look you up."

"Well," said Ian, "That is quite a tale, I look forward to meeting him."

As they sat, Ian's wife placed her handbag on the table, it was a beautiful crocodile skin bag with solid gold chain and trimmings. Rita and Janet commented at the same time, "that is the most beautiful handbag we have ever seen."

"Yes," said Ian's wife, "Ian bought it for me some time ago when he was in Johannesburg. I've been looking for some crocodile shoes, as accessories, for years and have shot many crocodiles but still haven't found one with shoes."

Everyone burst out laughing and that set the tone for the evening.

They ate a beautiful meal, then settled down for the serious part of the evening. The ladies spoke about how nice it was to see all the shops and all the whites, something they missed in Kenya. Ian and Frank reminisced about the old days and Jack was busy reading the contents of the folder Ian had brought with him about Sabi River Farm. It even contained an aerial photograph of the whole area, clearly showing the boundary fences, the roads, the buildings, the different paddocks, and the irrigation. Plenty of water, he thought, as the property backed onto the Sabi River.

There were homesteads, three of them, large machinery sheds and the African compound. On the far side of the river lay the private game reserve with a note indicating that there was plenty of game in transit and permanent all year round. Jack took off his glasses and exhaled, this, he thought, was too good to be true. He couldn't wait to have a look the next day.

***

Everyone rose early the next morning, Frank was always a plague and pain first thing, niggling at Janet, "Come on, sweetheart, pull a finger, we don't want to be late."

They finished breakfast, the women were still putting on their make up as they were dragged through the main doors and to the Landrover, waiting just as Ian had said, with the same driver as the previous night. His name was Enoch, and he greeted the Munros with a hand clap and a good morning. It was an hour and half drive to the farm entrance, through beautiful rural country. Once they left the city limits, the roads were not at all busy. They pulled up at a sign over the main entrance which read, 'Sabi River Farm'. There was no gate, just cattle grids made from railway lines concreted into the ground. On the right-hand side was another sign, 'Absolutely no hunting! Trespassers will be shot; survivors will be prosecuted'. This raised a smile from everyone.

They crossed the grid onto a sandy road, game tracks were everywhere. It was about three miles to the main homestead; only once did they see a glimpse of a brown stripped buck disappearing into the bush. The Rhodesian bush was different to Kenya, here it was thick with bushes denser making it harder to see the game. Eventually, they came out into a lovely lawned area, on the left were two beautiful, thatched houses, set well apart, at least one-hundred yards, the third home was well behind. As they pulled up, an African came running out clapping his hands, "Good morning," he said, in good English.

"Good morning." The Munros returned, and Frank asked who he was.

"Ah!" He replied, "Master, I am Wilfred. I cook and look after the house."

Rita noticed something moving in the bushes to one side and said, "What is that?"

It sauntered out, it was huge white rhino, must have been five feet at the shoulder, "Oh," said Wilfred, "her name is Lee-Anne, she lives here."

Everyone looked, even the driver, who was back in the driver's seat and refused to come out. Lee-Anne sauntered towards Wilfred who held out a carrot, she poked out her top lip and accepted it greedily, then turned and made her way back to the bushes.

"Well," said Janet, "that is different."

The homes stood on a slight rise and Janet wondered at the skills it took to build such beautiful homes and again the thatch work would put professional thatchers to shame. She wondered why and how Africans, with all these building skills, never built similar homes for themselves. They were quite content to live in a one-room round Kia or House with a shoddy thatch roof. Oh, she had heard the humour, 'it's so they don't get lost at night' or 'they can't get stuck in the corners.'

The view on the other side was spectacular, it looked down on the Sabi river, winding its way into the distance with beautiful sandy patches or beaches, and rocky areas.

"Frank, darling, I could live here."

Rita was talking to Jack, "Get back into town, Jack, buy it."

"Like it?" asked Jack, "done deal. He wants a bit too much for it, that's why it's still available. Let's look around and when we've had enough, we'll head back."

Wilfred interrupted "Sirs, Madams, I have made lunch."

The driver heard 'lunch' and fell out of the car. This meant he could fill his guts as well. The family ate well, thanked Wilfred, and gave him a nice tip, he cupped his hands and thanked them. It was early afternoon when they headed back to town, and they arrived in Salisbury at five that evening. They had discussed the property at length on their return journey and had decided this is definitely where they wanted to live. What a wonderful place it was, like Kenya all over again, when they had first arrived.

***

Chapter 18

Harari township was not far from the outskirts of Salisbury, mostly Africans lived there, and it was quite well set up, with regular bus services that ran until late at night. There was a modern hospital that provided a top-class health service, free of charge, there were schools, and the Africans even had their own university, but there were rumblings of discontent amongst some of the Africans. They were low paid while the whites had large houses and drove motor cars. This bred discontent; this was their land and they wanted it back. There were three main political parties vying to take over the country, Zanla, Zipra, and Zanu.

This evening, in the beer hall, three young African men were standing drinking beer. Botswari Ncube, David Mabuna, and Lovejoy Muringani. They were approached by an old African man, he was smoking a pipe and he smelled of Marijuana, his hair was grey, and his eyes were bloodshot. In his left hand he held a stick which he used to help himself walk. He stopped and looked at them then Botswari said, "Mad Ala, what is it that you want?"

They spoke in Shona, then the old man spoke, "It is not what I want, it is what you young warriors want. Do you want to be the white man's slaves forever?"

They looked at each other, then the old man asked, "Have you been badly treated by the white man?"

They nodded, "Sometimes," answered David, "sometimes they call me a stupid Kaffir."

The old man asked, "would you like what the white man has?"

"Yes."

Now the old man had their attention. "Do you know who I am?" he asked.

"No."

"I am the Zanla headman, I am looking for young warriors to fight and take back our land."

Lovejoy asked, "How can we do this? The whites have an army and air force and the police, we have no guns to attack the whites."

"What if I told you I have these things?" said the old man.

"Where do we get these guns?" asked one young man.

The old man went on, "We have new friends to help. The whites from Russia, and the yellow ones from China. Now we have many young men like yourselves, training, getting ready to attack the whites. But you must journey far and cross the Zambezi. Will you do this? There will be money and food and women in the camps. What you must do is think on this. Tomorrow night at this time I will be here."

David Mabuna was the strongest of the three, they discussed it till late in the night, "If we do this thing, we will be true warriors."

The others nodded in agreement, neither of the young men had anything to say. Botswari's sister worked for a white family in the city, and sometimes she gave him money. His mother was dead, and he never knew his father. Lovejoy's father was a drunk who beat his mother often, he could not live at home, and he did odd jobs for the white man in their gardens or washing their cars, but they called him black bastard and said, "Fuck off, Kaffir", he hated them. David's father was a Policeman who made sure his son went to school, learned to read and write the white man's language. They all agreed that they would do this.

The next evening, they were at the beer hall when the old man appeared in the doorway, he stared at them, then slowly limped towards them, his stick tapping in front of him and he shuffled on behind, tap, tap, left then right. He stopped in front of the young men, blue smoke billowing from his mouth and nostrils, and he smelled of sweat.

"Well, young warriors, I see you are all here. Are you all ready to fight for the new Zimbabwe?" He turned and said, "follow me."

He led them to the bus station; it was filled with Africans. Women holding babies, others leading youngsters by the hand, some carried chickens, others, plastic bags of fresh meat. On the far side, a row of painted African women plied their trade, they came and went into the darkness with their customers. There was a row of yellow buses, at least twenty, the old man stopped in front of a bus and indicated to the young men. On the front of the bus was a sign that read, 'Kariba'.

"Here," he said, "this one is for you. You must travel to a place call Chirundu. There you will leave the bus and you are to wait. Someone will meet you."

The boys boarded the bus, they had only the clothes they stood in, and wondered how they would survive.

The old man saw their worried looks, "Do not worry, young warriors, there will be food at the other end."

They took their places, then the bus started, and they were gone.

***

Chapter 19

It was Monday morning when Frank and Jack made their way to the Standard Bank, with them was the agent handling the sale of Sabi River Farm. They had agreed on a price, and they would pay a $5000.00 deposit. The ladies had decided they would spend the morning shopping in Salisbury and agreed to meet the men back at Meikles for lunch. As the ladies walked back towards the hotel, they passed a movie house.

Rita was the first to comment, "Oh! Look, Jan, the pictures. It's been years since we went to one of those."

Outside it had a huge sign, 'Latest Release, starring Peter O'Toole: Lawrence of Arabia.'

Jan looked at Rita. "It's a must see, Rita, all we have to do is convince the boys."

The sign indicated that the first evening showing would be at six, so, that evening at six, the four were at the theatre. It was a thrilling movie and they all commented on how much they enjoyed it.

On their way back to the hotel, they stopped in at the Ambassador Hotel for a beer and the discussion turned to the sale of the Sabi River.

"Well," said Jack "it's all done and dusted, we are the new owners of the farm."

Everyone smiled, "That's wonderful, darling," said Rita, "we will all love it here."

Then Frank interrupted, "I also have a surprise for you all."

Everyone looked at Frank with puzzled faces.

"What can that be?" asked Janet.

"Oh, how about, on the way home, we spend two days at Victoria falls. How does that sound?"

"How on earth did you work that?" the others asked, "it sounds wonderful, heard a lot about Victoria Falls. When do we leave?"

"Tomorrow afternoon, I have to say goodbye to Ian and Janet and thank them. I haven't seen much of him, but he has been very busy. I heard people talking, he is tipped to be the next Prime Minister."

That night they met up for a farewell dinner, Frank and Jack had discussed what would happen to Benjamin and his family and Jack had asked Frank to speak to Ian and ask if it was possible to bring them to Rhodesia.

Frank was about to approach the subject as Jack listened in. "Ian," Frank began, "you have been so helpful so far. I have one last favour to ask you."

Ian Smith turned his head towards Frank and shuffled his feet then said, "Ask away, old friend".

"Well, Ian, we have one staff member and his family, a total of six. The man, Benjamin, his two wives and three children, can we bring them with us? Benjamin has been with Jack almost thirty years."

"Ah! Frank, we have six million of them here, another half dozen won't really alter the balance. What I will do is write you a letter from my office instructing immigration and customs to allow you your family and house staff to enter

Rhodesia unhindered. Six Africans, you say? Done deal. You will have the letter tomorrow."

"Ian, you haven't changed a bit, always looking out for your mates."

Jack leaned over. "Ian Smith, I thank you kindly dear sir. Now let's have a whisky."

The evening grew late, and it was time to wind up. Ian was the first to stand. "Well, folks, it's time for bed".

Everyone stood. Ian spoke to Frank and extended his hand, during the evening Ian had told Frank that he couldn't make it to the airport to see him off and Frank had understood, but Ian had assured him the Landrover and staff would be there in the morning to ferry them to the airport. Janet and Rita sat and talked late into the night, they said that they would miss their home in Kenya, but both were excited about the move. Jack and Frank had said the move shouldn't take longer than three months. They were looking forward to mixing with Europeans again and said that they were a friendly bunch, the ones that had met so far. They knew there was no future under a black government, the health service was beginning to suffer, the boys would have to go to boarding school in the UK and be away for six months at a time and the security situation in Kenya was becoming worse by the day. No, this was the place.

They arrived at the airport, boarded the aircraft and it wasn't long before they were in the air and the rumbling of the undercarriage could be heard as it lifted into place. Jack again looked as if he had messed himself and his knuckles were snow white from the death grip he had on the armrests.

Rita leaned over and patted him on the chest, "Relax, darling," she said, but he couldn't speak so she just turned away. The two women changed seats and sat together. The conversation turned to Victoria Falls.

The cabin speaker crackled into life, "Good afternoon, ladies and gentlemen. This is your captain, Ross Greenwood. Welcome aboard. Our flight time to Victoria Falls is approximately three hours. We have to make a stop at Bulawayo in Matabele Land. You will not need to disembark, as we are only discharging passengers and taking on more. Now please sit back and enjoy the flight. We will be serving lunch shortly."

In the back of the seat in front was a folder, it had some leaflets about Bulawayo and Victoria Falls.

Bulawayo was also known as the city of blood. Mzilikazi was a southern African King who founded the Ndebele Kingdom, now called Matabele land. His name means Father. Originally a lieutenant of Shaka, he revolted against the Zulu king in the year 1823 and took his people to the north to what is now known as Matabele land. Lobengula Khumalo was the second and last official king of the Northern Ndebele people called Matabele. In English, both names mean men of the long shields, and reference to the Ndebele language, the use of the Nguni shield. Shaka Zulu had chased Mazilikazi out of Zulu land, now part of South Africa. He had taken his tribe, the Matabele, and moved north where they established themselves around Bulawayo.

All went well, and when Mazilikazi died, the new chief Lobengula took over. It is rumoured that he sent some of his young men to work in the Kimberly diamond mine in South Africa and when they returned, they brought back uncut diamonds. When Lobengula died, his body was covered in animal fat and the diamonds stuck onto his body, then it was loaded onto a wagon and taken to the Matopos Range, not far from Bulawayo, and there it was hidden away amongst the boulder mountains and has never been discovered, although plenty of people have searched. The Matabele problems began when the white settlers arrived, they came in covered wagons and brought modern weapons, the most feared was the maxim machine gun, and when the war began, the Matabele were slaughtered in huge numbers. Eventually, a truce was reached, and as they all began to get along, trading took place.

Often the settlers would take their wagons back to South Africa and load up with supplies and trade goods. The natives wanted axes, knives, blankets, and of course, salt. The pamphlet spoke of a Doctor Jameson, who appeared to have been a bit of lad and of Courtney Selous, another Englishman. It said he had killed eight thousand elephants in his lifetime. Janet wondered why anyone would do that, and then she thought of Jessee and how gentle she had been. How she raised her trunk and nuzzled her ears, then Rita's then Rosie, yes, poor Rosie, she had loved Jessee.

It wasn't long before the speaker crackled again, "Ladies and Gentlemen, please fasten your seat belts," and then they were on the ground. It wasn't even an hour and the new passengers had embarked and they were back in the air, the speaker crackled into life and the captain came on, "Ladies and Gents, in thirty minutes we will be at Victoria Falls, please sit back and enjoy the flight."

Janet and Rita were reading through the information leaflet about Victoria Falls. It stated that the first white man to discover the falls was a Scottish missionary called David

Livingstone, back in the year of 1855 and he named them after Queen Victoria. As they flew closer to Victoria Falls, a lady with an American accent was looking out the aircraft window, she said, "Look Brian, down there. The jungle is on fire. Look at all the smoke."

A young Rhodesian in a police uniform leaned across from the opposite aisle and said, "Madam, that is not smoke, that is the Victoria Falls. What you are seeing is water vapour. The Africans call it Mosi-oa-Tunya."

"Oh," said the American and asked, "What exactly does that mean?"

"Madam," replied the young man "that is Batonka, the two toed tribe. It means the smoke that thunders. When you stand near the falls you will understand why."

"Oh, thank you, young man. Did you hear that, darling? The smoke that thunders."

The undercarriage rattled into place then they were on the ground.

The airport was small but spotless. Outside were African traders selling their wares: wooden carvings, beads, all sorts of souvenirs, some with Victoria Falls written on them, but they boarded the bus straight away and drove off towards the hotel.

The hotel was a typical colonial type building painted white with the usual gardens. As they disembarked from the bus, an African of about thirty years danced towards the visitors. He was dressed in a white linen uniform and wearing a peak cap, his uniform was festooned with cap badges with all sorts of names on them and he blew a whistle. When he wasn't whistling, he said, "Welcome to Victoria Falls Hotel" and danced his way to the entrance. Jack extended his hand and gave him a tip, the African thanked him and danced away to await the next bus load of tourists.

As they walked towards the reception, Janet and Frank noticed the walls were adorned with horns: antelope, kudu, impala, wildebeest, and some Janet didn't recognise.

Frank said, "Jack, why don't you take the ladies through to the gardens, they say the view of the falls is fantastic. I'll check in."

Frank made his way to reception while Jack and the ladies walked to the gardens. In the distance they could see the vapour clouds hanging above the falls. In the cloud was the most beautiful rainbow and the women remarked at what a picture it was. Frank caught up with them and let them know that they were all checked in, rooms twenty-six and twenty-five. He held two sets of keys, and he handed one to Jack.

"Well," said Frank, "We are only here for two nights, let's make the most of it."

They ate well that evening and slept soundly, rising early the next morning, all keen to take a look at the falls. Parked outside the hotel were several complimentary tour buses, they jumped into one and the driver took off, it was a short distance before they came to a stop. A sign read, 'Rainforest track' with an arrow indicating the direction they should take. As they drew closer to the falls, the thunder grew louder, and a mist, almost like rain, fell on them, the vegetation was indeed thick and lush rainforest. Another sign had the words 'Devil's cataract' and an arrow indicating the direction. They made their way along the path until they broke out of the rain forest into a bare spot, the noise of the water cascading over the edge was deafening, so loud they had to shout to hear each other.

"My God," said Rita, "It's beautiful."

They all looked at each other.

Janet shouted, "Can you imagine how David Livingstone felt when he stood here over one hundred years ago."

Jack turned to the ladies and asked, "Why is it that so many Scotsmen leave Scotland and move abroad."

Frank answered him, "That's easy, Jack, it's the weather, the Scottish weather."

They all laughed, "yes," said Jack, "and all those English Lords and Ladies, they don't help."

Rita gave him a good dig in the ribs with her elbow, "All right," she said, "Don't start, sweetheart."

He took the hint and shut up for the rest of the day. They spent their time around the pool, lying in the sun, but Janet and Frank grew restless, they wanted to get home. Janet missed the boys and of course, the dogs. She could imagine the welcome they would get when they drove through the gates.

They spent the evening in the bar, it was full of tourists: Americans, Canadians, people from all over Europe. They began a conversation with an Englishman and his wife, he asked if Janet and Frank had they ever seen an Elephant in the wild and Janet said, "Oh, yes, we had one that stayed with us for nine months."

"Alright," said the Englishman, "no need to be sarcastic" and turned away.

Before long, they went back to their rooms as they had an early flight to Salisbury for their connection back to Nairobi, Kenya.

***

They boarded the flight to Nairobi, and it wasn't long before they were in the air. It was a late flight, eight in the evening, which meant that they would reach Kenya in the early hours, just as it would be getting light. This would work out beautifully and they could be back at Honeydew Farm by late afternoon.

Janet and Frank looked out the aircraft window, it was pitch black and as they looked down, they could see the lights of Salisbury disappearing beneath them.

They looked at each other, "Well," said Frank, "That's our new home. We should be back within weeks. All we have to do is drive from Biera in Mozambique and to our new home and life."

"I loved it down there, darling, and I'm sure the boys will feel the same. Oh, by the way, Frank, I'm pregnant again. Your fault. Yes, I blame you."

Frank didn't know what to say, so Janet said, "Just shut up and close your mouth. We'll talk about it at home."

An hour later, the hostess walked down the aisle telling the passengers that they were now crossing the Zambezi River. Frank and Janet nodded off.

Far below, on the bank of the Zambezi, were six long dugout canoes, each had two Africans with paddles, they waited, then out of the darkness emerged fifteen young men, led by an elderly African man.

He went to one of the men and spoke to him, "These are the new freedom fighter warrior recruits."

David Mabuna led the way, Botswari Ncube and Lovejoy Muringani were next in line. The rest were a mixed lot, no one spoke, and everything was silent except for the noise of the insects and the night animals in the distance, a hippo could be heard with its Whop-Whop-whop but none of the boys knew what it was. These were city born Africans and now they were being shuffled down the steep bank and into a canoe. It was dark, no moon, so they had to feel their way. As they pushed off and left the bank, they heard an aircraft fly overhead, going north. They disappeared into the darkness, David Mabuna looked back and said to his comrades, "look, look back, for we shall return trained in the white man's weapons and take back our land because it belongs to us, we will kill all the whites and drive them from our land." Then he fell silent.

It was early morning when the aircraft landed at Nairobi airport. They made their way to the terminal building, and Jack said to Frank, "You go with the ladies and fetch the baggage will you, laddie? I'll go and let the hotel know we're back, I just hope that beggar of mine, Benjamin, hasn't been out drinking all night."

Jack got straight on the phone and asked the staff to send Benjamin to the airport to pick the family up, but it was three hours before they located him, he was in the local Shabeene, drinking beer, and when he arrived, he looked like a Halloween lantern, his eyes were red, and he could barely walk.

"Right," said Jack, "you're in for it this time, just look at you. I don't know why I keep you on, now get in the back and sleep."

Benjamin staggered to the rear of the stud and fell in. Frank took over, they drove to the Norfolk hotel and settled the bill. It would be late afternoon before they reached home, they phoned Honeydew before they left and Adeena answered straight away, she assured them that all was well, and the boys were fine. It was four in the afternoon when they passed under the Honeydew Ranch entrance, they drove on up to the homestead. As they pulled in, the first thing they saw were the dogs, all sitting on the verandah. As soon as the stud came to a halt, they were down the stairs and onto which ever knee was vacant. Sophie, of course, headed straight to Frank and Janet.

Adeena and the boys heard the commotion and were now on the verandah. The dogs ran back and forth until Frank stepped in, "Right, you lot," he shouted at them, "Behave and settle down."

This made them worse, and it was twenty minutes before order was restored. Janet and Rita gave Adeena a hug and thanked her, then the boys got theirs.

"Have you two behaved for Aunt Adeena?" But both were in tears, this was the longest they had been without their parents and Jack and Rita.

Adeena spoke to Janet and Rita, "I have to run, Sam has been sulking because of the lack of attention," and she jumped on her scooter and disappeared in a cloud of dust, but before she left, Janet asked if her and Sam would join the family for lunch the next day. She agreed, then rushed off. Benjamin began to stir in the back of the Stud, he rolled out and fell onto the ground.

Jack went over to him and stood him up. "Ben," he said, "go home, get cleaned up, I want to talk to you tomorrow." Ben walked away with his head hanging low, he knew he was in trouble.

***

That evening, Janet and Frank broke the news about Janet expecting again. Of course, Jack and Rita were delighted, the boys didn't know what was going on.

As everyone began to yawn, it was time to turn in. Janet and Frank made their way to their bedroom, Frank made what he thought was a complimentary comment to Janet, but she barked at him, "that's enough from you," and changed and got into bed.

"Good heavens," Frank said under his breath, "What's that?"

"Don't mumble."

"Oh, sorry dear," then he mumbled again, "nine months of this!"

The next morning, Jack and Rita were up early, when Benjamin turned up, he hung his head.

Jack asked him, "What's wrong with you then?"

Benjamin raised his head and answered, "I know you are leaving, and I am to stay."

Rita went into the kitchen to fetch some fresh coffee.

"What are you talking about man?"

"You are going to leave me."

Jack looked at him and asked, "Ben, how long have you been with me?"

"A long time, sir, many years."

"Thirty-three years, you old fool. Thirty-three years. Do you think I would up and leave my friend?"

Benjamin stood upright, a broad smile across his face. He stepped forward and took Jack in a bear hug.

Jack tried to break free, then blurted out, "Will you let go?"

Benjamin released his grip; tears were streaming down the black man's face.

Rita had just turned the corner but turned back when she saw the two men, she heard Jack say, "Away with you. You great big Jesse. Away now. I would never leave you, Benjamin. You are part of the family, man."

Then Ben took Jack's hand and said, "You are my father, you are my father."

"Aw! Away with you," said Jack, "for Christ's sake man. Now go and tell your wives and children and start packing."

Billie was at Jack's feet, looking up at his master, Jack looked down and said, "You, Billie, and what do you want?"

At the sound of his name, his tail began to wag furiously and a broad smile came over the dog's face, then Jack called to Rita, "Come on, sweetheart, let's go next door, see what the other Munros are up to," and they made their way towards the neighbouring homestead, Billie trotting along behind. As they walked, Rita turned to Jack and told him she had heard him and Ben and said, "It's a very strange relationship between Africans and some whites, isn't it, Jack?"

"Well," replied Jack, "it is. That black man has been with me since I first came here. Through thick and thin, Ben was always there."

***

Jack had organised a working lunch at Frank and Janet's for all the management personnel of Honeydew. Tony had been informed of the goings on and was asked if he would please come to Frank and Janet's for lunch.

As they walked towards the homestead, Rita spoke to Jack, "It's going to be hard for you, sweetheart, isn't it?"

Jack looked at her and replied, "Yes, it certainly is beginning to sink in, I spent the best part of my working life setting this place up."

They chatted until they reached the steps, then Brian and Frank rushed down to see Grandpa and Grandma.

"Right," said Jack, "you two sit yourselves down, tell me what you've been up to."

Fifteen minutes passed, and the rest began to gather. The topic of conversation was, of course, the move.

Jack quizzed Tony on the progress. Tony replied, "All organised, Jack. All we have to do is pack up you and Rita's, and Frank and Janet's personal things and load them. I have booked passage for all on a Portuguese coaster in three weeks' time from Mombasa to Biera in Mozambique. From there it's one hundred and thirty-six miles to the Rhodesian border, a place called Umtali. We have three trucks, I have two Indian drivers to take us to Mombasa, I will drive the third truck, you'll be taking your Landrover and Frank the Stud. I imagine."

"Quite right. Well done, Lad. Next week I have the secretary for the Lands Department coming here with his Kenyan counterpart to sign the final papers. I believe the Kenyan is the new owner of Honeydew."

Adeena took the opportunity to jump in on the conversation. "Oh! Everybody" she said, "Sam and I have had some good news."

"What's that?" asked Janet,

"Well," she replied, "Sam and I have both been offered positions at Gaborone Hospital in Botswana, we are both so excited."

They all looked at Sam and Adeena, "That's wonderful. When do you leave?"

"We want to leave next week, we have already spoken to the powers that be in Nairobi, they said they were sorry to lose us, but they understood, they also said the funding for the clinic would come to an end soon, so it would seem all has worked out for the best, except for the Kenyans."

"Yes," said Rita, "That's the clinic and the school closing."

***

It was Monday of the following week, when a Landrover pulled up at Jack's home. Jack and Rita were expecting them, it was the new owners of Honeydew. Two whites were the first to get out, these were from the land department, one carried a briefcase, two Africans soon followed, and they made their way up onto the verandah. The Africans wore sky blue safari suits topped off with different styles of cowboy hats, each wore huge sunglasses, Jack shook hands with the two white men but the Africans made no effort to shake hands or extend any form of greetings.

The first words came from the larger of the two, "Well," he said in a loud voice, "this is our home now, white man, we want you out quickly."

Frank and Janet had just arrived and caught the end of the conversation. Jack kept his cool and answered, "will next week suit you?"

"Yes," replied the fat one, "that will be good for us."

This is a real Kaffir, thought Jack, each of them carried an umbrella and a briefcase. The men from the Lands Department looked embarrassed, the senior of the two presented Jack with some papers, "Mr Munro, please, sign here and we'll be gone."

Jack looked at it, moved to the table, signed it, and said, "There you are, she's all yours."

The fat Kaffir said, "We have great plans for this place and the rest of Kenya."

Jack just turned away and said, "Sure you have," and walked inside, he heard the Landrover drive off as he was pouring a whisky.

The four stood looking at each other, then Frank spoke, "Are you ok, Uncle Jack?"

"Yes," was his reply, "I've done alright financially, and we have a new life to live in Rhodesia, but I am putting my feet up Frank, you can take over the reins."

***

The week passed quickly and the day before they left, late in the afternoon, Frank poured a beer and walked to Rosie's grave, he stopped and looked down at the Rock Cairn he had built as a headstone, he had surrounded her grave with stones to mark her final resting place.

"Well," said Frank, "this is it, Rosie, we are leaving first thing tomorrow morning, so I am taking this time to say goodbye. They say dogs have no souls, but I don't believe that."

As he spoke, Sophie looked up at him, she was, as always, at his feet.

"I know, my girl, that you are watching over us, but I have to say goodbye, we both had a good life together and now I have this one to care for," as he went on, he began to scatter the stones which marked her place. When he finished Frank said, "Now none of the new people will know you are here. Rest in peace, Old Girl, until we meet again."

Janet had been watching from the verandah, but turned away when Frank started back, she could see the tears streaming down his face. Frank was a proud man, so she went inside.

The next morning, everyone was assembled ready to move, Jack and Frank walked to the front, Sophie and Billie followed on, Tony was driving the front vehicle, they stopped and chatted to him, "Well, Tony," said Jack, "Take one last look, lad and move off, when you're ready."

The diesel engines roared into life, one after another, with great clouds of blue-black smoke. Jack gave him the thumbs up, and they moved off.

"Ok, Frank, we'll follow on, you go first, Rita and I will bring up the rear."

Frank jumped in the driver's seat, followed by Sophie. The boys were both excited and waved to all their African friends who had come to see them off.

Jack had ensured that every employee received one hundred silver shillings as a bonus and they had all thanked him, 'Go well, Boss, from all the staff' was printed on a makeshift sign.

Jack and Rita, together with Billie moved off, they waved goodbye. It was just over a mile to the main gate that held the sign Honeydew Ranch, as they left the gates, at the bottom of the small hill, was a small pile of stones about knee height, Jack stopped and looked back. Nearly forty years ago, as a young man, he had driven this same road, not as well kept as it is today, he had needed directions and he saw a young African standing here, Jack asked, "Do you speak English?"

The young man replied, "Oh! Yes, sir, and I can read and write and do sums."

"Really?" said Jack, "tell me, the homestead not far from the river, is this the right way?"

"Oh, yes sir," he replied, "not far,"

Then Jack asked, "are you looking for a job?"

The African's face lit up.

"Ok, can you cook and keep house?"

"Yes, sir, but I have a sister, she is very good cook."

"Ok," said Jack "bring her."

"And, Sir, I have two brothers, very strong, good workers."

"Ok, tell them to come next week. Now, jump in and I'll take you to the homestead."

The African jumped in, Jack extended his hand and the African did the same. Their hands met and they shook in the traditional African way, "My name's Jack, what is yours?"

"My name is Benjamin. Sir."

And so began a lifelong friendship between the two young men.

Rita could see the lump in Jack's throat, and he looked at her, "Well, sweetheart, there goes a lifetime's work."

She reached out and took his hand. "I know, darling," she said, "come on, take one last look, think of what you have to look forward to and try not to think too much about the effort and hard work you put in."

Jack climbed back into the Landrover and put it into gear, they reached the crest of the hill, drove over, and then they were gone.

***